D1795970

GREAT KILLS

GREAT KILLS

A KILLIAN COLLINS NOVEL

KEVIN FOX

SHADOW**LAND**

ISBN: 978-1-7331187-5-0

Published by

Cover design & interior formatting:
Mark Thomas / Coverness.com

"Memories are the lies we tell ourselves to make sense of events we've suffered through. Each of us crafts a story that we call the truth, telling it in a way we can bear. In the end our story may be fiction, but even as fiction, memories are the most honest form of expression we can aspire to."

~ The Fiction of Truth

"If you're going to live a lie – make it a good one."

~Graffiti on the wall of the

Great Kills train station, Staten Island

CHAPTER ONE

…The glass shards embedded in my face started to burn, and blood flowed warmly into my eyes, forcing me to blink.

Blinking didn't help.

I was half-blind, running headlong into the low hanging branches of oaks and maples that whipped my face and arms as my legs were torn open by the thorns of sticker bushes. There was nothing I could do about it, since I couldn't see the branches through the rain and darkness.

My head pounded, causing my vision to blur, and I lost my balance as sporadic vertigo set in. I stopped for breath and inhaled the pungent smell of wet leaves, damp earth, and the musty odor of swampy ground that mixed with the scent of decaying rot that wafted over from the nearby Fresh Kills garbage dump. As I tried to breathe, I gently touched behind my ear, where I felt a deep gouge, tender and soft. When I pulled my hand away, it was warm and sticky with blood.

I was getting tired, but I had to keep going. The cold, sharp rain helped me focus and thinned the blood enough to wipe it away from my eyes so I could see. The only dimly consistent illumination was from behind me – from the headlights of the car I had run from, parked awkwardly off the shoulder of the road. Given the violent severity of the accident, the car should have been totaled, but it just appeared abandoned, with one window shattered. Just then a lightning strike illuminated the night with the sudden impact of electric blue daylight, giving me a momentary glimpse of the path ahead.

The lightning complicated things. I wanted to be able to see, but knew that I didn't want to be seen. Keep running. That's what I had to do. I had to get away from that car, and find somewhere warm to hide, but it was getting harder to run. The ground beneath me was waterlogged and gripped my feet, tripping me with uneven roots and rocks as I heard something snapping twigs and crashing through the underbrush –

– That's when I saw the shadows to my right move. I tried to run faster but only wheezed and choked, giving myself away as a hulking figure emerged from the shadows, the shades of darkness resolving themselves into the silhouette of a man, twice my height and at least three times my weight. I turned to get away, never feeling the sting of the branches on my face nor the thorns that pierced my legs, now too numb to care. Everything blurred, and then, in that way it can be in dreams, I was somehow deeper into the woods, falling to my knees, listening to the metronome of the softly insistent rain, and the rustle of leaves in the dark. I turned *to look for the source but only caught a glimpse of a lithe shadow as it fled into the woods, too small to be the man.*

Then flashlights ripped through the dark, their beams broken by the trees, reaching out to find me. They were coming. Again. I tried to stand –

– Too late. The bright lights caught me in their glare, blinding me. I screamed, heart pounding, unable to move…

*

…And the sound of my own scream startled me as I woke up in a confused panic. I tried to sit up but the blankets, twisted around me, held me bound. My throat was raw. I could taste my own blood… But it didn't matter. The dream was over. For now.

I knew this routine. I've had night terrors since I was seven. First, I had to unwind myself from the blankets, and then wrap them back around me to ward off the inevitable chill after sweating through my t-shirt. Next, I counted twenty deep breaths to get my heart rate back to something close to normal and identified all the shadows in my bedroom as ordinary. It took a moment for each of them to coalesce into their concrete forms – from the menacing man by the window into the suit hanging on the curtain rod, the gleaming knife into a belt buckle, and the half open closet door revealing not an eye gleaming in the darkness, but my detective shield hanging from a lanyard.

After my heart rate slowed, I forced myself to listen to the sound of rain on the roof for almost a minute. It was the same rhythmic sound of tension that underscored my night terrors. As I listened, I used the self-talk a child psychologist had taught me almost twenty years before: 'It's just rain, just water. Just a dream, not a memory. None of that ever happened. Nothing bad happens in the rain.'

It's always raining when the dreams come, and in spite of the words of reassurance I use to calm myself, rain isn't just water. Rain comes with hurricanes and tornadoes and floods, and dreams are more than dreams when they can make your heart pound and throat bleed from screaming.

That headshrinker I once had, he knew jack-shit.

He was only right about one thing, that while it was just a dream, it was based on something that actually happened – a car accident on a rainy night when I was seven years old. I was thrown from the car and my 'Uncle' Joe Corrigan, the driver – a man who was not actually an uncle, but worked with my father on a Federal narcotics task force made up of the NYPD, FBI, and DEA – was killed on impact. As my father's best friend, Joe was closer than family, and the trauma of his death radiated through all of our lives.

But I can't remember any of it.

I also can't remember anything from before the day of the accident – the night of October twenty-third, 1985. Today they call it 'Traumatic Brain Injury', but as a kid growing up in Staten Island, the other kids called it 'fucked in the head'. Both terms are accurate.

I've tried to recover any memory I can, sifting the facts from the dreams and I've learned to discard any recollection that doesn't have corroborating physical evidence, since my memory can't be trusted. My mind deals with things by creating these dreams, elaborate fictions that the psychologist claims I use to heal traumatic sense memories and take control of what I can't control in my waking hours.

The most factual detail I've come up with about that night is the sound of the rain, drumming on the roof of the car. The National Weather Service confirmed that for me. In my dreams the sound is distinct and clear, full of the musical tones and complex rhythms of raindrops on real metal – not some alloy that banged dead flat like modern cars would now. It was also confirmed when I tested the memory on an old Volkswagen Beetle that I borrowed, made the same year as the car Uncle Joe was driving the night of the crash. I sat in the borrowed car for ten minutes in the rain, getting chills, feeling my heart rate spike as I forced myself not to flee, until finally I hyperventilated and almost passed out. The sound of rain on a metal roof still makes me cringe and sweat.

In spite of the sound being a genuine memory, that sound somehow feels the most dream-like. The rest of it, from the car tires on the wet road, to the windshield wipers rubbing the glass, and even the last image I remember, a bright flash of red, white and blue light followed by a painful deafening sound, well, that's all debatable. Psychologists have told me that the light and sound are my mind's way of interpreting the lightning flash that they theorized startled Uncle Joe, causing him to pull the wheel of his 1973 VW Bug too sharply making it hydroplane off the West Shore Expressway, near Sharrotts Road.

The rest of what I know about that night comes from what the accident investigators pieced together afterward. I was thrown from the car, landing in the cattails that lined the highway. Two days later I was finally found. Somehow, I'd managed to get up and walk away, disoriented and bleeding. I still have a scar that runs from behind my left ear to the top of my forehead, made when some piece of metal went through my skull, creating a groove that hugged the inside of the bone until it exited at the soft hollow of my temple.

It's no surprise that I can't remember much.

The two days I wandered through the woods after the accident are lost to me, but it rained the entire time, and late on the second day the temperature plummeted from sixty degrees to the low thirties.

I guess I'm lucky they stumbled across me when they did – wedged under a tree, covered in fallen leaves, clutching some costume-jewelry ring that I must've picked up while wandering in the woods, which was one of the former illegal dumps that used to be common in Staten Island. The ring was faux gold – one of those fake, overly ornate signet rings with a sword and star over a red shield – the kind that always seem to be featured on the retro-antagonist in graphic novels. My dad calls it my *memento mori*, which he thinks means it's a memento of when I almost died. I looked it up. It's actually a phrase that means 'remember that you *will* die'. Cheery.

Eight days after they found me, I was released from the hospital, and the next thing I remember after that is two months later, at Christmas. It rained that Christmas, and I stayed inside for three days, too afraid to step out the door.

The doctors tell me it was the traumatic brain injury and post-traumatic stress disorder that caused my memory loss and hatred of the rain. Both still cause me problems, but they're manageable and every once in a while, when I'm stressed, I lose some time. I have over thirty years of memory that plays like a silent film, scratched and missing a few reels. Chunks of the year I was ten have gone missing, fourteen is a blur, the entire summer I dated my first girlfriend is gone (God how I wish I could remember what we did in her parent's basement), and my first year of college amounts to three months of time spent at bars and parties. I've been told that kind of memory loss is almost normal, but for me it's been that way my whole life.

I know that if I could find a way to remember the accident and the person I was before that night, the night terrors would end. I just need the facts. Maybe that's why I became a homicide detective with the NYPD, so I could learn how to turn facts into a coherent story, to control my dreams by knowing what really happened. I guess that was one reason, the other being that police work was a family business, since my father had been a detective as well. My best friends from elementary school, Charlie Pederson, and Tony Guinta were cops now as well and even Tommy O'Connell – the brains of our group –

was working at the U.S. attorney's office. That's the way Staten Island was – if you weren't a cop, you were a fireman, or worked for the MTA – if you didn't join the other side and get yourself involved with the mobbed-up service industries like private carting, or construction.

Either way, being a detective helped me piece together who I was. It still does, and I use those skills to piece together the last memories of the dead, of homicide victims, forever lost when they were murdered. So, I guess my curse is in a way a blessing, because even with my issues, I'm more effective than most on the department. Not that I've told the department I have memory blackouts. No, they're not aware of my problems. Thank God for HIPAA laws.

I was still lying in bed, trying to remember if there was anything in this dream that was different than the rest and was trying to get my heart rate back to normal when my phone buzzed. I didn't need to look to know it was a text, and I didn't need to read it to know what it said. I did anyway, hoping to distract myself.

'U dead? Heard u scream like a little girl'

Typical Kat. She was a sweet but damaged woman just a year or two younger than me. I had rented the upstairs apartment in my little Cape Cod to her on the recommendation of Charlie Pederson, who I'd known since the year after the accident. Charlie told me that Kat was some kind of charity case, a native Staten Islander and friend of his sister who'd come back from serving two tours with the U.S. Army's Criminal Investigations

Division in Afghanistan with PTSD and a bad attitude.

At the time it didn't matter to me what her issue was, I needed the rent. Then I met her, saw that she was beautiful and charming, and felt like I'd known her all my life. She would've been a serious temptation to me – if I hadn't discovered pretty quickly that she was completely bat-shit crazy.

I'm not sure if Kat was always unstable, but after she got back from overseas, she was in rough shape. Kat never talked about it, but from what she hinted at, whatever had happened to her involved serious retribution from a well-connected Colonel who didn't appreciate Kat's apparently career-ending investigation into his sexual kinks with unwilling junior officers.

Despite her PTSD, Kat never hesitated to jump in where angels feared to tread. In fact, the first time Kat heard me scream from the night terrors she broke into my place with a butcher knife to come save me.

I almost shot her. That's when we worked out the texting procedure.

'Just had a dream about you and a butcher knife. Go back to sleep.' I texted back, then turned on the radio to keep me company until the sun rose. Unfortunately, all the talking heads wanted to yammer on about was the rain and whether or not 'Sandy' would be a tropical storm or a hurricane by the time it made landfall. The only thing I got out of it was that the rain was going to fall for a long time.

Good thing I had the next few days off. I could hunker

down, turn on my television and pretend nothing was going on outside. I found a classic rock station and turned it up loud to drown out the sound of the rain, wondering what memories had been washed away so long ago, not aware that in less than twenty-four hours Sandy was going to bring them back in a flood…

CHAPTER TWO

Once the sun rose, I fell back into a dreamless sleep, until even the radio wasn't enough to drown out the storm. The gutters were rattling and the windows whistling as the wind forced its way through their seams into my sixty-year-old Cape Cod in Great Kills – the unfortunately named town in Staten Island. Apparently, the Dutch that originally settled Staten Island called streams '*kills*' in their native language and the name stuck. Apparently, no one ever thought enough of the real estate here to try and rebrand the neighborhood.

I ignored the din until they announced the time on the radio: 6:30 P.M. I'd slept the day away, so I dragged myself out of bed. I was about to go prep the nachos and beer for a *Game of Thrones* marathon on the big screen, when my heavy oak front door slammed open, the handle denting the sheetrock behind it. The wind brought rain spraying into the foyer, followed by Kat – all five-foot-nine of her, pierced and tattooed, with her hair dyed jet-black and her wide blue eyes looking for some excitement.

I didn't want any.

"I've come to save you from your misery," Kat announced, dripping all over my hardwood floor.

"Not in the mood, Kat."

"You're never in the mood. I think it's low testosterone, but I have a cure." She grinned, coming in, sweetly sweaty and only slightly less pungent than usual. Her long, glistening hair was plastered as tightly to her head as her spandex was to her trim body.

Kat, maybe from being a woman in the military and living in close quarters with men, seemed to be very comfortable in her own skin. Or maybe she just liked to keep people off balance. Either way, in addition to having PTSD she's an exhibitionist, bi-polar, and bisexual (which I only know about because she broke the water bed in her apartment one night and after saving my television from the flood that followed, I rushed upstairs to find a disturbing scene that included a man, a woman, and a knife, but that's another story). She also hints at her dark past before she signed up and other things that happened later, while she was stationed in Afghanistan. I once asked Charlie about it, but all he would say is that she enlisted to leave the series of foster homes she grew up in behind. My background check didn't turn up anything worth noting except that two of Kat's former foster parents were currently incarcerated and that she had a sealed juvenile record. Lucky for Kat, it was expunged when she volunteered for the Army.

"Let's go play in the rain, Killian. It's the storm of the century."

"I'm having nachos. Beer. The rain stays outside, I stay inside," I told her, looking pointedly at the puddle she was leaving as she ran a hand over the spandex, flicking off the excess water, spraying it everywhere.

"You have your own entrance, my door was shut, and you smell like the gym." I looked away. Kat likes it when people stare. I wasn't about to give her the satisfaction.

"So what? I did two hours of Jeet Kun Do and I'm just getting warmed up. You like the way I smell." It wasn't exactly true. She smelled like a healthy woman, and in her spandex, she looked soft and curvy in all the right places and like she could kick most guys' asses – but a little less pungent would have made her a lot more attractive.

"Go take a shower."

"Fuck that. Come shower outside with me. It's fuckin' fantastic out there. The wind could blow a truck off the Goddamn bridge. Trees are crackin' in half. The *energy* of it is tremendous."

"They closed the bridges – and you're out of your mind. It's dangerous," I said, stopping three feet from the door. I hate the rain. I hate when people tell me how beautiful the rain is even more. It's wet. Cold. Makes my skin contract wherever it touches me and makes every muscle in my body tense.

"Christ on a cross. You're an NYPD detective. Six foot three, two hundred twenty pounds of muscle and you're afraid of getting a little wet? Is that why you're here all alone?"

"Fuck you," I said, giving her the standard Staten Island answer for everything. I moved further away, taking refuge in my old ultra-suede couch, turning on the television as I did.

"Not likely. You're too good for me with all that Viking-red hair and piercing blue eyes. I used to think you were holding out for some Valkyrie, but maybe you're just scared." Kat teased and flopped onto the couch next to me, her damp hair brushing my cheek. Her assessment wasn't too far off, but it wasn't fear that kept me away. I stayed away because I was pretty sure she'd reject me the minute I tried anything – and because Kat *was* my friend.

I could play *Call of Duty* with her for days on end (even keeping up with her on good days), talk shit, admire the same women in a completely inappropriate and carnal way, spar in the middle of my living room as she showed me her new Jeet Kun Do moves, and enjoy meals she cooked for me just because she hated to eat alone. Why would anyone in their right mind fuck that up by starting a relationship? Kat snuggled in closer and I hit 'play' on the remote, trying to ignore the warmth of her.

"When was the last time you brought somebody home? Hell, when was the last time you went *out*?

"I go out."

"Yeah, to The Annex, with Charlie Pederson and guys you've known since Little League – where the only women you might meet one, or all of you, already screwed in High School."

"Maybe it's not all about getting laid for me."

"Right. You like being alone, hiding from the rain. You know, for a guy named Kill, with that scarface of yours, you're a real pussy," Kat muttered through a smirk. I ignored her, although I appreciate the fact that Kat likes my scars. Maybe they remind her of her own. She has two I've seen, one that runs two inches under her left breast through a groove between her ribs, and another on the outside of her left thigh that is long and deep and that she seems to display proudly whenever she can. It accents the muscular beauty of her lean legs – not that I'm looking – and is a badge of honor from her time in the Army.

Once, when we both fell asleep on my couch after a thirty-six hour tour de force on *Call of Duty*, I woke up to her fingers gently tracing the scar on my left temple. The scar makes me look tougher than I am, and Kat thinks that somehow my name, Killian Collins, matches the scar so well that I must have been born with it. I've told her it's from the accident, but after reading my astrological charts, she called me a liar and claimed that there were no accidents in my life.

"My name's Killian, not Kill," I corrected her. "It's Irish and doesn't have anything to do with murder."

"Well, it's Irish *and* ironic. Look at my name – Katherine D'Angelo. Katherine means 'pure' or 'chaste' and D'Angelo is 'of the angels'. You believe that shit?"

"Someone has a sense of humor."

Kat ran her hand up my leg, stopping at the scar on *my* thigh, a half dollar-sized, spiraling blemish that my mother says was due to my own stupidity. Apparently, I pulled out the cigarette lighter in our old Chevy Nova and burned myself. Kat traced that scar too, trying to get a reaction. She did. I stood, pretending that I was getting up to get a beer.

"Seriously, Kill. The storm of the century, Frankenstorm, Stormzilla, it's out there and you're going to stay inside?"

"Now you've got it. Because I'm not crazy."

"And I am?" she asked, and I just rolled my eyes. "It was Tommy, wasn't it? I explained that," she said, looking at me with wide innocent eyes.

"You stabbed him. A guy stumbling down the stairs with a fork in his 'nads makes anybody think twice about your sanity."

"I told him no. He tried anyway. You'd never do that to me."

"And Veronica?" I asked, popping open two beers.

"She *fell.*"

"Your 'friends' – seem to have a lot of accidents. I'd rather play it safe."

"That's the only thing you play, isn't it? Is that why you've got food and sump pumps and generators and gas stockpiled?"

"I'm prepared," I admitted. My house was well out of the evacuation zone and I wasn't one of those recent immigrants from Brooklyn that had built on swampland, so I felt safe. Being a former Boy Scout and the son of a semi-paranoid conspiracy-theorist cop, I also had four ten-gallon cans of gas in the garage, a generator, water – both to drink and in the bathtub for flushing – and guns. I didn't really expect any trouble, but there was looting during Hurricane Irene and this *was* Staten Island.

"If it becomes a zombie apocalypse, will you let me have one of your guns?"

"No."

"Come on, you've got like three," she pleaded. I had four actually – my on-duty Glock 19, my off duty .40 caliber Glock 22, a sawed-off twenty-gauge shotgun, and my father's old .38 special with the ivory handle. As with most cops I knew, my general attitude was 'loot me. I dare you.'

"I'd be murder with a shotgun," Kat argued, swilling her beer.

"I have no doubt. In fact, you're one of the reasons I have a gun safe."

"I'm well-trained. By the best Goddamn Army in the world."

"And not licensed in the State or City of New York."

"Fine, see how quick I leave you behind when the zombies come... And why are you hiding out here anyway? Shouldn't you be out on the streets doing some police thing? Evacuating evacuees? Taking on looters? Saving stranded *stunads* who didn't evacuate?"

"I have three days off." I'd barely finished speaking when the lights went out, leaving us in utter darkness except for the emergency flashlights that lit up automatically when the power went out. In their glow, I saw Kat smile.

"Locked in for three days. Lights out. No TV. No video games. No heat..."

She moved closer, grabbing a second beer. That's when my cell phone rang. If I had bothered to look at the caller ID, I might have risked three days alone with Kat.

"Collins," I answered.

"Kill. Hate to bother you, but two of my best Detectives just rode out to sea on their townhouses and my patrol guys are in it up to their asses – literally," the voice of Lieutenant Demetrius, from the precinct in Tottenville, came through the phone. I owed Demetrius big time, since he'd saved my ass from a couple of white supremacist gunrunners and had never called in the favor. Until now.

"I'm off duty, Demetrius."

"Nobody's off. It's a State of Emergency. Besides, it's an easy call. It's your neighborhood. In fact, you were requested."

"What the hell does that mean?"

"That same sultry sounding piece that's been calling in tips for you for the last two years called."

"She's a stalker. I've never even met her. I'm not going out in this shit storm based on anything she called in," I told him, determined not to leave the house.

"Right. Never met her. Sure. Then why'd she asked for the tall 'killer' who hangs at The Annex? Why'd she say she didn't trust any other cops? And why'd we get a nine-one-one that confirmed her call two minutes later?"

"That was probably her too. Some cop groupie is lonely on a stormy night – that's all this is."

"No, it's not. The nine-one-one was from the guy, you know the guy, a 'friend of ours', lives around the corner from The Annex, 502 Holten, right on the water there. The one with the classic Mustang. He backs up what your off-duty booty said. Added that he heard shots. Even thought he saw bodies outside his house or something."

"Give it an hour and maybe the bodies'll drift out to sea. It'll be the Coast Guard's problem," I said, trying to weasel out of going anywhere in the rain.

"Yeah, I know, but if I don't send somebody, everybody's gonna know and then, you know… They said shots fired, Kill."

"Yeah, I get it. Shots fired. There's no more free beers at The Annex when this woman starts complaining I didn't show."

"Exactly. Not that I take the free beers or nothin', but it's community relations and such." Demetrius didn't need to explain to me. I grew up in Staten Island, and in spite of its size, the island still operated like a group of small towns. Everybody knew everybody else, or at least a sister or a cousin of everybody else.

"Fine. I'll go look, but if it's a mess you're gonna have to get somebody else out there."

"Perfect, Kill. You do me a solid, I'll have your back," he said quickly, and then hung up without a good-bye. I turned to find Kat glaring at me, half her second beer already gone.

"You're going to leave me alone in the middle of 'Stormzilla'? You'd rather potentially get shot at than be here with me?"

"It's less scary," I said, going to the closet with my gun safe.

"Damn. That's cold."

"Let yourself out. And don't eat all my chips," I called over my shoulder as I strapped on my gun and grabbed my gold shield off the shelf.

"Can I have a few beers?"

"A few. Like less than three." I grabbed my Columbia raincoat and started to put my boots on. I hate the rain, but I'm ready for it.

"Less than three is a couple. A few is three or more," she said.

"Drink what you want," I told her, knowing she'd drink enough to piss me off, and no more. In spite of her issues, I understood and empathized with Kat. I once spent three months on loan to the Manhattan Special Victims Unit, and never did I have a more miserable time. I met a lot of women like Kat while I was at SVU. They were survivors, but fucked up enough that you could see that they went through some bad shit. Kat as much as admitted it to me on one of my bad nights. I think she wanted me to know that she understood what it felt like to wake up screaming.

Homicide was easy in comparison to Special Victims. The people you were standing up for were dead. They didn't cry on you. Not that Kat would ever cry, or that she was somehow 'damaged goods'. She wasn't. Kat was stronger and smarter than any woman I knew – but she was complicated and I couldn't be that sensitive guy that got her through things – not when I couldn't even get myself through a rainy night.

I walked out without saying good-bye. Kat didn't like good-byes anyway. She felt they were too final. The most you'd get out of her was a 'see you later' or 'until the next time'. She made 'good-bye' bad juju somehow, and now that she'd planted the thought in my head that every time someone said good-bye it might be for good, I rarely said it.

As I opened the door to my '73 Nova SS, I looked back to find Kat staring out the window at me. After a moment, she let the curtain fall, leaving me to wonder what might have been different if I'd met her a long time ago, or if neither of us had ever been damaged by life.

I didn't wonder long. The wind was whipping the rain into my face like a spray of liquid needles, sharp and cold, reminding me that I'd just left a warm, safe place for no good reason. I decided not to think about it.

I was getting wet.

CHAPTER THREE

Sandy was a bitch. I was driving through a maze of downed trees, sparking power lines, and flooded streets as rain pounded my windshield like it was trying to shatter it. I almost missed the left onto Wilbur from Seguine because my visibility was something like ten feet, but once I got on Wilbur the houses that stood between me and the ocean diminished the wind. Sticks and branches littered the ground, and I could hear the trunks of trees moaning to the point of snapping. When I made the right onto Holten the Raritan Bay was within ten feet of the road instead of its usual one hundred and fifty, and I saw the waves already pounding against The Annex, crashing seven feet up against its walls. Even then I knew the bar wouldn't last the night, and wondered if someone had saved the grappa and the Macallan's.

What a waste.

Rain. Enough said.

I slowed down, debating whether or not I'd be better off retreating to higher ground when two locals ran in front of my car, wearing garbage bag ponchos and waving their arms like lunatics. The guy, probably in his late forties but looking like a Medicare recipient due to what he'd undoubtedly call 'good living', was wheezing and out of breath. He could have been excited, or scared, or maybe just winded from the extra hundred pounds he was carrying around.

The woman was in worse shape. Apparently, she'd put on her makeup before leaving the house and it had run all over her face and sheer white blouse. Her hair, which was probably blown out at any other time, was plastered to her head and thinning. She was also wearing heels in the rain. I tried not to look directly at this Staten Island incarnation of Medusa, fearing that looking directly at her would damage my psyche permanently. Knowing my luck, my malfunctioning memory would choose that unfortunate image to hang onto. Hoping they wanted a ride to the shelter and had called in a bogus 'shots fired' call just to get it, I leaned out the window.

"What's the problem?"

"The problem? You blind? It's the Goddamn apocalypse out here," he answered.

"Besides that? You called in gunshots? Bodies?" The woman looked at me in shock, then at my car, as if the two didn't match.

"Oh, shit. You're the cops?"

I'd forgotten that I was in my own car and pulled out my gold shield, wondering what other moron besides a cop they had expected to show up here on a night like this.

"Detective Collins. Did you or didn't you hear shots?

"Well, yeah, but that was like an hour ago. Take a look," the fat man said with a tone of accusation and pointed down the block. Through the rain and darkness, I couldn't see anything.

"I don't see nothin' but water."

"Goddamn, he's either blind or fuckin' stupid. Go closer," the Medusa-woman screeched. I got out reluctantly and walked to the edge of the water, flowing up the middle of Holten, avoiding the kids' toys, bikes, and an entire Playskool kitchen set that the tide had washed up. The darkness beyond the house at 502 Holten suddenly took on a shape and became clear.

It was a ship – a yacht really, over one hundred feet long and taller than any of the houses –definitely not the kind of boat that usually made port in Staten Island.

"Fuck. That's a nice ride," I muttered, summing it up as best I could.

"Yeah. There's a problem for ya. Waves breakin' against my bedroom window and a Goddamn boat in my yard, slamming up against my house. I can't go inside – and I can't leave with that monstrosity tryin' to wreck my house. I want to know what gazillionaire owns it so I can file a claim. He can buy me a new Goddamn mansion. That's my fuckin' problem in a nutshell," the fat man cursed.

He had a point. His whole house was swaying to the rhythm of the waves, groaning and creaking. Every tenth wave would send the side of the yacht crashing against the house so hard that it looked like it might slide off the foundation.

"What am I supposed to do about it?" I asked. I mean, I'd be happy to stay and watch the inevitable tragedy, but what else could I do?

"Listen," the fat man ordered, waving his hand as if he could silence the storm. I heard the house groan, the wind, the constant white noise from the rain, and some banging. There was nothing... and then there was. Maybe. It was almost drowned out by the storm, but it was distinctive enough to make chills run up my spine.

"Was that...?"

"Give it a second. You'll hear it again." The woman shivered, and I understood why as I heard the high-pitched and terrified scream of a young girl.

Shit. I looked at the fat man, still unable to look at his wife in her sheer shirt, which by now had been painted in vibrant colors by her melting face. The Fat Man looked grim. He knew I'd heard it too.

"She's been screaming since right after I heard them gunshots." Perfect. This was just what I needed – gunshots and screams from inside an enclosed space that was pitch dark and was being pounded by waves in a hurricane. I'd have to deal with a possible shooter, a victim, medical issues, and the floor moving under my feet, all while being in the dark on a wet, slick deck.

"Are you sure there were gunshots?" I asked hopefully.

"I know gunshots when I hear 'em. They weren't fired

professional-like though. No three shot bursts. Just random, like somebody didn't know what they was doin'," the fat man answered, confidently. I wondered what family he was connected to, but I didn't doubt him. There had been gunshots. There was someone on that yacht...

"And the bodies you saw?" I asked, procrastinating.

"That many shots, there's bodies. Didn't need to see 'em."

"You call the Coast Guard?"

"Tried them. Told me to go fuck myself." I contemplated following their lead, but then I heard the screams again.

"You know how to swim?"

"I look like I exercise? Fuck you," he answered. Like I said, 'fuck you' was the standard Staten Island response to just about everything.

I was on my own.

Glancing up the street, I looked for something to inspire me. The house looked like it was the only way to get up high enough to get onto the deck of the yacht, but it wasn't a great option since the house was swaying from the force of the waves and would be torn off its foundation if I didn't move... quickly.

"Can I go through your house?"

"For what? You got a warrant?" asked the fat man, suddenly suspicious.

"No. I'm gonna climb out that window and jump to the deck."

"What are you, *oobatz*?" He asked, looking at me like I'd lost my mind.

"You want to come with me and find a ladder instead?"

The fat man looked at me for a minute, weighing his options.

"Go in the house, see if I care." He shrugged, probably betting that I'd die before I stumbled across whatever it was that he was afraid I might find. I put out a hand for his keys, knowing a guy like this would have his house locked up against potential looters. He handed them right over.

"Help yourself."

I went to the car, grabbed my Maglite and extra ammunition, double-checked that my 'LifeProof' case was secured around my phone and walked into the waves without looking back. I knew that if I stopped now, I'd freeze and go no further. The other times I'd gotten caught out in storms I'd lost whole days of my memory. If anything was going to cause a relapse – this was it.

By the time I reached the stoop at 502 Holten, I was up to my thighs in water and could feel the riptide trying to pull my feet out from under me. I grabbed the rail and hauled myself up the steps, looking back to see where Medusa and the Fat Man stood, but they were lost in the rain.

I unlocked the front door and pulled, but the wooden frame was cockeyed from the pressure of the waves. I put one foot on the wall and tugged, managing to force it open, then stepped inside. In the light of my Maglite I saw white leather couches, a white rug, and a gaudy, red-tiled gas fireplace that smelled as if it might be leaking.

A fire to go with the flood, that's all I needed.

I headed upstairs, taking them two at a time as the ocean pounded on the walls, making the house rock in a disconcerting rhythm. I was down the hall in four long strides, getting my sea legs as I moved toward the bedroom whose window faced the ocean and the yacht.

The rest of the house had been neat and organized, but the bedroom was a mess. There were men's socks and underwear strewn around, and bits of leather and lace I never would have expected those two outside to have. I was almost to the window when the yacht crashed into the house again and I was nearly knocked off my feet, staggering and stumbling against the silk-sheeted bed.

Regaining my balance, I went to the window and pulled it up, looking out to see the yacht's hulking mass right beneath me. The deck was less than three feet below me, but rocked away each time a wave hit. In constant motion, the deck was slick, and wet, and not an ideal surface to land on. I'd have to time my jump carefully or slide off and get crushed between the yacht and the house.

That might hurt.

I almost said 'fuck it' and turned around, but over the waves, the wind, and the grinding thump of fiberglass on wood, I could still hear sporadic and desperate screams. I knew I'd start hearing those panicked shrieks in my dreams if I didn't try to help.

Goddammit.

I squeezed my head and shoulders through the window

and squatted on the sill, bracing myself with my arms as the rain burned against my skin. While working up my nerve to jump, the tide suddenly thrust the yacht up and a wall of shining mahogany came right at me. I reacted instinctively and jumped. I was mid-air before I realized what I'd done – the deck was moving out from under me, floating out to sea. I caught the rail, my shoulder muscles screaming as my weight almost pulled my arm from its socket. My hip slammed into one of the uprights and my ribs compressed as I hit, hard. It was impossible to breathe for a moment, but I had the presence of mind to fall forward, onto the deck, rather than backward and over the rail. My right knee hit the hard mahogany as my left leg gave out, but I was onboard.

The yacht rolled and I almost slid back under the rail. I stopped myself by hooking my left leg around an upright, grabbing it with both hands. Catching my breath, I took stock of my situation – I was on the exposed deck of a grounded yacht in a hurricane, it was slamming up against a house, could break free at any moment, and I had to cross an open deck in the torrential rain. Everything was slick and cold, and the waves and water coated everything with unpredictability.

Basically, I was fucked, and I'd done it to myself.

CHAPTER FOUR

The only way off this boat was going to be to find the screamer, get her to dry land, and go home. That was my motivation – a warm dry house where hopefully I'd find a few beers left and Kat relatively sober.

I stood, stiffly moving toward the raised pilothouse where dim lights were still on, powered by an emergency generator. When I reached the hatch, I pulled it open and went down a few steps, noticing the beautiful woodwork that gleamed in the dim light. I took it all in quickly, in case I ever lived to testify about what I saw. The yacht was a Hargrave Custom Capri Series and nicer than any home I'd ever been in. I almost had a chance to appreciate it when the girl screamed again. As it died out, I could hear her trying to catch her breath and muttering in an accent I couldn't quite identify.

"Oh, God oh God oh God, someone get us out of here… Please," She begged, and then chanted something that sounded like the rhythm of the Catholic confession I'd grown up hating, in a language I didn't know. "*Bozhe miy, ya shchyro shkoduyu za te, shcho obrazyv Tebe, i ya znevazhuyu vsi svoyi hrikhy cherez spravedlyvi pokarannya Tvoyi...*"

She screamed again, and I shuddered. I needed to find that girl just to shut her up. As the yacht rolled, I was knocked off balance and caught myself awkwardly, pitching forward toward a set of narrow stairs. There were no lights on down below, so I put my Maglite between my teeth and brought my Glock up to its ready position.

I was beginning to miss my nightmares.

Moving as fast as I could without falling on my ass, I reached the narrow galley with its granite countertops and stools bolted to the deck. There was food that had been tossed around the room, as if someone's meal had been interrupted, but there were also boxes and crates. Quickly scanning them, I could see that they had been vacuum-sealed in plastic before they had been roughly torn open. As I shined my light on one of them, something inside reflected the light – clear plastic packages in bricks with a pure white powder inside – heroin.

A lot of it. Hefting one package, I felt the weight and knew it was both pure, uncut, and worth a fortune on the street. Then the boat pitched again, reminding me that I was on a tight clock. I kept moving, but as I passed the next crate, I noticed something in the stainless-steel refrigerator in the galley – a distorted reflection that looked like a face – a horror show face out of my nightmares, with its left temple collapsed, bone shattered and melted into scar tissue, obliterating what had once been an eye socket. I turned quickly, pulling up my gun as I did –

– But there was no one there…

Fuck. My heart was racing so fast I could hear the blood in my ears, crashing like waves. I get like this in the rain. Paranoid. Freaking myself out so much that my night terrors bled out into the false nights of a stormy days as the rain made my mind play tricks on me.

I took a deep breath and went back to work, quickly taking pictures of the drugs with my cell phone – a habit ingrained from gathering evidence at crime scenes. I might have kept snapping photos if the girl's piercing shriek hadn't startled me back into action. I headed back down the narrow hall, past the stairs and into the main salon – a room that was bigger than my living room, complete with a wet bar, leather couches, and a table that sat eight.

Somebody was going to be very pissed off if this thing sank.

I started across the salon, but stumbled over something bulky and dark in my path – a body. I fell over it into a warm dark mess on the carpet – blood. Startled, I whipped my Maglite around on the dead guy. He was maybe thirty, with close-cropped hair and the ruddy, rough skin and blocky teeth that marked a certain class of Eastern European criminal. The stab wounds that sliced open his lower abdomen and face didn't really help improve my impression of him.

His friends were less than ten feet away, on the other side

of the couch – three men in their late twenties or early thirties, none of whom had been stabbed. All three were shot in the face. Their blood had drained all over the expensive carpet. Leading away from the pool of blood were footprints, headed out of the salon, as if someone had lived through this massacre and gotten away.

I kept a firm hold on my gun and headed out the sliding glass doors at the rear of the salon, hearing pieces of the house snap off as the yacht slammed into it. The rain and the sea had wiped out any trace of blood out here on the deck, but there was a hatch cracked open there. It led down into the engine room. Water was pouring in as each wave crashed, but I could see that water was also coming up from below. The hull was compromised somewhere.

This night kept getting better.

The girl was close now, and I could hear her muttering in that sweetly guttural language, working herself up for another good blood-curdler. It never came. Instead, she went absolutely quiet. That could mean a lot of things. She may have passed out, or whoever killed the four men was still on board and could have killed the screamer.

Halfway down the ladder the smell hit me – a rotting, moldy, and fetid smell that had a tinge of rotten meat to it. The odor had a sharp edge, a coppery tang like the taste of blood turned to vinegar. It's a scent that any cop who's been on the job long enough will tell you is the smell of death. Even with a memory like mine, it wasn't something easily forgotten.

I played my Maglite across the darkened space and in its limited glow found pale, floating shapes that looked like thick albino eels. At first my mind refused to recognize them, but after a moment it hit me that they were naked limbs, bloated and bobbing in the dark water. Shining the light on them, I finally found their faces – dead faces, all with the distinctively unhealthy skin tone that's an indicator of carbon monoxide poisoning.

I counted three girls and four boys, all fair-skinned, Northern European-looking, and in their early teens, clothed in shorts and t-shirts. Each one was handcuffed to a pipe that ran across the engine room. Fighting the urge to bolt, I started doing a visual record, the way I was taught at the Academy, but my eyes started to tear from the foul odor and my stomach tightened, ready to purge itself.

There's a reason death smells the way it does. It's wired by evolution to inform every instinct you have to run from whatever killed the people you're looking at. It makes sense, since whatever killed them has a high probability of killing you as well. The odor also makes you want to puke, just in case whatever killed them has been ingested or inhaled. The fact that death is ugly, has a horrendous stench, and very often oozes out at you is a marvel of evolution, nature's way of trying to protect each of us by tapping into our most basic instinct for survival.

I didn't listen. I was too pissed off. Given the age of the victims, I knew this might be a trafficking case – and if I was ever going to catch who did this, I'd need evidence. A few quick pictures – call it thirty seconds – and I'd be gone. Then I heard the girl moan again.

Son of a bitch.

She was losing volume, but managed to emit a low keening wail, holding a bone-chilling note. I was going to have to go all the way down into the hold. Fuck. I hesitated. If I didn't get off this boat soon, I'd get swept out to sea. The smart thing to do would be to leave. Now.

I didn't. I couldn't. My father always told me that stupidity and bravery look identical in the moment, and only the results tell you which is which. I seemed to err on the side of stupid whenever someone was in trouble, which is why I became a cop.

Climbing down into the hold, I landed in dark water that made the pale flesh that floated in it seem luminescent. I scanned the faces of the dead, searching for the source of the moans, finally turning my light toward the darkest corner, where the water was deeper. I expected to find her alone and scared, handcuffed like the others.

She wasn't either of those.

The screamer was a slight girl with dark auburn hair that contrasted sharply with her translucent skin, and in spite of her size and current condition her attitude made her look both intimidating and dangerous. The girl's clothes were hanging off her body and scratch marks, most likely defensive wounds, were etched into her arms. She also had a gun pointed right at my face. I had made a slight error in judgment.

The killer of the men in the salon was still on board. She was right in front of me.

"Stay away..." she hissed in the strange accent that was somehow both similar and different than the Russian I heard on the North Shore of the island. It was thicker – as if English was an acquired second language. Whatever it was, it was hard-earned, and there was a toughness about her that could only came from experience. Her eyes reflected the light, shining green, with blue and gold flecks and a healthy dose of crazy and they narrowed as I tried to step closer.

"I said don't move—"

"Actually, you said 'stay away,'" I corrected her as I noticed a second girl behind her, her near twin, handcuffed to a pipe. The water was rising quickly around all of us, but I clearly couldn't rush this girl. She needed to trust me before I got any closer, so I tried to distract her, shining the light on the girl that was still handcuffed. She appeared to be older, since her face was more angular and her body less so.

Sisters. Had to be.

"Are you all right?"

"Do I look all right?" the handcuffed girl muttered, her voice trailing off weakly.

"She's your sister? Can you tell her to put the gun down?" The older girl nodded, staring me in the eyes, and then finally looked toward the younger girl.

"Put it down, Dariya. Can't you see he's not one of them?"

"All I see is a man with a gun."

"Dariya? I'm a policeman. You've got to get off this boat."

"And what was your first clue, genius?"

"You can't get off without my help. I can get her handcuffs off."

I saw Dariya's eyes shift to her sister, her weak point. If I could establish a connection, I might have a chance to talk her down.

"What's your name?"

"Alina," she said, shivering. She pronounced it with a stress on the 'i' and a lengthened 'n', with an inflection that I couldn't quite imitate.

"Dariya, Alina's going to drown if I don't help her. Soon. Put down the gun." I started moving forward again and her grip on the pistol tightened. "…Or, shoot me and drown. Brilliant plan. Who's the genius now?"

It was a standoff, and I could see Dariya's finger go white on the trigger. It crossed my mind as the storm battered the yacht and the water continued to rise that it might be a quicker death to have her shoot me –

CHAPTER FIVE

"Dariya. If he doesn't help, shoot him later," Alina ordered. Dariya grudgingly complied, lowering the gun and stepping back behind Alina so that I could get to Alina's handcuffs. It was a start, but Dariya could still shoot me if she decided to.

I was impressed. These girls were beautiful *and* practical. Somehow they'd killed four Eastern European Mafia-types, possibly wounded another, and had me dead to rights if I wasn't careful. Carefully avoiding the stressed-out, traumatized, and hormonal teen girl with a gun, I holstered my own weapon and reached for my keys.

The first order of business were the handcuffs. I was lucky on that account. Whoever had cuffed them had used generic handcuffs and my keys opened them easily. As they slid off, Alina stumbled forward and I caught her, feeling her slick, wet, and very cold skin. She was close to hypothermic, but there wasn't much I could do about it as I saw Dariya behind her, the pistol now raised to my face.

"Don't touch her!" I took my hands off of Alina slowly, making sure she didn't fall, and then held them up so Dariya could see them.

"Can you walk on your own?" She nodded. I stepped aside, giving her room to pass. She trudged through the water and I motioned for Dariya to follow – and as she did I tore the pistol from her grip.

I almost regretted it as her knee glanced off my thigh, barely missing its target. Before I could pull away, her teeth managed to take a piece of my forearm out. Thankfully her fatigue worked in my favor and I was able to take her legs out from under her, pushing her down in the water, close to her sister.

"I told you. I'm on your side – but I don't want to get shot in the face by accident. Understood?"

"You mess with us, I'll kill you," she promised, her stare pure venom.

"I have no doubt, but you'll kill us all if you don't get moving. Go." She didn't, not until Alina took her arm, gently, pulling her toward the ladder. I tossed the pistol in the rising water and followed them, hoping Dariya didn't decide to slam the hatch in my face. I kept a close eye on her hands and feet as she scrambled up the ladder, almost expecting a kick to the face, but she was in too much of a rush to get out onto the deck.

The weather had gotten worse while we were below. The wind was howling, and it carried lawn chairs and patio umbrellas through the air, discarding them in the waves. I thought about trying to get off the boat through the house again, but when I looked, I noticed that the peak of the Fat Man's roof was four feet off center and the whole place was leaning landward. It was going to collapse at any moment, and Dariya wasn't waiting for any man to save her. She was at the stern, untying a life raft that had already been inflated – as if someone had tried to leave earlier.

"We could use a hand," Alina called out.

"Just get in," I told them, putting the muzzle of my gun to the rope. It's a stupid way to cut a rope, especially when it means you're putting a hole in a yacht, but it's efficient. The shot snapped the rope and sent it lashing out, whipping across my arm and slicing open the taut, cold skin. It hurt like a motherfucker, but the raft was free. I was pushing the raft off the deck and into the water when Alina suddenly yelled, looking past me at something with wide, terrified eyes –

"—Anton, NO!"

I turned in time to see a teen boy, six-foot tall, muscular and soaking wet, with blood streaming down his face from a scalp wound coming at me. His shoulder caught me in the ribs, causing me to lose balance and slip –

– Free-falling over the side. My weight took Dariya and the raft with me, tumbling twenty feet down into icy waters. The salty wetness felt like acid and I was unable to get a breath before I hit the frigid waves. My lungs went into spasms almost immediately. I kicked, desperate to get to the surface, feeling my right foot connect with someone's body.

I hoped it was the idiot Anton and not the girls. A moment later I broke free from the sea's wet grasp, gulped the air and swallowed salt water as another wave hit me in the face. The raft was being pounded by surf that covered the flimsy craft in salty spray and I reached for it. Dariya was already in it, holding on valiantly as it was tossed, at the mercy of the waves.

Anton was nowhere to be found, but I caught a glimpse of Alina swimming toward the shore. The waves were determined to help her, thrusting her at the shoreline as violently as possible. The last few feet would be the most dangerous for her as the waves smashed against the hard pavement below, but it looked as if she'd make it.

Exhausted, I swam without making much headway. Dariya was screaming, furious at the universe and cursing me for some reason. It didn't last long. Two large waves brought us to within twenty feet of solid ground, and then a third, larger wave caught us –

...And the world turned upside down again.

The raft was flipped upright and over by a sudden surge, and I caught a glimpse of Dariya going headfirst into the water before I was pummeled by debris. Something jagged and sharp caught me in the stomach as I struggled to orient myself. I flailed, slammed a heel into the bottom, then slipped and went deeper until I felt the rough surface of the paved road. It scraped my torso and tore my skin as the waves tried to pull me back under, but I fought back, clawing my way out.

...I might have blacked out.

I know I'm missing pieces of what happened next...

The next clear memory I have is lying flat on my back, shaking water out of my eyes. The street was lit up, brighter than before. It was a sporadic, flashing light, illuminating everything in a shocking-blue glare. I turned my head to find what I knew I would, but hoped I wouldn't –

– Downed wires, dancing like electrified snakes as they put everything within thirty feet into stark and brilliantly lit contrast. I knew that if the wires landed anywhere near me, all of this water would conduct that energy perfectly and the voltage would finish me off. I got up carefully and saw him.

Again. One-eyed Willie. The guy with the collapsed left temple and no left eye, standing in the shadows beyond the downed wires, only illuminated when they sparked. I knew that I'd seen him somewhere before, but of course I couldn't remember where – or if it was just in a night terror. I moved toward him, but as I started to he pointed behind me. That's when I heard her shriek and turned to find Dariya walking out of the waves, legs bloody and a gash on her head. In spite of the punishment she'd taken, she still looked as if she were ready to take on the world, but was shrieking as if it had already ended.

...Then I saw Alina lying motionless in the middle of the street, her legs still being lapped by the waves. Even from where I stood, I could tell that she wasn't breathing. I glanced to see if One-eyed Willie was coming to help, but he was gone. It was all on me. Looking back, maybe I should have told Dariya what I was going to do, but even if I had, I doubt

I could have prevented what happened next.

I only did what I was trained to do.

I went to Alina, dropped to my knees, made sure her airway was clear, and started CPR. It took a few seconds of blowing air into her lungs and pounding her chest, but Alina coughed once –

– And then there was a sharp blow to the back of my head. The pain disoriented me and my vision dimmed as I rolled over expecting to find Anton –but it was Dariya, swinging at me, her arm coming down at my chest. I didn't have time to react –

"I said don't touch her!"

The scream landed at the same time as a sharp blow to my ribs that hurt more than it should have. As Dariya went to pull back, I tried to grab her arm, but she was wet and slick and slipped away. As I tried to go after her, I found I couldn't breathe. That's when I looked down and saw the walnut hilt of the Karatel knife protruding from between my ribs.

Dariya had stabbed me.

I'd fucked up. I should have known. Should have pieced it together.

Of course, it was Dariya. She was the killer. I knew when I saw her with the gun, but I'd forgotten about the first dead man, the one who had been stabbed. Dariya must have gotten the knife first, stabbed him, then took his gun and killed them all.

"Why?" I asked her, confused. Why stab me after I'd saved them?

"You're just like them. You, you tried to rape her... as soon as... you could." She stammered. In spite of the rain, I could see that Dariya was crying, a victim, trying to be a survivor. I admired her for that, at the same time that I wished I could pull out the knife and give her a taste of what it felt like to be hurt for no good reason.

The anger only lasted for a second... I knew that this girl already knew what that felt like.

I crumbled to the ground, losing my sense of time and place for a moment. In my peripheral vision I noticed movement, dimly aware that Dariya had helped Alina up. I couldn't focus on them, only on the knife – and my blood, seeping out around its blade. It occurred to me even then that it was a beautiful knife, an uncommon knife, unlike the ones I used to take off perps when I was a uniform. I didn't know then that it was designed specifically for the Russian FSB, the successor of the Soviet KGB, but I knew even then that it was a knife used by professionals to kill.. In the sharp electrified light from the downed wires that hissed and danced, my focus on the knife didn't seem irrational, just hallucinatory. As if this was another night terror and I'd wake up any moment, throat raw from screaming. I didn't.

I closed my eyes as I lay on the pavement, realizing too late that the heavy rain falling on my face would make me feel like I was drowning again. The water was encroaching on me, crashing closer and closer as spasms of sharp pain radiated through my chest. My vision was fading inward and it was getting darker all around me as I heard footsteps splashing in puddles nearby, running toward me.

I prayed that it wasn't Anton or Dariya coming back to finish the job, as whoever it was kneeled at my back. I tried to turn to see if it was the creep with the damaged face, but couldn't. It was then that I heard a woman's voice, humming and mumbling something.

"*Cuimhnigh, a Dia go léir, nár chualathas trácht ar éinne riamh a chuir é féin faoi do choimirce ná a d'iarr cabhair ort ná a d'impigh d'idirghuí is gur theip tú air.*"

The voice had a rich treble tone, and the rhythm of this language was once again that of a prayer, but much sweeter, and gentle. Soft hands reached around me and gently laid me flat as the sound of the incantation went on. The shadowy silhouette of a woman in a hooded raincoat hovered over me, her face almost invisible in the shadows until intermittent flashes from the downed wires illuminated her hazel eyes. They met mine, reflecting the sparks of electric light, giving her an otherworldly air and opened wider, startled as she saw my face.

"The girl stabbed *you*?"

I nodded, catching my breath as I placed her sultry voice – she was the woman who'd been calling me, giving me tips over the phone for the past few years. My stalker.

Christ, she was the reason I was here.

"…It wasn't her fault. She thought I was…" My voice trailed off. I had to stop, catching my breath to try again. "…She didn't… mean to."

"I'd hate to see what she does on purpose," she said, even as she put one strong arm around my shoulders, getting ready to lift me.

"Who are you? Why'd you call me here?" I asked.

"Now's not the time. There's too much to tell and you're bleeding. Can you help me?" She asked, leveraging my weight, helping me to support myself. Once I was on my feet I looked back down at the knife, my free hand unconsciously drifting to its hilt, wanting to free it from my chest.

"Don't touch it. It looks like it missed your aorta and the superior vena cava."

"You're a doctor?"

"No. But I know that if I move it the wrong way, the blood will flow and you'll die," she advised.

Good to know. I kept my hands away from it, stumbling one painful step at a time to my car. I don't remember all of the next few moments, but one brief bit of clarity is the image I had of her face as she took my keys and laid me out on my own back seat. The wind whipped off her hood and her silky auburn hair streamed out over her shoulder for an instant. She caught my eye, and despite the seriousness of the situation, she smiled. In that moment, I'd swear I'd known her before – seen her like this, soaked through by the rain.

CHAPTER SIX

I could hear the pure tones of rain drumming on the metal roof of my Nova as I opened my eyes to near darkness. The woman in the front seat was a dim silhouette and was driving cautiously around fallen trees and through deep water. In spite of her caution, water was seeping in the doors as we made our way up Holten Avenue, moving toward Staten Island University Hospital.

Keeping my eyes open was difficult, but I tried to focus on the woman who saved me. I felt like I should remember her from some class or summer camp – but I didn't. Typical. This happened all the time with my memory issues. Sometimes the person I thought I should remember was a stranger, other times I'd spent a year or two in school with them.

"I know you," I finally said, hoping she'd fill in the blanks.

"You didn't last time we met," she said simply, confirming that we'd met before.

"Sorry, my memory is… terrible," I said, struggling. It was getting harder to breathe. "If it was college, I'm …sorry. There were …whole months …I lost. Did we…?" I asked, worried, but she just smiled.

"Don't hurt yourself talking. It's all right. I'm 'Rigan," she told me.

The name didn't sound familiar. At all. I nodded, too tired to speak and now able to see the emergency lights of the hospital. Chaos was swirling outside the doors as injured people walked or were carried in, soaking wet through knee-deep water. If the tide surged much further, even the hospital's emergency generators would be under water.

Rigan pulled the Nova up near the ER and I took out my phone and slid it under the seat. The photos I took would be evidence and I wanted to keep them safe. It was hidden by the time Rigan opened the back door and I had sudden and startling sense of déjà vu. I'd seen her before, like this, leaning down into a car over me… I recognized her hazel eyes. I was sure of it...

And then I wasn't…

Pain shot through my chest as Rigan tried to move me, and she was a stranger again, just helping me out of the car. The exertion made my head spin, I stumbled and then it all went dark for a while. Sounds lingered distantly, disconnected in time and space as the splashing, overlapping metronome of the rain and the voices of doctors and nurses and EMT's, disjointed and without meaning, filtered through.

...And then I was gone. One moment Rigan was with me, and the next...

*

...I was freezing, shivering in the cold and the darkness, a fine misty fog gathered around me. The moon cut through it from above, illuminating the shallow water that I stood in, so bright that it threw the shadow of a gnarled oak onto the still surface in dark contrast. All around me were cattails and marsh grass, like the ones I remembered being everywhere in Staten Island when I was a kid. Every muscle and joint in my body was swollen and stiff as I knelt in the pond, thrusting my arms into the darkness of it, digging my fingers into the thick gray clay. The tendons in my hands were stretched to the point of agony as I noticed a face in the disturbed reflection of the water. It was my face – when I was seven years old.

After a moment, my fingers scraped something below the surface. It was hard and flat, about two-foot square. I grabbed the edges, dragging up a box wrapped in some kind of waterproof oilskin, when I heard the rustle of leaves, too steady to be the wind. Startled, I put the box in the oilcloth and shoved it back in its watery grave, covering it quickly with heavy clay. I'd barely hidden it when I saw him, moving out of the mist with a shotgun in his hands, raising it as he strode toward me – a dark-haired man with a mustache and sideburns.

— Before I could move he was standing over me, the barrel of the shotgun pushing down on my chest with a sharp pressure.

I couldn't move. Could barely breathe…

"Where is it?" He asked, his trigger finger twitching.

"I'm…" I tried to answer him, but my breath gave out.

"Tell me or die here." He said, shoving the gun into my chest harder, forcing my face under the frigid water. I tried to hold my breath, but I could feel my lungs spasm and I choked, coughing…

He let me up, smiling coldly. Beyond him, hiding in the dense cattails, I saw the moon reflecting off familiar eyes that looked black in this light but weren't. I knew who they belonged to, and I knew that they wouldn't look away until it was all over.

"If your friend has it, tell me where," he said, leaning once again on the barrel, threatening to send me under. I struggled to speak, but my mouth was full of water and all I got out was something that sounded like 'dool hun if', before the man pushed me under again and my chest felt like it was going to burst –

*

—The pain was excruciating as I regained consciousness to find a nurse pressing down on my wound, trying to stem the flow of blood. Rigan was still talking to me, as if I hadn't been lost in my nightmare for long.

"Hang on. You'll be fine."

"Stay…" I told her, knowing that she knew more about than she was saying, but she pulled away, shaking her head.

"I'm sorry. I am. But I have to find the girls before they do. You'll understand when you remember."

"Remember what?"

"Everything," she said softly, so only I could hear as the stretcher rolled down the hall. "...And don't trust anyone. If they know you remember, they'll kill you," she said. I felt her warm sweet breath on my face, and then she kissed me and whispered, "*Go dtí an chéad uair eile.* I'll be in touch."

Rigan had barely finished speaking when the stretcher slammed through the doors of the O.R. and she was left behind. A moment later there was a mask coming toward my face and I was gone again, dreaming fevered dreams, full of hallucinatory images that made no sense...

*

...The next thing I remember there was a haggard and care-worn face that I recognized, but couldn't quite place, watching me from the chair next to my bed. I couldn't find a name to match the face, but the man helped me out as he leaned over me with a smile I recognized as the 'good cop' smile.

"Hey, he's back. Good to see you, Detective. I'm Detective Lieutenant Michael Burke. I just have a few questions about your attack," Burke said pleasantly, as if asking for gardening tips.

"I know you..." I tried, but I'm not sure how it sounded to him, because the words were mangled and a dark look crossed behind his eyes for a moment. Maybe he didn't recognize me, but I'd finally placed him. He was a pallbearer at Uncle Joe's closed-casket funeral. I was only seven at the time, but he looked vaguely the same, with his close-cropped hair now completely gone and the addition of crow's feet around his eyes. I was sure that I'd changed more than he had.

"You've got an interesting memory. Last time we met, I was probably your age."

"…At the funeral, right? You were on the task force with…" I struggled to finish. Whatever drugs they'd given me made my mouth feel like it was filled with glue. "…my dad and Uncle Joe," I finally finished.

"I was. We can catch up sometime. Right now, I need you to tell me everything you recall. I'll catch the woman that did this. You know who she was?"

"No," I whispered honestly. A door slammed somewhere nearby and I heard a deep male voice, angrily addressing Burke.

"Lieutenant, I told you – not now. He needs to recover. He's still feeling the anesthesia."

"He's fine. Aren't you, kid?" Burke asked, leaning in closer. His features were blurry and I was fading again, trying to focus on him but only seeing –

*

-- *A rippling image of the barrel of a gun and the bright light of moon, shining down through water, blood-tinged from my wounds. The shotgun pushed harder on my chest and the moon receded, fading behind a cloud. Rain fell on the surface, causing the moonlight to ripple –*

– And then suddenly I was struggling toward the surface, hearing voices calling my name from nearby…

*

"…Killian. Come on. Talk to me. Who was she, Detective Collins?" Lieutenant Burke asked. I tried to sit up and focus. I was unsure of how long I'd been out, but Burke hadn't moved.

"Who did this to you?" He asked again as I tried to clear my head.

"Some girl. From the yacht. Maybe fourteen."

"Nurse said it was a woman that brought you in. Got the impression you knew each other. What about her?"

"Good Samaritan, that's all," I told him. He knew I was holding back. I got a good look at her – could have described her hazel eyes and the asymmetrical freckles on the bridge of her nose, but I wasn't ready to share her with Burke just yet.

"What's the damage? Did I win the line-of-duty lottery?" I asked, changing the subject as I realized that I wasn't feeling too badly, considering I'd been stabbed in the chest. Other than a sore itch between my ribs and a dull oppressive headache, I felt better than I had most Sunday mornings in my early twenties. Burke smirked and shook his head.

"No such luck. You'll be back to work in a few days. The blade she used was sharp, made a real clean cut, and she didn't get it all the way in. You bled a bit, but the loss of consciousness was from 'stress.'"

"What's that supposed to mean?" I asked, not liking the way he stressed the word 'stress'.

"Hey, I'm making no judgments, but the docs said you were freaking out about the rain and it was just eight stitches. My little girl got more than that when she fell off her bike."

"So make her a detective," I told him, trying to not sound as bitter as I felt.

"She already is one… can we get on with this?" Burke asked, and I could see the judgment in his eyes.

"It wasn't a panic attack or PTSD. I was stabbed."

"Sure. I get it. I don't like the rain either," he said. "…Now, the woman who brought you in, did she say anything to you?"

'I remembered the phrase she'd used in the car, '*go dtí an chéad uair eile*', but I said nothing to him, unsure if the words were real or hallucinated gibberish. Burke must have seen my hesitation and he pressed the issue.

"So, she did say something to you. Do you remember what it was?"

"It wasn't even English."

"Was it Russian?"

His question put me on edge and tipped his hand. Burke had no reason to guess that it was Russian or anything like it unless he already knew about the yacht. Something wasn't right, and as I grew more lucid, I started to see the shape of what it was – Burke was here, interrogating me, but why? Why would an old hairbag of a detective that had worked with my dad and uncle show up in the middle of a hurricane? Combined with the anonymous phone call luring me out to investigate the boat, something wasn't kosher.

"It wasn't harsh like Russian. It was sweeter. Singsong. But why does the woman matter?" I asked.

"She's a material witness. The girl who stabbed you was probably just scared, but the other woman was there for a reason and I heard it was a woman that requested you at the scene," he said bluntly. It was an accusation, pushing me to admit that I knew more about her.

"How do you know that? And why? Me getting stabbed in the middle of Frankenstorm isn't important enough to send a detective, so stop bullshitting me."

Burke smiled coldly and decided to shift gears.

"To be honest, I was already investigating that yacht. Was waiting for it where it was supposed to dock in Brooklyn. When the storm hit I realized it would complicate issues. Thought I got lucky when I heard it ran aground," he explained.

"Why were you investigating?" I asked.

"Am I being interrogated now?" Burke smiled, as if he enjoyed my paranoia, then leaned back and settled in. "That yacht you were on? Belongs to a Russian billionaire whose son was supposed to be on it, but isn't. A missing billionaire's son is a crappy way to start a day."

"That doesn't answer why you were looking into it before he went missing?"

"Yeah, well, after I worked with your dad I stayed in narcotics. Long story, but you know how it is with the NYPD. You work a couple of big cases, you learn a couple things, you become the resident expert. This yacht's owner, Alik Markov, he's been known to traffic drugs, and girls, and arms, and anything else that keeps him in the black."

"So why are you here and not at that yacht. Or out looking for his son?"

"Because missing Russian billionaires are enough to get the Feds attention. You know that."

"The Feds?" I asked, missing something again.

"Yeah. Them. To be honest, I wasn't even going to talk to you. You getting stabbed is a side note. But by the time I got to the yacht it was grounded and the Feds were swarming like the nest of WASPs they are. Wouldn't let me on board."

"So, you don't know that there are at least four dead Russians and probably seven dead kids on that thing?" I clarified. Burke shrugged, being brutally honest, not blinking an eye at the mention of the dead kids.

"You know the Feds. They don't like to share. So, do you mind? I'd like to get ahead of the Feds and not cover up anything just because daddy Markov owns too many shares in the big oil companies. …So, what'd you see?"

"Hang on a minute. Something stinks. It's no coincidence I was the guy called out by some crazy woman – and that you knew my father?" I asked.

"Doubt it. I don't trust coincidences. You shouldn't either. All I know is that your dad and uncle were working on international smuggling way back when. Narcotics mostly – but like I said, some trafficking – even arms crimes bled over into it. Maybe there's a connection. If I were you I'd ask the woman that called you. Who is she?"

"I wish I knew," I told him truthfully. Burke stared,

waiting for me to give him more. I couldn't.

"Okay… How'd you end up on board?"

"…The boat was slamming up against the house. All I wanted to do was get on and get back off. In the galley there were some crates. I saw some packs of what I'd bet were heroin."

"Your phone was missing from your personal effects. Any chance you got photos?" He asked, quickly, trying to catch me off balance. The question rubbed me the wrong way. What the hell was he doing going through my personal effects?

"Must be floating somewhere. I wasn't sightseeing anyway. There were no photos." Screw him. If he was going to go through my stuff, I was going to lie to him. I knew it was probably a bad idea, but one of my many child psychologists once told me I had ODD – 'Oppositional-Defiance Disorder'. She said it was the inability to do what I was told or to take anyone's word for anything. I was proud of that – why would I ever take anyone's word for anything, and why should I do what I was told unless it made sense to me? It made me a good detective. Trust no one. Only facts.

"How many crates were there?" Burke asked, impatient.

"I didn't stop to count. Maybe fifteen, from about a foot square to about four-foot square."

"Damn. That's a lot of pure skag."

"Well, at least you caught it before it hit the street, right?"

"No. None of it was recovered. Feds claim that by the time they got there it was all gone. My bet is that's why the woman who brought you in bolted." Burke stopped there, leaving me to infer the rest.

"You think she went back to get that stuff off the boat?"

"Maybe."

"In a hurricane?"

"Well, it's gone. Somebody just lost a shitload of Afghan Albino and had four Russian Mafia soldiers killed in the process. The Russians are going to hunt down whoever did it and get rid of any witnesses, pronto. Either way, I need to find that woman. Fast."

Burke made a good point. Stealing from the Russian Mafia was stupid, but making the son of one of their billionaire capos disappear after killing his friends was straight-up suicide, but I doubted the woman who saved me had it in her.

"What about the two girls?" I asked, knowing they'd probably be killed on principle alone.

"Two girls?"

"And possibly a teen boy. They got off the boat as well."

"Good for them. What makes you think they're worth anything to anybody?"

"They're worth something because they're people. Kids… Somebody should be looking for them."

"Love your idealism, Collins, but they're better off staying lost. If the Feds find those kids, they'll send them back to whatever hell they were in before, or put them in danger of becoming witnesses – or targets. Your best bet is to walk away. Let 'em go. Consider them lucky." Burke stood to go, stopping at the door and looking back for a moment.

"Go home, forget about this. I owe it to your father and the memory of Joe Corrigan to keep you safe. I can't do that if you get in the middle of it. Trust me." With that Burke stepped out, letting the door close softly behind him.

I wish he hadn't said that. Any time someone tells me to walk away, it seems to me the request itself is a good enough reason to stick around.

A half an hour later I'd found my clothes, signed myself out against medical advice, and got sample painkillers from the hospital pharmacy. If I wasn't going to develop a whole new series of night terrors, I needed to find those lost girls and the woman who saved me.

'Rigan'. That was the name. I remembered that much…

CHAPTER SEVEN

The waters had receded and fourteen hours had passed since I was admitted, but it was still raining as I exited the hospital to find my car where I left it. The engine sputtered a few times, but eventually the moisture burned off and it caught. Power and tree crews were visible working on Seguine Avenue, clearing it, so I headed that way to get back to Holten. It still wasn't easy. Cars had been abandoned in the storm and blocked the lanes where fallen trees and power lines had cut them off from whatever destination they had once dreamed of reaching, and I saw no signs of power anywhere. There were no lights in houses, no traffic lights, no sounds of music or movement other than the chain saws and diesel engines of the power crews.

I'm not sure why I felt the need to return to the wreck of the yacht, but after talking to Burke, I was sure that I'd missed something about this whole event that was critical. To be honest, given the stress of last night, I wasn't sure how much of what I remembered actually happened and how much was part of the fevered dreams I had in the hospital.

The first blue and white I saw was parked at the end of Van Wyck, blocking the way to Purdy Place, its lights flashing lazily as the patrolman reclined in the passenger seat. I parked on what was once somebody's lawn and walked down to the RMP, catching sight of the yacht, further inland than it was when I left it. After the Fat Man's house collapsed, I guess there was nothing to stop it from floating over where The Annex once stood to where it now sat, wedged upright by debris. In the daylight, I could read the yacht's name clearly – '*Chistota*' – which I found out later means 'purity' in Russian. Nice.

Outside the crime scene tape, volunteers, firemen, and uniformed cops combed through the wreckage, looking for survivors as the odor of decay and the musty smell of ocean rot, fishy and organic, rose from all around. Seaweed and dead fish were lying on top of clothing and toys and pots and pans. The level of destruction was impressive, but I was focused on the decks of the *Chistota*, where I noticed a Crime Scene Unit doing all the technical work that I never had the patience for.

The details of the scene stood out to me – the crime scene tape was taut and in neat symmetrical lines; guys in matching blue raincoats who looked like they got their hair cut at SuperCuts were moving through the CSU guys; and nobody except those two groups were behind the tape. Feds, obviously. NYPD crime scene tape always flutters in the wind and goes from convenient point to convenient point – practical, not

Federally anal – and we have better haircuts.

The patrolman in the car struggled to roll down his window, as if moving that index finger was outside of his contractually obligated duties. He was about to tell me all the reasons I couldn't be here, so I flashed my shield.

"Middle of a natural disaster, we get no FEMA, but the FBI shows up right away? What's the crisis?" I asked, playing on the natural distaste every street cop had for the Feds.

"Somebody called in the destruction of a mansion and a yacht and said there were bodies in the street. For all I know, Elmer Fudd washed up on shore."

"Bodies? Really?"

"Feds are denying it, but some dimwit detective got here first, so we know it's true. Too bad he got himself stabbed or it'd be our case," he told me with a cop's usual cynicism.

"Must be a big deal to bring out the Feds. Especially in the rain. Feds melt in the rain."

"Don't I know it. You shoulda heard the hissy fits they was throwin' about the detective that got himself stabbed. They were pissed he ever got on the boat in the first place. Way I heard it, guy was tryin' to arrest a local who was lootin' the boat. She didn't appreciate it and stabbed him. Shoulda let her drown, you ask me," he told me, just making conversation.

"He rescued a woman?" I asked, beginning to see the outlines of what the 'official story' might become.

"Ask me, we should charge her with piracy. Bet we could make that stick. Probably the only time we could."

"Thinking like that is what'll get you your gold shield, officer. Who's in charge from our side?" I asked, looking around at the sodden and miserable cops and volunteers moving over piles of broken two-by-fours and siding that had once been homes.

"Kill – I heard you almost added an 'ed' to your name," I heard from behind me, before the patrolman could answer. I turned to find Lieutenant Demetrius stepping over the detritus of the storm. He looked miserable, wet and unshaven. "Get it? 'E-D', like in past tense?"

"I got it – and it's no thanks to you, Demetrius," I said, hoping that I didn't look as bad as he did. Up all night with no sleep and no shower had aged him about five years.

"Wait, this is on me? All I did was ask you to come for a look-see. No one asked you to go play hero. What happened out here, anyway?"

"They're not keeping *you* in the loop?" I asked, even more wary now.

"Feds ain't tellin' us shit. They claim Maritime is their jurisdiction."

"Maritime? It's in the middle of Purdy Place."

"I'm gonna argue with Feds that want to take a headache off my hands? You really get stabbed? I heard it was just a panic attack."

"You talked to Burke?"

"Of course. He said it was a scratch." Demetrius said. I glared at him, my chest still sore. "C'mon, Kill, don't be mad at me. It was chaos out here. Ten minutes after I called you, I got a call from the Chief of D's telling me that the yacht of some Russian billionaire had run aground. We were to secure the scene but not go on the boat. I tried to call you—"

"By then I was probably on board."

"Exactly. Why would I think you'd get on the damn thing? Go on a boat in a hurricane? *Fog* is too wet for you." I let it go. Time to change the subject.

"So, Burke responded as soon as he heard the name of the boat?"

"Yeah, guy's obsessive about this Russian billionaire and his drugs – but the Feds say there were no drugs. No bodies either." Demetrius looked over his shoulder toward the FBI guys, lowering his voice. He nodded to me and moved further away from the uniformed officer in the car.

"...And don't ask me nothin' else, cause I know nothin', Detective."

"Cut the crap, I won't quote you," I said, but nothing about this felt right. It reeked of a cover-up – but why?

"There was heroin on board," I prodded Demetrius.

"You're mistaken."

"And kids. Teen boys and girls."

"You had a rough night and were sedated. I'm sure it's all muddled, Killer," Demetrius said, as if quoting a script.

"All right, play it that way. What'd the Feds say about why they're here if there are no bodies and no drugs? National Security again?"

"They didn't even bother to make an excuse this time. They

said 'you don't see anything', so I don't see nothin.'"

"Why would the Feds cover up a boat full of drugs and kids?"

"Between you and me? The Russian billionaire it belongs to, Alik Markov? He's got a hired army that'll poison a reporter for daring to say his toupee is for shit, never mind ones that accuse him of being the drug-dealing piece-of-shit criminal that he is. It was before your time – mine too – but his brother Mikhail, a KGB guy, disappeared here back in the eighties. The KGB, still around back then, thought he defected. Put Alik Markov in Lubyanka prison for seven years just for being related to him. Since then the guy's been nuts – blaming the CIA, the FBI – even the NYPD for his brother Mikhail going missing. I hear the Deputy Director of the FBI got a personal call from Putin on Markov's behalf this morning, to make sure the guy's son was on the first plane back to the motherland. Guess he's afraid they'll put him back in jail if his son pulls a disappearing act too."

"So, you found the son?"

"No. Still missing. They were sending a message that they don't want him held or questioned. Anyway, Markov's kid, Josef, he's got a record of his own and is accused of some pretty nasty shit."

"Like?"

"A teenage girl was found in his hotel room last year, raped and beaten. By the time SVU showed up Josef Markov was on a plane to Moscow. Case died on the vine and the DA was told to bury it. Markov Junior's passport was flagged and he was asked not to come back, but he doesn't seem to care. He just pulls up in his yacht and doesn't deal with customs."

"I can see why you're staying out of it," I said, trying to wrap my head around all the moving pieces. If the son, Josef, was free in a country where he was wanted for a brutal rape, wandering the streets in the middle of a natural disaster after losing his daddy's precious cargo, he'd be desperate and dangerous.

"Probably better for everybody if Markov Junior washed up somewhere along Holten or Purdy," Demetrius muttered, looking at the chaos around us.

"The Feds really think they can cover this up? That they can send the son back if we find him? There are still witnesses. There's a dozen dead and molested kids on that thing."

"If the ones on that boat are dead, putting a guy on trial and making an international incident out of it isn't gonna happen. Let it go, Kill," Demetrius advised, glancing away as one of the blue raincoats approached. It was a Special Agent, and he tried to stare me down as he got closer. He made it to within ten feet of me before he looked away.

Jackass. Never try to eye fuck an Irish cop or a rabid dog. Neither has the good sense to back down.

"What if I don't let it go?" I asked Demetrius, purposefully letting the Fed hear me.

"Detective. You're Collins, right?" the Fed interrupted, taking the bait.

"Last I checked. Who are you?"

"Special Agent in Charge. I wanted to—"

"Special Agent in Charge who? Is this like a knock-knock joke?" I asked, cutting off that bullshit. That's one of my rules. If you can't tell me your name, you're automatically full of shit.

"Stevenson," he answered reluctantly. "I wanted to thank you for your help. I understand you tried to assist last night but were unable to get on board, so you reported the boat stranded. Too bad a looter attacked you."

"I *was* on board last night. She *wasn't* a looter," I clarified. Stevenson forced a grin, speaking more slowly, as if he thought I really didn't get it.

"I don't think you understand. You never made it onto the *Chistota*. You don't want to be a witness to this."

"Why not?"

"Witnesses to Russian mob business have statistically shorter lives. You never made it onto the ship."

"That's the official story?" I asked, wondering if Special Agent in Charge Stevenson realized I had ODD and that because he told me I *couldn't* investigate he only insured that I now *had* to investigate this whole sham.

"Already filed. I read your preliminary report."

"The one I haven't made yet?"

"Yeah. That one. By the time we got here locals had looted the ship. According to your report, it must have been one of them that you ran into…"

"She wasn't a looter. Neither were the two girls who came off that ship. I saw them. Two girls, half-naked, scared to death—"

"Sounds like most of the girls from this neighborhood," Stevenson said with a smirk. I should've hit him then, defending my hometown, but I'd been working on being a grown-up and using my words instead. I didn't want to ruin my 'haven't-hit-a-fucking-moron-in-a-month' streak.

"They barely spoke English."

"Again, sounds like the locals. What do you call them now? Is it still guidettes? Cugettes? Glitta-chicks?"

I said nothing, but took half a step forward, ready to break my streak. Demetrius stopped me with a firm hand on my shoulder. It was probably for the best. Getting stabbed and arrested within twenty-four hours might've been a black mark on my permanent record.

"Are any of your people out looking for these 'looters'?" I finally asked, setting him up.

"What looters?"

"That's what I thought. What about the missing heroin?"

"What heroin?"

"Got it. So, if I find either one, I get to take credit for breaking the case?"

"I don't know what you're talking about."

"Glad we have an understanding," I told him, and turned away, starting back toward my car. I hadn't gotten three steps when one of the young muscle-bound volunteers called out from a pile of shingles that had once been the roof of The Annex.

"Lieutenant! We got something here—"

Demetrius heard the tension in the guy's voice, the same way that I did. We both knew what he'd found even before we saw what it was and raced to the top of the debris pile to confirm it.

I saw the pale patch of flesh that poked out from beneath a dresser, puckered and bloated from the salt water as I reached the top. Then the dark hair came into focus and I could see the distended and hirsute stomach of the Fat Man I'd met last night. A heavy gelatinous leg was draped over his stomach – a leg that was not his own and still wore the heels she'd been wearing when I saw her last. Medusa.

I strode toward the Fat Man before Stevenson could stop me and knelt down, looking behind the dead man's ear. The hole that was there was dried and crusty and so dark red that it looked black. I was sure Medusa had a matching one. This shooter was a professional. I'm sure if he were still with us, the Fat Man would have appreciated his killer's work.

"Son of a bitch..." I muttered. "They're getting rid of the witnesses."

"What are you talking about?" Asked Stevenson, just catching up.

"The Fat Man and Medusa here. They made the second call. The one that brought me here. They saw something they shouldn't have."

"Maybe they drowned," Stevenson shrugged, still not getting it.

"Flip him and show the boy genius, would you?" I asked an officer who had already started to lift the dresser off the bodies.

He nodded unhappily, but squatted down and pushed the fat man over onto his side to reveal the hole just behind his left ear.

It was precisely placed, the kind of hole a twenty-two caliber leaves. At close range, a twenty-two breaks through the skull but isn't powerful enough to come back out. It just bounces around inside, tearing up brain matter, making it a perfect executioner's weapon.

"…You think Markov did this?" asked Demetrius, putting it all together.

"Could be. It's professional. Clean shots." I told him, turning to look at Stevenson, who had gone pale and looked confused. "I'm going to ask you once, Stevenson, and I want no bullshit. Lives depend on your answer, got me?"

"Screw you," he said, trying to recover his composure. I asked anyway, knowing his face would give me his answer.

"Was Markov, the owner, alerted to what you found on that yacht? Did you tell him how many bodies were on board?"

"It's his yacht," Stevenson answered, trying to avoid the question but answering it anyway.

"You fucking moron. You told him there were witnesses still alive."

"How do you figure?"

"If he can count how many dead bodies there are, he's already got people looking for the survivors." I told the idiot as I turned to Demetrius. "What's the nearest storm shelter?"

"Tottenville High School, why?"

"Because I didn't come out in the rain and save two girls

only to have this numbnuts get them killed."

"Why do you suddenly care so much?" Demetrius asked.

I didn't have any good answer. Dariya had stabbed me. Her sister left me bleeding in the street, and it was still raining. I had no reason to care. I could be home and warm...

But I did care. And I was curious – I'd been called to this boat for a reason and I wanted to know what it was. Or maybe I cared because I understood what it was like to be wandering and alone in the rain, and that after what they went through, those girls' dreams would wake them up to the sound of their own screams for the rest of their lives.

If they lived long enough to dream.

"Kill, stay away from this one. The Feds have ordered us off and I'm ordering you off. You're on sick leave, as of right now," Demetrius told me as I started back toward my car.

"Got it. Call it PTSD – that way anything I do can be connected to my mental health later. Thanks, for the excuse," I told him and turned away just as he flipped me off.

"I warned you," he added, knowing that I would ignore him. It was just my personality. Couldn't be helped. Maybe that's why I felt a connection with those girls, especially the one that stabbed me. I liked the way she dug in and fought against it all, saying screw the world with every fiber of her being...

...Or maybe the connection went further. The reflection in the stainless-steel refrigerator and of the man behind the wires – the one who'd somehow stepped out of my night terrors and into the storm – came back to me, as did the familiar hazel eyes of Rigan. They made me wonder what connections my brain was making that my memory was keeping from me. I was called here last night. Requested. Fuck me… maybe Burke was right, maybe there are no coincidences. It didn't matter. There were questions that needed answers and those answers might help find two girls who were lost in a storm, half-naked and wandering around in a foreign country. Statistics said if I didn't find them in the next twenty-four hours they'd be dead or sold off into the sex trade.

Have I mentioned that I hate fucking statistics almost as much as the rain?

CHAPTER EIGHT

I followed Hylan Boulevard past Wolfe's Pond Park, headed for Tottenville High School. I was in the middle of a six-lane boulevard without a building in sight, looking at downed trees and storm damage as steroid junkies and their usually well-coiffed counterparts cleaned up the mess, looking like the *Walking Dead* version of themselves. They were dirty, unshowered, with day-old make up streaking their faces and day-old hair product congealed in their hair. Still, they attacked the detritus of the storm with manicured-but-damaged nails and bulging biceps streaked with dirt. Only in Stankin' Island. It was clear that the balance of base brutality and civilization hadn't really been changed by Sandy – the storm had just washed away the trappings and camouflage to show that the essence of both would remain no matter what.

I had once left Staten Island to go to college, but even there the island never left me, since everyone could hear the forgotten borough in my accent and attitude. I didn't mind that most people dumped on the island – everyone did. The granite that made up Todt Hill was a barrier between the East and Hudson rivers and the ocean, so we caught all the garbage and debris flowing out. So I guess it was no coincidence that the island was also once home to the world's largest garbage dump, collecting trash from points all over the city. But it all just made the island stronger. As my grandfather used to say, excrement and adversity make the best fertilizer.

I think that was part of the reason I hated Agent Stevenson. He had no right to talk shit about Staten Islanders. Its people were like weeds: impossible to get rid of, resilient, and adaptable and when you tried to kill them, they just came back stronger. In spite of its notoriously blue-collar reputation, Staten Island's produced world class lawyers, brain surgeons, NASA scientists, film producers, musicians with platinum records – and of course people who ended up on death row or as porn stars, but that's my point. Screw Stevenson.

I made the left onto Luten Avenue, seeing the chaos outside Tottenville High School almost as soon as I did. Thankfully the school was not actually in Tottenville, which had been hit hard by the storm, but was in Huguenot – obeying a logic that only a native Staten Islander could explain.

I abandoned my car halfway up Luten and walked up to the gate in the fence that was closest to the gyms, snaking past volunteers bringing in pizzas from Goodfella's for the newly displaced and homeless that were now living in the school.

We were all tracking in water and mud, but the mess wasn't the real issue. The real issue was the palpable anger that the people were venting at the Federal government and the Red Cross, imagining them to be these all-powerful organizations that failed to swoop in and save them. I'm not sure they realized that both were groups whose primary function was to write checks to empower local organizations, and that they were only as good as the locals they supported.

The second big problem also emanated from the people. They smelled.

It wasn't their fault, but the humidity and the humanity packed into the gym combined to create an odor that should've been arrested and charged with assault. The Axe Body Spray, Aussie hair products and other scents used to hide their natural fragrance were apparently left behind in flooded houses. I needed to get what I came for and get out quickly, so I looked for somebody with a clipboard who was yelling about something besides FEMA or the Red Cross. I found him in the middle of the hardwood in a wife-beater t-shirt and veins popping – a side effect of steroid addiction.

"One slice apiece until I say so, you mooks." He told his audience, who pushed toward folding tables that were stacked with fresh pizza.

"Anthony," I called out. He turned, along with about fifteen other guys. I had gotten lucky, but I'd taken the odds. The name 'Anthony' had about five to one odds of being right in this neighborhood, followed in some order by Jimmy, Vito,

Sal, Frank, Nicholas, Michael, John, Victor, and Carmine. The derivatives of Tony, Ant, Tone, Nick, Nicky, Mikey, John-John, Vic, Sally-boy and the rest made it easy since all of them answered to their full name in case it was somebody's father calling them.

"Who's askin'?" This particular Anthony asked, one foot planted, ready for fight or flight.

"Detective Collins," I told him, flashing my shield. I saw him relax once he knew I wasn't out to kill him or settle a score, but his eyes narrowed as I got closer and he had to make an attempt to use the one atrophied muscle between his ears. You could almost see it flexing at the temples.

"Wait. You're Kill Collins, right? I heard a you. You used to go here."

"So did most of the people here right now," I said, nodding to the people in the gym. A decent majority of Staten Islanders never leave the neighborhoods they grew up in and a lot of the faces in here looked familiar – or at least bore a family resemblance to people that I knew.

"I think you was my brother's year – Vic DiBenedetto," he said. This was kind of a Staten Island 'bona fides' test. We'd ask each other who we knew until we could find out our degree of separation. The closer we were to the same people, the greater level of trust there would be, even if we were on opposite sides of the law. Fortunately, I knew Anthony's brother Vic, although he was one of the biggest pricks you'd ever want to meet.

"Yeah. I knew Vic. Changed the game 'kill the man with the

ball' to 'Kill Collins'. Thought he was a comedian."

"Yeah. That's him," Anthony said with a smile, proud of his asshole brother.

"Hope he said nice things about me."

"He said you always fought dirty."

"I guess that's nice, coming from the guy who was on top of the pile on. Where is he now? Elmira Correctional?"

"You're a funny guy," Anthony snapped, his face clouding over. "He's on parole with one a them ankle bracelets. Can't even go to Jersey to the strip clubs, and my cousins Dom and Vin are upstate 'cause a you people."

"My apologies. Sorry you're related to guys stupid enough to get caught."

Luckily, Anthony laughed. Most guys appreciate the truth when it's delivered without spite or judgment. Anthony was definitely brighter than his brother.

"You got a point. Morons, all of 'em. But I'm tryin' to get these people fed. Fuckin' government ain't doin' it, so what the fuck you want with me?"

"I'm looking for a couple of girls."

"Who isn't? But I ain't in that line a work," he said, turning back to the pizza dismissively. "Talk to my cousin Jo-Jo. The one in Stapleton, not the one in New Dorp." Damn. Jo-Jo. I'd forgotten Joseph, Joey, Joe, Jo-Jo, Seph and the rest of the Joe nicknames. The anesthesia must have still been in my system.

"Not that kind of girl. I'm looking for two *lost* girls. Maybe Russian or Ukrainian or something. Redheads."

"Redheads is a specialty market. You might want to go to Jersey. There's a guy out there, Mickey, Mikey, Nicky – Mack. Somethin'. He's got them porcelain-skinned types. You want a slice? Best pizza on the island," he volunteered, slapping a slice in my hand before I could refuse.

"You're not listening. I'm not looking for a 'happy ending'. I'm looking for two girls that came off a boat that washed up in the storm." Anthony suddenly turned back, a gleam of interest in his eye. He knew something.

"Is this that the Federal case?"

"What Federal case?" I asked, not wanting to ask leading questions.

"The one that generic looking guy from Ohio came in talking about. He said there was body bags everywhere, dead strippers – and that them two girls knew somethin'. He had real a bug up his ass about 'em. Never mentioned that they were redheads though."

"Did you tell him anything?"

"Fuck no. I lie to Feds on principle."

"You see ID?"

"Didn't need to. He was in a bad suit, a cut-by-numbers haircut and thought his shit didn't stink. His face might as well been branded F-B-I – fuckin' big idiot. Moron – like anyone here'd help a Fed find witnesses without findin' out who they was witnesses against? You could get yourself in a jam that way," he told me, although we both already knew that. This was the part where I needed to ask questions carefully, since Anthony already told me he intended on lying if it didn't suit his interest.

"If I told you I thought those girls were in trouble, would you lie to me too?"

"Not on principle. Depends on why you want 'em and who they're in trouble with. What'd they do?"

"Stabbed me. But I don't hold it against 'em," I answered honestly. Anthony was trying to hold back laughter, assuming the worst as he projected his own degrading imagination on me.

"You dog... Two of 'em and you got 'em so hot they stabbed you?"

"It wasn't like that. They were locked up in the engine room of a yacht with a bunch of other kids who were all probably fifteen or under. They're the only two that survived. Four Russians were upstairs – all dead. The younger sister took 'em out."

"Damn... I knew it. She looked bad-ass," Anthony blurted out, and then grinned as he saw my reaction, knowing he'd screwed up. "All right, Kill – they was here. But not for long. The young one, like you said, she looked scary, but the older one was sorta hot. Not that I'd be inappropriate with her or nothin'. It's just a fact. They took some food. Loaded up and split."

"They were fifteen at best, Anthony," I warned him, just in case he was hiding them and had any illicit intentions.

"Yeah, right. Fifteen is the new twenty-five. Grass on the infield and 180 games a year with half these girls. Look at 'em, even in here. They want to score as much as the guys – not that the Lolitas are my thing."

"They're in trouble, with nowhere to go."

"There's a lot of that goin' around."

"I only want to help them. I don't want to find them with Jo-Jo from Stapleton."

"Jo-Jo's not really a bad guy, you know. He doesn't do that white slave shit. He's got a volunteer army. Figures a girl wants to make a living, she can fuck a donkey for all he cares as long as she cuts him in as her promoter. Still, he'd sure as shit never sell her to nobody."

"So, if you hear anything about these two… You'll call?" I asked, knowing that I was pushing my luck.

"What do I get out of it?" He asked, looking around to make sure no one was listening too closely to him making a deal with a cop.

"Me owing you a favor."

"A *legal* favor?"

"That's the only kind I do." Anthony sighed as if I was wasting his time.

"Yeah. Shit. I heard that about you. That why they call you 'Righteous Kill.'"

"Nobody calls me 'Righteous Kill.'"

"Maybe not to your face." He grinned, enjoying himself. I turned to walk away. Now he *was* wasting my time. I needed fresh, or at least fresher, Staten Island air than the human smog wafting through the gym.

"Hey, Kill, wait up. Maybe I saw them girls talking to this one woman." I stopped and turned back to see if he was messing with me. Didn't look it. "She's from down by Wolfe's Pond. She's some kind of Voodoo Queen or Wiccan or Kabbalah priestess or somethin'. Wanders the woods, eats the wild berries. You know the type. All of 'em live down by Wolfe's Pond, Lemon Creek – in mutant territory. Some people livin' near them swamps is old school Staten Island. Creepers. Boo Radley lookin' guys that might be keepin' all kinds a ugly in their basements. Maybe even them girls."

"Boo Radley?" I asked, impressed by the reference.

"Hey, I *read*. Just 'cause I got this accent don't make me a fuckin' mental midget. No offense to the little people. But yeah, all sorts live out there. Creepy guys that got like limps, and hunchbacks and one-eyed wonders."

"You seen a one-eyed guy?" I asked, aware of the statistical unlikelihood that was a coincidence.

"Not personally, no. But you hear shit," he said, disappointing me. "Anyway, the Wiccan Woman, she was talkin' to them girls, next thing I knew they was gone."

"Describe the Voodoo Queen. The Wiccan."

"She's a fine piece, just scary. Sorta hot. Intimidating, like you'd never have a chance to fuck her – but she might fuck you."

"Got a cell I can borrow?" I asked, suddenly remembering that mine was under my back seat, where I'd left it before going into the emergency room.

"Where's yours?"

81

"Somewhere in the Atlantic Ocean," I lied. Anthony pulled out a cell phone, but didn't hand it over.

"This another favor?" he asked, negotiating. I was tired of the game.

"Sure. Here it is – I won't bust you for the 'roids in the trunk of your car," I told him, watching him go pale before he caught my bluff.

"You're guessing, right?"

"I was. But now I know. Get rid of the juice, before I have to do something about it." I put out my hand and he slapped the phone into it. I dialed quickly, hoping I could reach Kat. If anyone on this Island had an in with a Voodoo Queen, it would be her.

The phone just rang. Damn. I hoped my house hadn't gotten flooded. Anthony saw my look.

"Whoever she is she's probably fine. A lotta the phones ain't workin'," he reassured me. His accent certainly didn't make him stupid.

"What makes you think it's a she?"

"I dunno, what makes you get tense when it rings off the hook?" Anthony asked. His aptitude at reading me pissed me off. I handed his phone back and started to walk away again. Kat was probably just hung over on my beer with my stereo jacked up loud, hooked into *Call of Duty*.

"They really stab you?" Anthony called after me.

"Bounced off a rib."

"Still. I know guys that'd throw 'em a party."

"So do I."

I was almost to the gym doors when a familiar woman with a face that I couldn't quite place grabbed my arm. Maybe I went to school with her, maybe I arrested her. It was hard to tell the difference sometimes.

"Detective... Is it true they're using I.S. 24 as a morgue? Storing body bags in the basement? I heard there were bodies all up and down Yetman, Seguine, and Barclay."

"I wouldn't believe everything you hear," I said, gently pulling my arm away.

"Is it true The Annex is gone?" she asked, more desperately.

"Yeah. I saw that myself," I told her. Her eyes welled up with tears, and it occurred to me that they were the first tears I'd seen all day. I touched her shoulder gently and stepped outside, trying to give her the benefit of the doubt. A lot of memories had been made in The Annex, and a lot of the kids in that gym were probably conceived in the parking lot. Maybe there was good reason to shed a tear for the old bar...

Hell, I might have been more upset myself if I wasn't worried about the condition of my own house. Between Hurricane Sandy and Kat, I didn't know what to expect when I got there, so I got my phone out from under the back seat and kept trying her the whole way home. No luck. Hopefully when I got there I would find Kat hung-over, but sober enough to give me a line on this Witch of Wolfe's Pond so I could find Alina and Dariya before Josef Markov did...

There was a clock on it. All the bridges to and from the

island were still closed, but they could reopen any time. Once they did, Markov could get out. Until then, I still had a chance. The girls were on their own when they got to the High School, but two redheads with strange accents wouldn't get very far on Staten Island. They'd need help, and it sounded like this witch-woman of Wolfe's Pond had taken them in. I needed to track her down. Fast.

CHAPTER NINE

Nelson Avenue, Cleveland, and Hillside were all dark except for a few bonfires illuminating backyards. Branches littered the street and lifeless power lines stretched across standing water. The Island, always on the brink of being a dystopian mess, had lost all its pretenses. I was only going home for a moment, figuring that I could get a shower and dry clothes and see if Kat knew this 'Witch of Wolfe's Pond', I could get to her before Josef Markov. If anyone knew a Wiccan priestess, it'd be Kat.

I wasn't worried about getting a hot shower or having power either, since I had generators and gas. My oil heat I had was old school and didn't need electricity to function – but as I trudged up the sidewalk, I noticed that the front door wasn't latched.

I approached slowly, pushing it open slightly and saw what I expected: A puddle in front of the door, and smaller puddles leading away from it into my place. Kat had gone out to play in the rain. I could hear the shower running and felt the heat hit me like a wall, carried on a stiff breeze. She must have turned it all the way up and then opened a window to 'take the edge off and get some real air', which was a phrase I'd heard far too often. Goddamn Kat with her 'real air'. I followed the footsteps toward the bathroom, noticing that all my beers were gone, nacho crumbs were everywhere, and the television was turned cockeyed, almost pulled off the wall.

I stopped as I got far enough in to see the kitchen.

The refrigerator and freezer doors were open and everything that had been in the freezer was on the floor. I glanced back at the living room, noticing now that I'd gotten in this far that my couch cushions had been sliced open and there were holes in my sheetrock every few feet.

My hand went to my gun, and I stopped to listen.

I heard nothing except the shower and the wind.

I tried to put the pieces together – it wasn't looters – my television, computer and electronics were still here. It couldn't be Kat, she'd never make this mess without taking credit for it immediately. The place had been tossed. Someone was looking for something specific – but what?

I reached for my cell, about to dial nine-one-one, but couldn't get a connection. The landline on the counter was also dead, so I took my gun out, moving quietly on the creaky old hardwood. As I slid along the wall toward the bathroom, I tried to take a quick inventory, but couldn't find anything that was missing. I opened the closet where the gun safe was kept. It was open – but all my guns were there.

This wasn't making any sense.

I did another visual, looking for signs of a struggle. There was no blood, thankfully. Looking down, I saw that the water on the floor had started to bleach out the wood. It had been lying there for a few hours at least, so there was a chance that whoever tracked it in was already gone. I hoped. Shooting somebody and filling out all that paperwork was a chore that I didn't have the energy for at the moment.

I made a quick turn into the hallway, sighting down my pistol, but it was empty. The doors to the basement, bathroom, and bedroom were all closed. The first door was the bathroom. I touched the knob to see if it would turn. It did. I hesitated. If Kat was in there, I didn't want to walk in on her naked in the shower. Knocking wasn't an option, because if it *wasn't* Kat in there, I'd just be warning them. The lesser of two evils was violating Kat's privacy, so I took a deep breath, readied my pistol and shoved the door open –

—Only to be blinded by steam, being blown into the hall by the wind from the open bathroom window. The shower was empty and the linen closet was ajar, with every towel I owned dumped on the floor. I backed out, leaving the shower on in case anyone in the basement or bedroom was listening, then turned to the basement door, opening it quickly.

There were puddles on the stairs, and the light from the hall illuminated a mess below. Storage boxes had been ransacked and ripped off the shelves that would have kept them above the water that now covered the floor.

If I found the guy that did this, I was definitely going to shoot him. I was about to go down into the stagnant water in the dark when I heard her ear-piercing scream, shrill and harsh, setting my nerves on fire –

– Kat was in the bedroom.

– Shrieking as if a hot branding iron had been shoved right through her. I ran, not thinking, pacing it out so my right foot hit the closed-door mid-stride, splintering the frame, sending the door bouncing back off the wall. I started to scan the room for threats, but stopped as I saw her tied face down on the bed, yelling bloody murder. She saw me and yelled –

"—Next to you!" I turned, catching sight of a shotgun butt just before it met my temple. A bright sharp pain radiated out from where it hit, sending arcs of throbbing agony through my head as my neck snapped back. I slipped on the wet floor, collapsing as everything drifted efficiently to blackness.

…It always seems to happen when it rains. My world melts and becomes a steaming, slippery brown mass of pain and complications that sucks me under…

*

…I couldn't have been out for long, because I heard the front door slam just as I opened my eyes. The blood was painfully pulsing through my retinas, causing my vision to blur with each excruciating heartbeat. I wanted to move, but my body was in revolt, not quite receiving the messages my brain was sending.

"Are you going to just lie there?" Kat asked, with just the slightest hint of concern in her voice.

"Why don't you get up and help me?"

"I'm all tied up at the moment."

I tried to get to my feet but slipped again, and the stitches in my chest started to compete with my head for attention as they stretched with the effort.

"You hurt?" I asked Kat.

"Not hurt, just pissed off."

"If you're not hurt, what'd you scream for? I could've had the guy if you didn't scream." I told her, reaching under the mattress for the hunting knife I kept there in case of emergencies. Like I said, I'm paranoid. I reached for her wrists and started to slice the rope.

"I'm here tied up half-naked in your bed and you're worried about getting a guy? You sure you're straight?" She asked. I was sure. Kat was wearing one of my t-shirts and not much else. I was so straight I had to keep my eyes on the knife – and *only* the knife – to prevent any accidents. Kat also looked at the knife and then at me, as if I'd betrayed her.

"Was that under the mattress the whole time?"

"It's for emergencies."

"Might've helped if I knew that."

"I couldn't tell you. One of these nights you might have been the emergency. Just tell me what happened."

"I was on COD mowing down some noobs with the headphones on when he grabbed me from behind. I managed to give him a glancing blow to the nuts before he tased me. I coulda kicked his ass if it wasn't for that thing."

"A Taser? Really?" I asked, shocked. "What kind of guy uses a Taser?"

"What kind of friend doesn't tell me about his emergency knife? If I knew it was there…"

"He might've shot you if you had a weapon. Besides, you and sharp objects are a dangerous combination. Did you see his face? Was it fucked up?"

"No. I don't know. He grabbed me and tased me. And it was dark, so don't give me shit. You didn't see his face either, did you?"

"Did he do… anything?"

"Yeah. Almost bored me to death asking questions about you."

"About me? Nothing else?"

"You mean did he 'have his way with me'? Do you see his blood anywhere?" The question was obviously hitting too close to something Kat was sensitive about.

"Then why'd you scream?"

"I was afraid he was going to kill *you*."

"Why would he kill me? Did he say something to you?"

"Yeah. He said he'd kill you if I screamed."

"Seriously? And *then* you screamed?"

"I figured he was gonna kill you anyway. Screaming was to even the odds. I knew he couldn't tase you 'cause he ended up using all his Taser cartridges on me," she explained, pulling up her shirt to show me the characteristic burn marks. "I wasn't exactly cooperative."

I was not surprised. I looked away quickly, trying to avoid the free show Kat was giving as I finally cut through the last rope.

"Where the fuck have you been anyway? Leaving me here all alone."

I didn't answer, but her eyes went wide as I straightened up, focusing on my chest where I'd torn my stitches and somehow lost the bandage.

"Oh, God – you're bleeding. Are you shot?" she asked, moving too close for comfort. I pulled open my shirt and looked down at the wound, seeing it for the first time without a bandage. Burke was right. It really didn't look like much of anything, even if it did hurt like a bitch at the moment.

"No, not shot. Stabbed."

"He stabbed you? But he had a gun."

"Not him. The girl. From the boat."

"What girl?" Kat asked, a hint of anger in her tone. "You went out on a boat in this weather? Like on a date?"

"No, Kat. Maybe your dates end in stabbings, but if I get stabbed – it's not a date."

"I was just asking. Anyway, she's obviously not gettin' a second date after acting like that."

I turned and left, headed toward the kitchen, not engaging Kat's insanity and she followed me down the hall, looking around my place as I walked through.

There was a half-full, warm and skunky beer on the counter, the last visible alcohol in the house. I needed it. Medicinally. I took a swig, ignoring Kat as I tried to wrap my mind around what the hell was going on.

"There was just one guy?"

"That's all I heard. The lights were out and the storm was loud, but that would be my bet."

"What was he looking for?" I asked, taking in the mess. Everything seemed to be here. In the wrong place, but not missing.

"Do I look like a fucking detective, Detective? I woke up hog-tied, face down in your bed. It was like all of my dreams but without the happy ending. The old bastard was tearing the house up, asking me about where you kept stuff."

"Old bastard? What makes you say he's old?" I asked, trying to swallow the fetid beer.

"He smelled old. Sounded old. How the fuck do I know? He was old. Didn't say much, and when he did, he muttered. Like he didn't want me to be able to ID him by his voice either. He was a pro. Maybe even ex-military." I didn't doubt Kat. She was hyper-observant in the way many survivors of abuse and terrible childhoods are, but I was curious about the old guy. Josef Markov was young. One-eyed Willie was old – if he was even real and not a figment of my fucked-up imagination.

"How long ago did he get here?"

"Jerkoff, I've been tied up, blindfolded and hung over – and you think I've been watching the clock?" She had a point.

"That's it? There's nothing else you remember?"

"Yeah. He took your decoder ring. Asked where you got it."

"My *memento mori*?" I asked, confused. A coincidence linked to my dreams and the past – but what did it have to do with me, Russian oligarchs, kidnapped kids and drug smuggling?

"*Memento mori?* Is that what you call it? That's grim."

"You know what it means?" I asked, surprised.

"Now you're insulting my intelligence? Four years of Latin, Classics Institute, Tottenville High School. Not to mention a Masters in Classical Literature from—"

"—You have a *Masters?*" I asked, astounded.

"G.I. Bill. And technically I'm four credits short. The Dean and I had a disagreement over what constituted obscenity so I showed him my performance art. After his wife walked in on us, I was asked to take a break. The idiot –"

"—All right, forget it. My apologies. Back to my... 'decoder ring'," I told her, afraid we'd go off on an hour-long tangent. We had that tendency. I needed to know why I had been called personally to the scene. It felt like a set-up, but a set-up for what? To get me out of the house so whoever was behind this could steal some trinket I found in the woods?

"He said the ring was stolen. That it belonged to an 'old friend' and that he'd get something out of returning it, but you'd have a lot to answer for. Like where you got it." So maybe that was why I was involved. Whoever took the ring thought I had a memory that would tell them shit even I didn't know...

"…Then he said to tell you he wanted to know where you put everything else," Kat added.

"'Everything else'? Like what?"

"How the fuck do I know? He just said, 'Tell the Killer I want the rest.'"

"And then what?"

"Then I bit his hand and he tased me again. Next thing I know, you're coming back in the door insulting me, my intelligence, and my observation skills. You know, if you gave me the gun when you left, none of this ever would've happened."

I ignored the comment, dumped the rest of the beer in the sink and headed toward the closet for clean, dry clothes. Kat was right, not that I'd ever tell her that. If I had trusted her, she might have had a chance with the guy. Instead, somebody made it personal and fucked up my house and my… friend.

"Should we call the cops?" Kat asked, following me.

"I am the cops."

"Maybe you should call Charlie Pederson or Tony Guinta," Kate suggested.

"Not happening. Every cop in the city is working on Hurricane Sandy right now. I'll deal with it," I told her, pulling out a change of clothes.

"Not without me. I get tied up in a guy's bed after he gets me drunk, I get breakfast. At the very least."

"Kat, not now—"

"No. Bullshit. You're not leaving me here alone. This place aggravates my PTSD. I'll freak the fuck out." Kat stepped in front of me, blocking my path to the door.

"Your PTSD? You're admitting to it now?"

"Don't be stupid. You know I admit to it when it suits my needs. That's a symptom of my issues. I'm self-serving. I'm also serious."

"I don't have time to baby-sit," I told her, rushing to get out the door before she made me feel worse. Kat timed it perfectly, waiting until I'd opened the door and had to face the rain alone. In that vulnerable moment, I hesitated, and she whispered behind me –

"Take me with you or I don't tell you the rest…"

"I'm not falling for this shit," I warned her, but I couldn't call her bluff. If she knew more, I needed to know what it was.

"He spent a lot of time in the basement looking for something."

She was telling the truth. As soon as she said it, I knew that it was true. It was the only thing that explained the mess downstairs. I'd seen a few of the photos that had been downstairs in boxes on the floor of the bedroom. I'd missed it because I was worried about Kat, and maybe because the photos didn't mean much to me. They weren't even mine. When I bought this house from my parents they'd left some of their stuff here in storage, since their new place didn't have room for all the crap they'd collected over the years.

"He sat on the edge of your bed with a flashlight, going through them," she went on, sure now that she had my attention. "…He was reading one, really interested, when your car pulled up."

"And?"

"He went to shove it in his pocket when we heard the front door open, but it dropped. He never had the chance to pick it up. If you knew what was in that clipping that was so interesting…"? Kat's voice trailed off, seeing the look on my face.

I moved back to the bedroom, scanning the floor – finding a yellowed newspaper clipping half-hidden under the bed. There was an old ad for 'Korvettes' on one side, a store that had closed in the early eighties.

I flipped it over and read the headline: '*Small Plane Crash Near Sandy Ground, Two Dead*'. It was a clipping from the Staten Island Advance, dated October 20th, 1985 – three days before the car accident that killed my memory. Three days before I found the ring that was just stolen. I read:

A fifteen passenger Beechcraft 99 Airliner operated by La Pureza, a Dominican company, crashed in a heavily wooded section of Sandy Ground late last night. Residents of Rossville reported that the small plane was flying extremely low in the fog and heavy winds that preceded last night's thunderstorms. According to NYPD Detective James Collins, the first responder on the scene, the Beechcraft had taken off from Santo Domingo, bound for Teterboro. Whether it went off course in the storm or was intentionally off course has yet to be determined. Detective Collins had no comment when asked if the plane could possibly be involved in the drug trade, which has been an increasing problem in recent years. The investigation is ongoing.

The article went on with suppositions and descriptions of the weather without adding any real facts, but there was enough in what I'd read for me to start asking questions. Why was the task force investigating a plane crash, and why were detectives with the Narcotics Task Force the first ones on the scene? I unfolded the last bit of the article, but there wasn't anything more other than a grainy black and white photo of a cargo plane, a twin-engine turboprop that looked familiar. It looked like something out of *Goldfinger* or *You Only Live Twice*.

"Is that a real clipping? From a real paper?" Kat asked, trying to read over my shoulder.

"No. Just the Staten Island Advance. From 1985."

"Who keeps a piece of paper that long? Why save it when you could just look it up on the Internet?"

"My dad's a guy who never trusted technology and was used to filing away evidence in storage boxes." He'd kept it for some reason, but why? Would he even remember if I asked him? I knew now that it was connected, all of it, from my ring to the Russian yacht, the plane crash – maybe even One-eyed Willie – everything. But how?

I had a lot of facts and a lot of information – but there were too many missing pieces. I knew that Burke was right and that there were no coincidences, only patterns and evidence and pieces that fit a bigger puzzle. I just need to see the big picture. Remembering the piece of the puzzle I'd originally come here to fill in, I turned back to Kat.

"You know some crazy lady from down by The Pond? Some

Wiccan, or Voodoo priestess or something?"

"Why would I?"

"You're into all that 'alternative lifestyle' stuff. You talk to dead people and told me you were into woo-woo shit like that, a cult or something."

"I said I was a *hedonist*. That's not a cult – that means I like pleasure," she said, defensively. So much for Kat's help.

"Damn. I was hoping you'd be useful."

"Thanks, now I'm useless?"

"I didn't mean it that way," I apologized, hoping to avoid a Kat-fit. "I'm just frustrated. All I've got right now is bad dreams, a twenty-five-year-old plane crash, and some guy that wrecked my house chasing two teen girls that were kidnapped and brought here along with millions of dollars' worth of pure heroin on a Russian billionaire's yacht."

"Sounds like a lot to go on. What's the issue?"

"The issue is that it all leads to the same place," I told her, frustrated.

"Right… To your father. And you don't want to go there," Kat said flatly. It wasn't a question. She knew me too well.

"You don't know what he's like…"

"Don't need to. Apparently, we both have 'daddy issues,'" she said with a smile, grabbing one of my jackets out of the closet.

"I love my father."

"I know. That's your issue," she said, stripping off her shirt to change. I turned my back – not that she cared. "…But are you really going to let some asshole catch up to those two girls just because you don't want to deal with your dad? Seriously?"

"He's got problems."

"Like you don't?"

"He lives in Tottenville. The streets are blocked. Cordoned off. I heard no one's allowed in or out."

"You have a badge."

"I'm injured. And the streets are dangerous."

"I've driven Humvees through Third World nations while avoiding sniper fire and IED's. I'll drive," she said, walking past me wearing one of my shirts, my jacket, and the same pair of yoga pants she was wearing when I left. "I need to go with you anyway. I'm not staying here alone again without a gun."

"No."

"Your choice – the gun or the keys."

"I said no, Kat." I wasn't going to let her pressure me, but she held out her hand, waiting for the keys.

"Really? Tell me, Killer, what's the statistical average young girls survive running away from the Russian Mafia? Twenty-four hours? Thirty-six? Tick-tock…"

I glared at her. She was right, I knew that, but I wasn't going to cave.

*

Ten minutes later, at the eighteen-hour mark, we were past the barricades set up at Page Avenue. They stopped all traffic to the Outerbridge and to Tottenville. The ghouls had already started to head down to see the destruction, and the NYPD didn't want to give free reign to looters.

Kat was also driving. We'd compromised. I let her drive, but she would have to wait in the car at my parent's place. A flash of my badge had gotten us past the checkpoint, and the uniform there reassured me that the bridges were still closed. That meant the girls couldn't get off the island, but neither could Josef Markov – for now. I still had time to find them all.

"See how easy that was?" Kat asked, smugly.

"I don't like rain, or water, or Tottenville, that's all."

"...Or bridges, or tunnels or anything that goes over or under water. In fact, you don't like anything that connects you to anything else. Like new experiences, or new people, or a simple kind word or touch," Kat lectured, reaching across the front seat to touch me. I pulled away and she jerked the wheel, almost sending us into a downed telephone pole.

"Stop."

"See? You can't even let people touch you. What caused *your* PTSD?"

"I'm fine. I connect."

"Yeah, over the Internet. By playing *Call of Duty* with a Dragunov sniper rifle and about three ounces of lead. It's not the same... Somebody really fucked you up when you were a kid, didn't they?"

"Maybe. I don't remember."

"Don't, can't, or won't? They're not the same." Kat said, and then sat in silence for a moment. "Must be nice," she finally muttered.

"What must be nice?"

"Not remembering. Wish I had your gift."

I left it at that. I have enough problems without arguing with Kat over the benefits of remembering or forgetting. I had enough issues to face today.

Like my parents.

CHAPTER TEN

We drove past Yetman Avenue and saw a half dozen houses that had been flattened, saw neighbors lifting roofing and siding and walls off of piles of building material that had once been homes, drove on as they lifted limp corpses from under water-soaked mattresses.

There wasn't much else we could do.

Whoever could be saved had been, except for Dariya and Alina. They still had hope at least. A few blocks on, inland, we turned up the street my parents had lived on since they sold me the house I grew up in. We found my mother sitting in a beach chair at the end of her driveway, as far away as she could get from her new pre-fabricated, Americans-with-Disabilities-Act-approved, two-bedroom bungalow and still be on her own property. A sun umbrella kept the rain off and a private cloud of cigarette smoke shrouded tightly around her. The Marlboro Menthol she sucked on glowed red in the dim light, and as she saw my car pull up, she quickly put it out under her foot. Five other butts were already there, but she waved away the smoke as if that was the only thing giving her away. The cigarette was her major concern as we parked. Not the tree on the house across the street, cutting in virtually in half, nor the smoking ash of the destroyed front porch three doors down, incinerated when a power line fell. Yes, my mother's priority was not getting caught smoking in the middle of a natural disaster.

Kat looked at my mom trying to disperse the smoke and then stared at me for a moment. "Crap, you came from that? I don't see it."

"I haven't smoked and pretended not to for over forty years. I also don't keep gin in the toilet tank. Keeps me young and pretty," I told her, taking a good hard look at my mother, Theresa Collins. Her skin was as soft as worn leather, and too tan for Irish skin due to years of abuse. The stress of Joe Corrigan dying and having her only son not remember who she was afterward drove her innate predisposition for grim pessimism over the edge.

"Sure you don't want me to come with you?"

"Positive. I'll get enough shit on my own."

I got out. By the time I was halfway across the street, Mom started laying down the ground rules for my visit.

"I don't want to hear a word out of you, understand? I'm not smoking in the house and I've got to deal with him twenty-four hours a day – with no help from you. I don't need your judgment."

"Did you hear me say anything?"

"You're thinking too loud. I can see it in your face. Might as well be screamin' at me." Her voice was slurred, like she'd been drinking already. "His nurse is in Stapleton. Says she can't come out because the storm was too bad and they won't let nobody in or out. Typical of her kind. And yet here *you* are. The boy who melts in the rain."

"Glad to see you too, Ma. And the police do have Tottenville shut down. I had to use my badge to get past the barricades, so I'd take it easy on Rosie if you don't want her to quit," I told her, trying to talk her out of firing another home healthcare nurse. She was especially hard on them, being a former nurse herself and one of the most critical women I'd ever met.

"If you wanted to help, you'd be here more often and you'd shut your mouth with all your judgment," Mom mumbled, then nodded over my shoulder toward my car.

"You gonna innerduce us?" she asked, slurring even more.

"You've met before. That's Katherine, my tenant."

"Kat," Kat corrected from six inches behind me, daring to smile at my mother, offering her hand.

"Right. I guess I didn't recognize you without the metal in your face."

"Nose ring," Kat kept smiling and shook my mother's hand. It was well played, making her feel guilty for being rude.

"Right. So, are you two finally a thing?" Mom asked, changing the subject.

"No," we both answered at the same time.

"Why not? Should I be worried about you? You're a good lookin' kid. Maybe too good lookin.'"

"Is he here?" I asked, nodding toward the house.

"Mentally or physically?"

"Either. Both."

"Hard to tell. The Old-timer's gets worse in the rain. He's like you that way. Just sits in the sun room with the shades down."

"I need to talk to him."

"Good luck. You might just be talking *at* him." Without thinking, Mom reached for the pack of cigarettes. I should have known the condition my father was in from the way she was chain smoking in the rain. I didn't blame her – part of the reason I didn't come to visit was the tension created by his illness. I started for the house, wanting to get it over with. Kat followed me, and I didn't even try to talk her out of it.

"Take off your shoes when you go in, I just vacuumed," Mom called out after us, lighting another cigarette.

I did take off my shoes, if I didn't she'd remind me every time I saw her for the next six months. Kat followed suit, catching up to me about halfway down the hall to the sunroom.

"Is she always like that?"

"No. She used to be better, when my father was well enough to take care of her. She resents him now, almost as much as she resents me."

"Why you?"

"My mother thinks I don't appreciate what it cost to raise me, give me food and clothes and take care of my 'mental defects'. She also thinks that I should be here every day working off my debt to them. It's probably because I didn't remember who she was after the accident."

"Damn. Harsh. You get fucked in the head and your own mom holds it against you. I'm starting to see why you're so fucked up."

I stopped at the door to the sunroom. The dim light coming in through the drawn shades was refracted by the rain-soaked window, bathing the room in wraithlike shadows that danced across the floor in the gloom. My father, the former NYPD Detective James Collins, sat in his leather recliner with a Guinness. He stared out the only window that didn't have a drawn shade, watching the rain fall.

"Hey," I called out, a bit sharply. He didn't even blink. "Dad," I said, a bit louder. Nothing.

"Is he dead?" Kat asked, echoing my grim thoughts. As if in answer, he silently sipped his stout.

"We never should have come," I muttered, taking a step back to get out, but Kat was in the way, blocking the door.

"Stop bein' a wuss. Go ask him. I didn't drive out here for nothing." I tried to step around Kat, but she just shifted her weight, like she was ready to wrestle me into submission.

"Ask. Now."

"Why bother?" I whispered, as if he'd understand, even if he heard us. "He's got Alzheimer's. Half the time he thinks I'm his father, or his old partner."

"So? Just means his head's in the past. Your questions are

about the past, right?" Kat asked with a grim logic.

"You want me to fuck with his head?

"His head's already fucked. You're just playing inside the delusion. Hell, it could be less confusing for him. Kinder..."

"You're so full of shit."

"Ask," she said again, putting one hand on my chest, pressing me back into the room. I gave up. It was worth a shot. I turned and walked up slowly behind him... laid a hand gently on his shoulder.

"Hey."

He jumped, turning to look at me, his right hand coming up toward me. That's when I saw it – his old service revolver that was in his lap – and was now pointed at my face.

Christ, I thought, he better recognize me this time.

"Damn. Don't sneak up on me like that," my father said, his hand shaking as he lowered the pistol. What the fuck was Mom thinking, letting him have his gun?

Then it hit me.

She was giving him the decision. Literally putting it in his hands. In her mind it was probably a kindness, an opportunity to end his misery

"I called your name. You didn't hear me," I told him, keeping my hands where he could see them, reminding myself to swipe the gun at the first opportunity.

"You've got a soft voice. Always have. If you didn't you'd be in charge by now," he said quietly. I assumed he thought I was someone else, because I never had a soft voice and was nowhere close to ever being the guy in charge.

"You know me," I told him, trying to plant an idea in his head. His eyes narrowed and I could see the confusion in them.

"'Course I do," he lied. "What the fuck are you doin' here?"

"I came to talk to you about that plane crash," I tried.

"Dammit, Joe. Theresa's in the other room. I don't want to talk about this. You know how she feels about keeping them here this long," he answered. It had worked – he thought I was Uncle Joe. I glanced at Kat, hating that it was her idea. To her credit she was only slightly smug.

"Sure. We'll keep it quiet," I told him, playing along. "But we need to figure out what's going on. Tell me what you've got so far."

Dad sighed and nodded, but then noticed Kat behind me. His eyes narrowed with suspicion. "Who's the piece of ass?" I turned to Kat, who was suppressing a grin.

"Kat, you mind waiting outside?" Kat blew me a kiss and then walked out, smirking. My father watched her go, enjoying it until Kat was out of sight.

"A little young for you, but you could bounce quarters off that," he said with a gleam in his eye. It was always strange when my father treated me like one of his old buddies, especially when he got raunchy.

"She's just a friend."

"Yeah. Like the last three."

"She's gone now. We need to talk about the plane." I tried to redirect him. I felt badly, lying to him, but my father was the one that taught me to do anything to solve a case. A lie was just one tool in a detective's arsenal.

"No shit. Damn right we need to talk about that plane. It's been three days. Theresa's getting nervous about havin' them here," My father got up, with more nervous energy than he'd had in years. He went to the windows and pulled aside a shade, peering out into the backyard, as if looking for someone in the trees behind the house. The gun was still in his hand, his finger on the trigger. "Maybe you can take them for a couple of nights until we can find the guys who are looking for them."

"Take who?"

"Don't be a smart ass. You know who. That plane was full when it hit the ground and they think we took the cargo."

"What cargo?" I asked, but he was too wound up to answer directly.

"I'm tellin' you, Joe. We never should have taken it, even if they ended up getting it. Now all of it is missing and the guys who are going to come looking for already proved they'll kill anyone who messes with their business."

"If we know where it is, it's safe. Right?" I asked, just to keep him talking. The story was starting to become more clear every time he spoke. It revolved around the plane crash and whatever was on it, and somebody who needed to be saved. It was starting to sound damn familiar.

No coincidences. That's what Burke had said.

"*We* don't know shit. You hid it while I took them kids out of there," my father muttered. "Now they're looking for it and anyone who might know where it went – they're killing people to get their stuff back. They want them kids. They're going to figure out we took the kids in, and they're going to think we have the rest. …That's what Theresa is afraid of. Guys with guns showing up at our door."

"You think they'd come after cops?"

"I think guys willing to deal kids to the highest bidder are willing to do anything. We should've called the task force in…"

"You know why I didn't do that," I told him, trying to keep him talking.

"Yeah. Because someone on the fuckin' squad is dirty. Probably the same one that killed Tompkins and Germanario," he said, obviously agitated.

Damn. That came out of nowhere.

Tompkins and Germanario were two New York City cops found shot, execution style, on a pier in Brooklyn after a buy and bust apparently went bad. The general consensus was that they were good cops, and after Internal Affairs admitted Tompkins had called them to ask for a meeting hours before his death, suspicions ran rampant that it was an inside job – that they'd been killed by dirty cops. The case was still technically open, although no one pursued it after a group of Columbians who were in possession of the murder weapon were killed during a raid in East New York. Everyone seemed to agree that it was better public relations to blame the Columbians than to investigate the elite Narcotics Task Force.

"We gotta do something, Joe, but who can we trust?" my

father asked, clearly worried. "We either have to turn over what was on that plane and give up on finding the corrupt motherfucker who's behind this – or find out who on your squad is dirty – and damn quick. Otherwise they'll find us and those kids done like Tompkins and Germanario," he said, popping open the cylinder of the revolver to check his load.

It was full, and he was agitated. I couldn't play around with him like this much longer without setting him off, but it was now pretty damn clear that there were two crimes, decades apart, connected by a cache of stolen art and smuggled kids. But how did I fit in? And why was I called to the scene? Did someone know that my father worked the original case? And what else did my father know that he wasn't telling?

"Let's go back a bit. Maybe there's something we missed. How did we find the plane?" I asked my father.

"You. You brought me into it, Joe, you know that."

"I know. But maybe hearing it out loud will help me figure out if I missed anything."

"Fine… You told me you'd gotten a tip from your cousin in Ireland, Declan – the one on the Corrigan side. He told you how they were bringing the stuff in, doing some kind of triangle trade – cash for drugs, kids, and then guns to the IRA on the way back. Declan said the route out of Boston was compromised when Sean O'Callaghan turned informant and they intercepted the seven tons of weapons on the *Marita Ann*. To get the next shipment through they were going to try for a night landing at the old Miller Field, off load the payment and load up the guns... This is on you and your damn side investigations. I'm only in this because I did you a favor goin' out there."

"Okay, blame it on me. What should I have done differently?"

"Kept me out of it. You saw those kids. They know something – and the guys who took them know that they know. ...You still meeting with that informant tonight?" He asked.

I shrugged, unsure of what to say. What informant was Uncle Joe supposed to meet, and what night was he referring to?

"I guess," I finally answered. "What's today?"

"Thursday. The twenty-third. Why?" – The twenty-third. The night Uncle Joe died. Damn.

"Yeah. I guess I should meet the informant. We gotta know what's going on, right?"

My father nodded, as if that was the right decision. I wished I could figure out a way to ask him who the informant was or what the informant might know without giving away the fact that I wasn't really Joe, but he changed the subject before I could.

"Maybe you can take them kids out of here before that," he said, nodding toward the other room. "Theresa's hanging on by her last shred of sanity, chain smoking like a fiend and standing out in the rain so she don't need to be near them."

I had been trying to remember what kids he was talking about. Of course, I had no memory of any kids in my house before the accident, and my parents rarely spoke about that time except in the most general terms. I always thought they didn't talk about that time because the death of Joe was so difficult, but there was obviously a lot more to it.

"What about Killian?" I asked, hoping to clarify how I ended up in the car that night.

"Why do you think Theresa's so freaked out? They remind her of him. It's breaking her heart. They gotta go. We gotta keep them safe, then figure out who was behind this horror show."

"Of course. We'll get them."

"Damn right we will. You saw those kids. You saw what somebody did to them. All tied and bound, shoved in like old luggage, abused," he said, his voice trembling, eyes welling up. "...All them other kids dead. These ones'll be dead too if they find 'em."

My father turned away, wiping his eyes. I'd never seen him like this. As he looked out the window I saw him try to pull himself together, then look up at his reflection. I saw the confusion in his eyes as he saw his own face, decades older than he remembered being at the moment. He stared for a few moments, and then slowly turned around, suddenly coherent, in the present again.

"Killian... What are you doing here?"

"I came to visit. We were talking about Uncle Joe," I told him. He touched his eyes again, as if that made sense of the tears he'd found there.

"Joe? You sure? What'd I say?" he asked suspiciously, suddenly on guard.

"You started talking about a plane crash."

"The fuck I did," he snapped, angrily.

"You did. It was what you and Uncle Joe were working on before he died, wasn't it?"

"Before he died, right… I don't remember what you're talking about," he lied. He remembered twenty-five years ago better than he did twenty-five minutes ago.

"You're full of it."

"Now I'm full of it? You call me feeble-minded most days."

"Why won't you talk about Uncle Joe? Or anything that happened before the accident?" I asked, putting the pressure on. It didn't work. My father had the same sharp look he always used to have when he was interrogating me as a teen. He hesitated, but didn't break, the slightest hint of a smile revealing itself at the corner of his mouth.

"Accident, huh? That's what we were talking about?" He asked, and I got the impression that he relaxed, as if I'd missed something, and whatever secret he was keeping was still safe.

"I'm going to reopen that case."

"Don't mess with shit you don't understand, son. The last time you went messing around, the bastards broke my—" he stopped, cutting himself off.

"The last time I went messing around with what?" I asked, but he shrugged, looking away. "Go ahead, Dad. Finish."

"Finish what? Don't remember what I was going to say," he lied again.

"It was about the case Uncle Joe was working on when he died."

"Let the dead stay dead, Kill. That case needs to stay buried. Every time it comes up again, somebody gets hurt," he said, going back to his recliner and sitting with the gun in his lap. He seemed to notice it for the first time, but wasn't surprised that it was in his hand.

"I found two girls on a yacht. Seven other kids dead in the hold and one boy that drowned trying to get off. Heroin on board. I can't ignore that."

"Whose yacht?" He asked sharply, an edge in his tone.

"Alik Markov's. Why? Does it matter?"

He turned to look at me then, genuine fear in his eyes. "Jesus… Kill, promise me. Don't get involved. Not you. Hand it off. Get anyone else on it, just not you. It's dangerous," he said solemnly. It made no sense. I'd spoken with my father about dozens of cases. Dangerous cases, including murders and undercover organized crime cases. He was never scared for me before.

"Why? Is it Markov? Is that what's so special about this case? Why is it dangerous?"

"No, it's just… Because I said so. That's reason enough."

"What are you afraid I'll find?"

Dad shook his head, looking out the window as if he were about to slip away again. "It's raining, Kill. You can't find anything in the rain."

"Can't find what?"

"What you've been looking for. The same thing they want. You can't find it in the mud and the rain. It's gone, buried.

Better off forgotten. If you find it, they'll—" my father suddenly stopped, looking at the reflection in the window. His eyes glazed over and he looked back at me with that confused look he'd perfected over that last few years.

"Killian? Is that you?" he asked, feigning dementia.

I knew what he'd seen, and I knew he was faking it. My mother was reflected in the window. He wasn't going to talk with her listening. I turned to see her in the doorway, staring at me with disapproval.

"Is everything all right, Jimmy?" My mother asked, her tone insinuating that I was the problem.

"Everything's fine, Ma."

"Leave him be, Kill, he's not a suspect you can interrogate." I ignored her, moving so I could look into my father's glazed eyes as I spoke to him.

"I'm not going to stop looking. You should know that someone broke into my house and tore through your old photo albums. They stole that old ring I found when I was lost in the woods."

I saw his eyes flick toward me for a split second and even thought I heard my mother catch her breath. They were *both* hiding something.

"Does that mean anything to you, Dad?"

"It doesn't matter. It means nothing. That ring is just a piece of trash you found. I don't even know why you held onto it. It's not part of some Goddamn conspi—," he muttered.

"– James Collins," my mother warned from the doorway,

although whether she disapproved of his blasphemy or the fact that he was giving me information was impossible to tell.

"Christ, give it up, Theresa. It's all so long ago. It doesn't matter. It can't possibly be related to the case that took Joe from us," he said.

"It's not? Then why did you react when I said it was Markov's yacht? Why tell me to stay away? And why is your old friend Burke so interested in it?"

"Burke...?" My father muttered, as if trying to place the name. "God, I haven't seen him in a while. He was so broken up when Joe died... We all were."

"I don't want you talking about this anymore," Mom snapped, interrupting.

"In a minute, Mom," I told her sharply, sure now that they both knew something more than they were willing to share. "There was a woman at the yacht. She took me to the hospital. Five-nine, maybe five-ten, auburn hair, hazel eyes, about my age –"

"About *your* age...?" My father looked concerned, shocked even.

"Let it go, Killian," my mother interrupted harshly.

"She knew me from somewhere," I went on before she could stop me. "She's involved."

"The one that talked to Sean..." my father muttered, glancing at my mother. I swear they both looked worried. Before I could press further, my mother stepped between us, her hand on my chest, angry.

"He doesn't know what he's talking about, Killian. He's sick."

"I am sick. You're right…" The moment had passed, my father was looking out at the rain again. I've been sick since the night I let Joe go out there driving in that weather. We should never have gotten involved in that case," he said quietly, and then looked up at me with clear eyes, holding out his revolver toward me. "Better take this. It's yours now. Get it out. I'm a confused old man who's a danger to himself and everyone else… You better go."

"What if I won't?"

"Suit yourself. It won't matter. I'm done. I won't give you anything more. It'd only encourage you to do something stupid."

"Like he needs encouragement," Mom sniped from the doorway.

"I'm not letting this go—" I warned them both.

"Killian, it's time. You're upsetting him. Confusing his memories," my mother said, motioning for the door. I looked between them. I wasn't getting anywhere with them today, that much was clear. I started to go, but my father stopped me again, grabbing the hand I held his gun in.

"Kill. Come here," he told me, waving me closer and opening up his arms. This was his way of dismissing me over the last few years. I was about thirty when he started to hug me good-bye, and now it had become his way of kicking me out.

I leaned down and noticed that his eyes seemed to be on the verge of overflowing again. I couldn't hold his gaze, and instead looked at my mother as I hugged him, watching her as she defiantly stood guard. That was when my father shocked me, whispering quietly enough so that Mom couldn't hear.

"Sean Corrigan. Ask him about Ireland. About Declan – and the woman who was looking for your Uncle Joe..." I squeezed his arm to let him know I understood, then strode out the door, brushing past my mother with a barely a wave.

"That's it? You're going? Leaving me alone with him in the middle of a natural disaster without even a temp nurse?" Mom asked, calling after me.

She might have said more, but I let the door slam and kept walking. I didn't have time to argue with her. My father, in his addled way, had given me a lot more facts and a ton of information, but all the extra puzzle pieces just made a bigger mess to sort through – and I was no closer to finding Alina or Dariya.

We were going on the twenty-four-hour mark and all I had was a brief understanding of an almost thirty-year-old case and a lead on a woman with hazel eyes that I couldn't remember. It felt as if I was running out of time. The only hopeful note was that as I looked for the Outerbridge through the gloomy rain – I couldn't see it. The lights were still out. There was no way off the island. For any of us...

CHAPTER ELEVEN

I stepped out into a gentle rain to find Kat leaning against the Nova. A soft dewy mist had settled over her, as if she hadn't moved the entire time I was inside. She looked magical, her skin glistening, matching her eyes.

"You know it's still raining?"

"It's misting," she said dismissively, still looking me in the eye.

"It's wet. That makes it rain. You could've waited inside," I told her, dragging my eyes away from hers.

"I'm not sure your mom and I would've lasted together in that small of a space."

"Why, what'd she say to you?"

"Asked if I was a lesbo and if we met because you arrested whoever it was that abused me," Kat said with a smirk.

"She's very subtle."

"And observant. Likes to use what she sees against people, doesn't she?" Kat asked as we got into the car. I turned the key and put it in drive as she slammed the door.

"S'all right. I gave it back to her. Told her if she was even ten years younger I'd be lookin' at her instead of you."

"Lovely. Glad you're sexually harassing my mother."

"We have an understanding now. She can be mean to me and I can piss her off by being nice back. I feel like part of the family already. What'd your dad tell you?"

"Nothing. Just confirmed that these two cases are connected and that woman at the yacht is involved. Hinted that it has something to do with what I might've seen the night Uncle Joe was killed."

"Your Uncle Joe?"

"Well, not really my uncle. He worked with my father on the Federal Task Force. They were close. Really close. Joe was driving the night of my accident. My Dad also said something about 'the last time I went messing around', and about 'the bastards breaking something.'"

"Breaking something? What does that mean?"

"The only thing I ever remember getting broken was my father's jaw, but I don't see how the two are connected."

"What *do* you remember about 'the last time you went messing around'?"

"Not much."

"Well, *there's* something we all can count on. Killian Collins' memory," she muttered, but it wasn't quite true that I didn't remember. There *were* some things... and talking it out might do some good –

*

It was the summer I had turned thirteen, and I'd gotten interested in both the accident that took my memory and my life before it. My mother wouldn't talk about it, and my father gave me either vague descriptions of baseball games I'd played when we lived on the North Shore, or stories about what my now-dead grandparents were like. None of it filled in the blanks for me, and the less I knew the more I felt the need to find out what had happened to me during the two days I'd been wandering in the woods.

I'm not sure why I needed to know more that summer, but it might have been because that past May, Valerie Marie Salerno, a twelve-year-old girl just a year behind me at Totten Intermediate School, had gone missing. Her body was found on the last day of school in June, at the end of Maguire Avenue in the woods between Parkwood Avenue and Bloomingdale Road.

The crime scene was only about two miles from where I had been lost after my accident. When I read about it in The Staten Island Advance, my night terrors had come back. Of course, Valerie wasn't the first girl to go missing only to be found later, half eaten by the wild dogs and raccoons that still roamed in the woods of Staten Island. Holly Ann Hughes was a legend by that time, and Judy Somerville was still a recent tragedy, found buried in a shallow grave behind Tottenville High School just a few years before. I had started collecting articles about all of them, becoming obsessed with young girls disappearing in the woods where I had wandered. I knew that I was obsessed because my night terrors had returned, this time with horrific images of a girl in danger – and that the dream was a way to control reality. According to my doctor – it was a way to right the wrongs I couldn't otherwise. Some days I wondered if the same impulse was what drove me to become a cop, but back then, the dreams just scared the shit out of me – and I was having more trouble sleeping than I ever had before.

If there had been anything else that summer to take up that space in my brain that was occupied by morbid thoughts and dark daydreams, maybe I wouldn't have gotten caught messing around in the frames of the homes under construction where the woods I had grown up in used to be – but Charlie Pederson, Tony Guinta, and even Tommy O'Connell were all gone for the summer. Tony and Charlie were away at camps, and Tommy was in summer school for failing math.

So there I was, reading lazily on the second floor of a half-built house on a Saturday. I was in the middle of Robert Heinlein's story *"All You Zombies"* when I noticed that the words were drifting away in shadow. I was tired because the dreams had been keeping me awake, and the sun felt so good that I shut my eyes –

*

…And I was running again, my legs torn open by the thorns of sticker bushes. My head pounded and I was getting tired, but I had to keep going.

That's when I saw the girl for the first time. She no more than eight, with her long auburn hair tied back, darting and dodging through scattered moonlight and the trees like a mythical deer that had taken on human form. My psychologist at the time said I'd created her from all the dead girls I'd been reading about, but she felt more real than that, and when I touched her in my dreams she was solid, soft, and smelled of earth and sweat and was running in denim shorts and t-shirt, which were useless for protection in the cold October night air. There was mud caked on her calves and her legs were scratched and bloody above the mud line. She never hesitated, running flat out, never stopping as her hair caught on the branches. I thought for sure she would get away –

Until I saw the shadows behind her move.

When I inhaled to scream and warn her, I only wheezed and choked. A hulking figure emerged from the shadows, the shades of darkness resolving themselves into the silhouette of a full-grown man. He didn't try to talk to her or warn her, he just extended his arms, holding what looked like an iron bar – and clotheslined her as she ran. Both of the girl's feet left the ground and her neck snapped back.

Somehow the man didn't hear me as I ran toward them, amped up on adrenaline and anger. Maybe he was too focused on the girl, kicking and clawing at him as he pushed her flat on her back in the mud, straddling her, ripping her shirt and backhanding her across the face.

"How do you like that, little bitch? Teach you to make me

run," he growled as he grabbed her by the hair and pulled her face close to his. His voice was muttered and indistinct in the rain, something about it different, maybe foreign.

I slowed, coming up behind him. The tire iron he'd hit her with was on the ground between us – but I hesitated.

The sour acid of cowardice made my stomach tighten and I stood absolutely still for a moment, afraid to grab the tire iron. In the silence, I heard his words, still muffled by the white noise of the rain.

"...break you in. Make you worthless," the man muttered, as he ripped open the young girl's shorts.

That's when I saw the scar on her thigh. It looked almost exactly like my own scar – a spiraling blemish the size and shape of a cigarette lighter from an old car. The only difference between the two was that her scar was on her left thigh and looked as if it were brand new and barely healed.

The scar gave me the courage I needed. With both hands I grabbed the tire iron and lifted it over my head, exhaling with a scream, swinging it like an axe, aiming for the soft spot at the base of his skull.

The metal struck, vibrating. It made my hands flare with pain and then go numb. Nothing happened for a second... And then the man turned and looked right at me, stunned, but unaffected by the blow. I tried to step back and away, I lost my balance. Falling, I lashed out with the tire iron, feeling the metal strike and stop abruptly, sending pain shooting up my arm. He'd grabbed me, and as I tried to keep his wet, slick hand off my *neck I felt it go slack and something slid off into my fist.*

His other hand must have still had a grip on the tire iron, because he was on top of me and had me pinned in the mud and I couldn't pull it back to hit him again. That's when something warm and wet dropped onto my cheek and oozed, slug-like, across it. I struggled against him, but the man wasn't moving.

At all.

The mud was forgiving and let me slip to one side, wriggling out from under him. When I glanced down at him I saw that he looked at me with only one eye. Where the other had been was the tire iron. He was dead. I'd killed him, but I felt nothing. Heard nothing. I saw nothing but his eyes and the tire iron for a long moment, my hands balled into fists at my side, something small and hard in my right one.

Then the sound slowly filtered back – first the softly insistent rain, then the rustle of leaves. It was the girl. I turned to look for her as I heard her move, wanting to help her, but I only caught one last glimpse of her as she fled. I can't forget that image as she sprayed mud up behind her, looking as if like she had been born to run wild. It was then that I heard distant voices – other men, looking for us. They were coming, and I was standing over their dead friend. I need to go –

*

– I bolted upright, chilled. As I opened my eyes, I thought at first that a cloud had passed in front of the sun, but then saw it was starting to dip below the horizon. As I looked out to see it, I noticed two men at the tree line, silhouetted. Both men looked like both *cugines* – in sweaty wife-beater T's, with gold chains and half dollar-sized Christ heads, tattoos on their biceps and the ripped muscles that were most likely from steroids, raising the specter of 'roid rage'. They each had shovels and a pickaxe and were digging at the edge of a shallow, seasonal creek bed. The shorter of the two men was in the shallow creek up to his knees. He was built like a fireplug, with a mangy mustache and thinning hair, but the taller one was a ripped V-shaped guy that looked like he was way too big to be messed with.

Of course, I thought they were burying a body – I was thirteen and having nightmares about dead men and tire irons and girls in danger. Morbidly curious, I walked through the framed-out wall to the next window opening and leaned out, not noticing a block of wood sitting on the sill. I must have brushed up against it and it clattered off the plywood exterior as it fell.

When I looked up again, my eyes found the two men in the woods, looking right at me. They saw me.

"Get to the front. I got the back," the shorter of the two men yelled as he dropped his shovel and started running toward the house I was in.

I ran. Instinctively.

My bike was in the weeds, closer to Sharrotts Road. If I could get to it, I knew some trails that cut off the corner and would take me straight to the one-way service road, Drumgoole Road

West. If I could get there, the two *cugines* wouldn't be able to follow me –even if they had a car close by.

Luckily, the big guy was muscle-bound and tight, and couldn't run. Definitely more of a fight guy than a flight one. At thirteen, I was all flight. I was fifty yards down Sharrotts Road on my bike before the big guy even hit the pavement and I was on the dirt trail before I heard the gravel churning up beneath the car's wheels.

I didn't stop until I made it out the other side and was coasting down the service road, listening for the sound of their car. I heard nothing. The car was gone. Relieved, I started pedaling steadily, in the orange glow of the setting sun that lit up the roadway behind me. The pavement was smooth and clear and the adrenaline was washing out of my system as I enjoyed the wind in my face, tearing ass down the hill.

…And then I heard the roar of a busted muffler, right behind me. A white pickup was less that forty feet back, coming down the wrong way. It had been coasting silently in neutral, but now it was racing toward me as I saw the big guy and his buddy in the front seat. I pumped the pedals as hard as I could.

It was no use.

The truck was suddenly alongside of me and the big guy's arm was reaching out the window. I tried to swerve, but the big guy caught my arm and the bike was pulled out from under me as the back tires of the pickup rolled over it, crunching metal and snapping plastic. My feet hit the ground as I yanked away from him, and then I was free…

...falling and rolling onto one shoulder, asphalt scraping away skin as I rolled. I finally stopped as my hip hit the curb. I didn't move. The pain was starting to throb its way into the whole right side of my body as the blood rushed to the surface.

The sound of the pickup's doors slamming motivated me enough to try and get up, but hadn't even taken a step when I felt a giant hand slam me hard between the shoulder blades. Falling face first into the weeds, my wrists caught my full weight, going numb as my right elbow collapsed. I kicked at his arm, flailing, but had no traction and nothing to hold onto as he pulled me backward by one ankle. I wasn't going anywhere.

"Motherfucker. Look at that," the smaller guy mumbled, and then casually kicked me in the ribs to stop me from fighting. With the wind knocked out of me, I saw what he was looking at – the scar on my thigh.

"Where'd you get that scar, Red?" He asked, calling me by a name I hated. My hair wasn't really red, but when I was a kid it was lighter, and in the summers the sun would bleach it so that the brown went a bit reddish/auburn.

"From your mother—" I muttered, answering his question about the scar as any Staten Islander would. He kicked me again, harder. Through teary eyes, I could see the bigger of the two men smile. He was missing one of his canine teeth and was at least six-five. Steroids was now a definitive diagnosis, and he had a bad case, including the 'roid rage that went with it.

I just lay there for a moment as he moved closer to look at my scar. When he was close enough, I snapped my other leg straight out, planting my heel into the bridge of his nose. I heard it crack a millisecond before I felt the warm spray of blood on my shin. The big guy roared in pain and was about to put a fist through my chest when I heard a familiar mechanical whine and a shout.

"Let the kid go or I'll blow your fuckin' head off," a deep voice said as I recognized what the sound had been – a tap on a police siren. The big guy let go, putting his hands in the air as a uniformed cop approached, his gun pointed at the bigger man. The cop's younger partner was flanking the smaller guy, who also had his hands where the cops could see them.

"Officer. This is just a misunderstanding," said the smaller guy, pasting on a smile under his thin and patchy mustache.

"He's full of it. They chased me down. My Dad's on the job," I yelled as quickly as I could. That phrase was like a magic incantation when recited to any cop in New York City. The older cop's eyes narrowed as he tested my bona fides.

"Where's he work outta?"

"The six-o. Coney Island Homicide," I answered, the way only a cop's kid would.

"I don't give a rat's ass who his father is. He was vandalizing the construction sites," protested the smaller guy.

"I wasn't doin' nothin' but reading. They were digging in the woods with shovels. Like they were burying something."

"That true?" Asked the older cop, obviously the senior partner.

"It's a construction site. People dig. Go look if you want," muttered the big guy. "I think the little shit broke my nose."

"That'll teach you to pick on someone your own size. What's this about digging? It's Saturday. Nobody digs on Saturday."

"We do. Ever hear of Swamp Pink?" the smaller guy asked, smugly.

"Swamp *what*?"

"Swamp Pink. It's a flower. An endangered species. *Helonias bullata*. Some damn tree huggers are making us transplant every last one of 'em before we can bulldoze." The cops exchanged a look and the junior partner shrugged.

"I buy it. Whose gonna make up somethin' like 'Hell-on-us Bulls-tatas'? "And you're really doin' that? Transplanting *flowers*?"

"We're paid to do it. Supposedly the damn weed'll go extinct if we don't. That's how we caught this kid in the houses. We were doin' our job," said the smaller guy, putting his hands down, starting to get irate.

"We had stuff stolen from the site. Then we see this little shit—" The Toothless Giant continued until the older cop held up a hand, interrupting.

"—So you go the wrong way down a one way and run him over?

"It was an accident. He swerved into us."

"Bullshit," I said, trying to make sure the cops didn't lose sight of the fact that these guys had been trying to kill me.

"Fine, I get it. It's a he said-he said, and everybody's wrong. Anybody want to go to jail today?" The cop asked, looking at all of us. Nobody reacted, so he went on, talking to his partner. "Write these guys up for reckless driving. I find you near this kid again, I will shoot you, understood?"

"Understood," said the smaller guy, before the big guy could say anything.

"And you, kid," the senior partner said, looking at me. "I catch you near them houses, I'll take you in, charge you, and then call your dad. Now get in the car. We'll take you home."

"I'm okay."

"I ain't askin', kid," he told me, and then helped me get the bike into the trunk of the patrol car as his partner wrote up the two guys.

I watched them, and they watched me. None of us watched the cops. Finally, I got into the car and told the cops my address. We had to go the long way around because of the one-way streets. The pickup followed us, about a half a mile back, slowing down as we turned onto my block. The bored cops didn't seem to notice, or care, probably assuming their warning as 'The Law', had put an end to the issue.

They were wrong.

I saw the guys in the pickup looking at me as I climbed out of the police car, and then they slowly continued past.

They knew where I lived.

CHAPTER TWELVE

I got lucky. My father saw the bike before he saw me.

That meant, of course, that he was worried that I was dead or permanently disabled by whatever accident had mangled it, so he was relieved that I was fine when he did finally see me and had already blown his ability to feign anger. Dad grounded me for a week.

I didn't really mind, because every night for the next week my Dad would arrive home to find me peering out past the heavy drapes, as if I was waiting for him. He thought I was bored, but to be truthful, I was afraid – watching for that pickup with the man with the mangy mustache and his giant friend. Worried that I was becoming a lonely, housebound loser, my father offered to take me to the movies, just the two of us, a week after my bike got wrecked. I even got to choose the movie. My mother must have felt badly as well, because she decided to go with us. The offer was almost worth the beating I took, especially since the guys in the pickup couldn't find me if I wasn't at home. I'd be safe at the movies.

At least that's what I thought.

We were in our green Dodge van on Hylan Boulevard, headed the movie theaters near the OTB when it happened. Hylan Boulevard, then and now, was an experience in Darwinian driving. Slow traffic could go as slow as thirty miles an hour, the fastest somewhere around seventy. Most did around fifty, and everyone constantly shifted between lanes, navigating between the slow and weak and the fast and the strong. One misjudged lane change and three or four families would be making a call at the funeral homes that seemed to crop up every couple of miles on the boulevard.

We were at the stoplight on Hylan and Keegan's Lane, in the middle lane behind a Black BMW, when the light turned green.

"It don't get any greener, genius," my father muttered, looking in his driver's side mirror to see if he could get around the car in front of him. He must have seen it coming, because my father pulled the wheel in the opposite direction as the van rocked hard to the right and there was a squeal of metal on metal, a shrieking high-pitched sound underscored by a deeper thud. It took me a moment to realize that the black Cadillac that had just passed had sideswiped us, shattering its passenger side mirror.

"Jesus Christ! What the hell was that?" My mother screamed.

"Hold on," my father told her, focused. He hit the gas,

chasing down the Cadillac, flashing his headlights at it while weaving in and out of traffic.

"Kill. Get the plate number," he said, but I already had it committed to memory. I wasn't a cop's son for nothing. I had the plate number, the number of occupants, the cross streets it happened at – everything. All we had to do now was find a phone to call it in.

We never got that far. The Cadillac pulled over on the shoulder where Great Kills Park and the woods come right up to the edge of the Boulevard. My father stopped behind it, one hand unbuckling his seatbelt, the other going to his ankle holster where he kept his off-duty gun, just to make sure it was there.

"What do you think you're doing?" Mom asked, worried.

"He stopped. We'll trade insurance, unless…"

"Unless what?"

"If he's drunk or high, I'm holding him 'til the sector car gets here."

"Jesus, Jimmy. Can't you let it go, just once?" she asked, pleading, but the door slammed in her face and we were left watching my father as he took out his badge and moved cautiously up to the Cadillac. He leaned into the driver's side window, identifying himself. The adrenaline from the cars colliding was already wearing off when I saw the driver lean out the window…

…He had a mangy mustache.

It took a minute to sink in, since I'd only seen him once

and didn't expect to see him here, now. Before I could react, my father said something to him, reached in the window past Mangy Mustache, and came back out with the Cadillac's keys. ...For a minute, I thought it was all going to be all right. My father had the guy's keys. He had the gun. He had the badge. But then Mangy Mustache was out of the car and walking after my father, angrily saying something at his back as the passenger door of the Cadillac opened. The Toothless Giant stepped out and then I knew the sideswipe wasn't an accident.

"DAD!" I yelled as loudly as I could, to warn him about the giant – but over the traffic and through closed windows, he couldn't hear me.

The Toothless Giant didn't slow down or hesitate as he walked up behind my father, spun him around, and hit him with everything he had. I didn't know it at the time, but my father's jaw was broken in three places and two teeth were lying on the asphalt in the center lane of Hylan Boulevard. We later learned that the Giant's hand was also broken in two places, but he was feeling no pain, since he was too high. Unfortunately, he *was* clear-headed enough to start patting my father down, looking for his gun.

"Oh my God. Jesus Christ, what the hell are they doing?" My mother screamed, panicking. It was pretty clear to me what they were doing –

– I reached under the front bench seat where my father kept his toolbox and pulled out his three-quarter-inch Craftsmen ratchet, almost twelve inches long and three pounds of solid steel. Clearly, I wasn't thinking clearly.

I opened the door anyway, focused and intent, striding straight up behind the Toothless Giant as he bent over my father, his hands just inches from the gun in his ankle holster. The soft spot where his neck and skull met was surrounded by knotted muscle, so I took two hands to swing the ratchet.

"Vince!" Mangy Mustache warned the Giant, but it was too late. The ratchet came down with every ounce of power I had in my thirteen-year-old arms. It was a solid hit, but I didn't hear anything crack. The giant just collapsed to one knee and shook his head, dazed.

"*Affanculo!*" the giant roared and stood, coming right at me, his face red with anger, his eyes bloodshot, his pupils dilated to utter blackness. That's when I did the only smart thing I did that day.

I ran – but he caught a piece of my shirt and slammed me against the side of our van. Facing him, I saw him pull back to launch his huge fist at my face. I dropped to the ground. Glass shattered above me, raining down as his fist went into the side window of the van.

"Fuckin' son of a shit-bitch!" the Giant screamed. I rolled to the center of the van, out of his reach, shaken.

"Come here, you little shit. I wanna snap your neck," he said, reaching for me with his bloody hand. I bit it. He screamed and I spit blood and grains of glass back at him as I tried to escape out from under the other side of the van. I never made it – a shadow fell over the pavement on that side. Mangy Mustache was looking at me from under the muffler, faking a smile.

"Come on out, kid. We just want some answers. We know that you know where it is," he said in a conciliatory tone. "We won't hurt you if you tell us where," he said, reaching under to grab me. I slammed my elbow on his fingers and heard one crack. It might seem sick, but it was a beautiful sound. He yelled from the pain and when he looked at me again, I gave him the finger. It felt good.

…And then he suddenly stood up, moving away. I watched his feet, thinking it was a trick, then turned to see that the Giant was also moving quickly back toward their car. I stayed put as I heard Mom yelling above me… and then I heard what they'd heard. Sirens. Somewhere close by and getting louder. I looked out toward the boulevard to see if I could spot their cars approaching, but all I saw was a 1973 Volkswagen Bug and a man that looked like the pictures I'd seen of Uncle Joe (I had no memories of him), on the opposite side of the street, looking toward the sirens. He caught me looking out of the corner of his right eye and glanced at me sideways for a long moment, smiled sadly, and then got back in his car – and left without ever fully facing me – as if once he knew I was going to be all right, he wasn't needed. I know it couldn't have been Uncle Joe, but he looked so familiar, and was right where I needed him, but he was gone before I could even see him full on.

The VW backfired as it weaved into the traffic… and then I must have closed my eyes, because I lost a few minutes. Either that or my memory went dark again. Whatever happened, I didn't come back until I heard my father's muffled and strained voice calling to me.

"Killian. It's all right. Come out," he said with a lisp, blood drooling uncontrollably over his lip as he knelt to look at me. When he offered me a hand I took it, and noticed that traffic had started moving, now that the show was over. The sirens, wherever they were, moved on, fading in the distance.

"Get in the car," my father ordered, already moving toward his door.

"Shouldn't we wait for the cops?"

"I am the cops. No one else is coming."

My father got in, calmly, and I heard his teeth rattle as he tossed them in the cup holder.

"Jesus Jimmy, your teeth…" my mother whispered, horrified.

"I have others. You got the plate number, Killian?" he muttered, barely moving his mouth.

"Absolutely."

"Good job," he told me, then put on his turn signal and pulled out into traffic.

"Where are you going?" Mom asked quietly, still in shock.

"I promised Kill a movie. He's going. Then I'm driving to a dentist. When we get there, you can call the precinct."

"But your teeth—"

"Can wait. Movies first. Besides, they'll be looking for this van, not him."

"Jimmy—"

"Let it go, Theresa."

His tone must have stopped her. We drove in silence until we pulled up outside the theater as if there was nothing different about this day.

"Give him money," Dad ordered, and my mother did, without a question. "Buy some candy, Kill. Tell me about it when you get home."

I nodded and stepped out, but I didn't shut the door right away. I turned back to look at both of them, knowing that something wasn't right and that this whole thing didn't quite make sense.

"What were they talking about?" I asked.

"Who?"

"Those guys. They were the ones who chased me and ran over my bike."

My parents exchanged a look. They hadn't known that, and it meant something to them. After a moment my father sighed, holding back the pain.

"No, they weren't. I've told you how bad eyewitnesses are, right? Two stressful things in a week, you just thought they were the same. You know how bad your memory is."

"Yeah, but…" I stopped myself. He was right. My memory was completely *fakakta*.

"Good. Then you understand. Now go. You'll miss the previews." I shut the door. He pulled away with a wave. My mother didn't even look back.

By the time the previews had ended, I was into the movie.

Jurassic Park. Escapism at its finest. By the end of the movie I barely remembered what had happened. It might sound strange, but anyone who grew up in Staten Island would understand. It's one of those places where 'nobody sees nothing' and casual violence is accepted. You get over it. If you don't, you don't last. I got over it easier than most, possibly due to the fact that my memories don't stick in the same way other people's memories do. I guess that's why I might remember events in ways that make no sense – like thinking Uncle Joe was on the boulevard or that some girl was in the woods the night of my accident.

...Sometimes I think I'd be better off if I remembered to just forget it all.

*

"So, you think the guys that broke your father's jaw were the same guys that chased you down?" Kat asked, obviously doubting my version of events. I couldn't blame her, since my history of recall was spotty at best. In fact, the first time I had the 'girl dream' after she moved in I was convinced that the girl in the dream looked like Kat – or was Kat. Of course I never told her, and knew that it was crazy and that my subconscious had probably changed the dream girl to look like Kat since the details of my dreams seemed to be fluid.

"...And if they were the same guys – why?" Kat asked as we approached the barricades that sealed off Tottenville. Thankfully they were still in place. That meant the bridges were still closed. Markov was still trapped somewhere on the island

and I still had time to find him and the girls.

"I don't know, I haven't even thought about them in twenty years. Not until my father brought them up today," I finally answered, trying not to look out the window.

"How do you not think about that?" She asked. I shrugged. Forgetting unpleasant events was my specialty.

"I probably stopped worrying because Mangy Mustache and the Toothless Giant were both arrested after a shooting in Brooklyn three months later. The three strikes law sent them away for a long time." Kat stared at me for a minute, suspicious.

"Who shot them? Guys that knew your father?"

"My father knew everybody."

"Right…" she muttered, as if confirming her suspicions.

"It wasn't like that. Those two guys were connected. They'd used Uzis to spray four storefronts, killing two people because they were dealing in a neighborhood owned by the Gambinos."

"Nice. But what the hell were they after you for? What were they digging up?"

"My father said there was something valuable on that plane. And kids."

"Like you found on that yacht."

"Yeah. And he acted all freaked out about my ring getting stolen, about Markov owning the yacht – and if I had to bet, he knows who the woman at the yacht was."

"Damn. And he didn't tell you?"

"No, the raving bitch from Bay Terrace stopped him."

"What was that bit about those guys noticing your scar?"

"I'm not sure where that fits in. Not yet."

Kat shrugged, excited. "Smuggling, drugs, plane crashes, kids being held captive, family secrets... Man, this is starting to get good. Where are we going next?"

"We? You know you're not a detective, right?"

"Details, details. Army C.I.D. is the same thing, basically. Besides, I'm smart. I think like a criminal. I could be good at this. Give me a gun and I'm set. We can track down that asshole that tased me and shove his cattle prod where the sun don't shine. Get him to talk," she said with an eager smile.

"You know there's no Tasers up the ass in civilian life, right?" I told her.

"Come on, I read the news. I've seen the movies. You can be honest with me, Killer. You guys like it rough, right?"

"Forget it. I'm taking you home right after we make one more stop. You think you can behave for another fifteen minutes?"

"Only if I can come inside with you this time."

"Fine. If you behave... And don't engage with the guy we're meeting. He's a little off. Sean Corrigan, from what I hear, is a flake, but you gotta be nice."

"Corrigan? As in Joe Corrigan, your dad's old partner?"

"Yeah. His father is Uncle Joe's cousin," I told her, and saw her do a double take.

"Wow. Didn't know they were from the Island."

"Yeah. Cousins all over the place. Cops, firemen, doctors. My family lost touch after Joe died. I think they blamed my dad for his death," I told her, wondering why my father would send me to talk to Sean. As far as I know, my dad hadn't seen any of the Corrigans since Joe's funeral, mourning over his closed casket.

"You know where this Sean Corrigan lives?"

"Right near the school. When I was a kid my dad would never drive past that house – so one day I asked my mom why. She told me whose house it was. He never went past there or the old mansion on Arthur Kill," I said.

"The abandoned and haunted place? The Kreischer Mansion?"

"Yeah. I think the Corrigans were groundskeepers there for generations, until after Joe died."

"How cool is that? I used to go partying in there after it was abandoned… Is this Sean guy cute?" Kat asked, and I could see where this was going.

"Don't even think about it, Kat. I've heard stories about him from friends he went to school with – he apparently went off the deep end after a trip to Ireland. He's obsessed with some girl he never met, and travels all around the world looking for her even though he's not sure what she looks like. He's written books about her."

"Sounds like every horny guy I ever knew. Maybe she looks like me."

I almost responded, but thought better of it. It didn't matter. I needed to know why my father sent me to talk to Sean. I had no idea what could he possibly know about this case – or the one my father and Uncle Joe were working twenty-five years ago – but if he had any pertinent facts I needed to know. Something tied these cases together, and the more information I gathered, the more likely it was that I could track down those two girls before it was too late.

The clock was still ticking, and getting louder every minute.

CHAPTER THIRTEEN

"Last thing my father said to me was 'don't trust anyone', and 'ask Sean about Ireland. About Declan and the woman who was looking for my Uncle Joe," I explained to Kat as we stood on the sagging front porch of the Corrigans' old Georgian style home.

"You think she's the one who has the two girls?"

"She was at the yacht. She matches the description of the Witch of Wolfe's Pond – and she knows too much. So yeah. Maybe Sean knows where she is."

"And who is Declan?"

"Not sure. But my father mentioned that name as someone my Uncle got a tip from about the plane -- so here we are."

I had to speak loudly, as the sump pumps were forcing water out through open basement windows into the swampy yard. Sandy had done some damage here. Trees were down all over the property and a few dozen shingles littered the lawn, but it seemed as if the house itself was relatively unscathed otherwise. Kat kept prodding, intense.

"You don't know anything about this Sean person?"

"A little. I read his book – well, the summary. On line. He's a little off his nut with conspiracy theories and 'hidden histories' – but he does have relatives who were associated with the IRA and gun-running. Just don't ask him anything about traveling the world to find a long-lost soul mate." I rang the doorbell again, impatiently. It was still drizzling, I was getting damp and moist all over, and I was suddenly very aware of why I hate both of those words.

"Traveling the world to find a lost love? That's sweet," Kat said with a dreamy look. I should've left her home, but I still felt guilty about her being tased. A little.

"Romantic, mental. Not much difference, is there?" I rang the bell one last time, then knocked loudly – remembering that they probably had no power like the rest of the island. I was about to give up and leave when I heard wet and soggy footsteps behind me.

"Killian Collins."

We both turned to see Sean, his hair too long and his beard looking as if he hadn't shaved in a week or more. He was carrying a long-handled ax over his shoulder, wore knee-high rubber boots, jeans, no shirt, and had mud covering his entire torso.

"You know who I am?" I asked, confused.

"Sure enough. You're the reason my Uncle Joe is gone," he shrugged. "I heard you were a little mental. Didn't go out in the rain or something?" We were off to a great start.

"And he heard you're a flake who believes in conspiracy theories and travels the world looking for his lost love," Kat volunteered.

"So, he's the one who read my book?" He smiled and held out a hand. I shook it, starting to like the guy.

"No. He read the summary, but maybe *I* should read your book," Kat said, offering her own hand. "Kat. And I'd love to hear about your work."

"Well, then, good timing. I only got home two days ago. I was in—"

I held up a hand, stopping him. "To be honest, I'm not that interested. My father –"

"– I'm interested," Kat piped in. "…A guy who's not afraid to get wet and dirty *and* travels the world? Damn, Kill. Don't stop him." Sean grinned.

"Kat, there are two girls missing." I stepped between them as I pulled out my phone and cued up the photos I'd taken on the yacht. "I'm here because my father sent me to talk to you. He seems to think you'll know something about Uncle Joe, what his death had to do with Declan and Ireland and some woman who came looking for him."

Sean looked around, uncomfortable suddenly. "Umm, right. Better come inside – this might take a while…"

*

The house Sean shared with his father, Joe's cousin, Aidan, smelled of seawater and humidity. Sean took off his boots and wiped himself down with a towel, oblivious to Kat's stare.

"You came to the right place. There are probably only about six or seven other people in the world that could tell you about the real truth behind gun-running during 'The Troubles' and how the Irish in Boston and New York – including the police – were complicit."

"You mean there's someone who knows more than you?" Kat asked, in her annoying and flirtatious way.

"Shocking, inn't it? Someone has more useless information in his head than my son," called out a voice from the living room. I turned to see what I had at first thought was an old grey cat sitting on the back of a recliner and realized it was the top of Aidan Corrigan's head. I could see the bottom of a beer bottle tip up as I watched, confirming that it was a human being and not an ancient cat.

"Hello, Mister Corrigan," I yelled over the television. He just lifted his beer in a half-hearted salute.

"Who's that?"

"Killian Collins."

"Well, bloody feckin' hell. The flood has disturbed the ghosts of the livin' dead. Your Da's not dead, is he?" Aidan asked, never turning around.

"No, sir."

"And yet you're here. It's a bad omen, inn't it?"

"It's fine Da. Go back to your show," Sean called out, leading us into the kitchen.

"Sure. But the dead are restless son. Bad portents. Look at this weather, and look what happened to The Annex. Now that was a *damn* shame. Think of all that good liquor, washed away..." he kept talking as Sean opened his laptop. Sean ignored him, leading us into the kitchen. He lit the burner, filling a teakettle as he spoke, more quietly now so his father couldn't hear.

"When I was in Ireland I met with the old rebels – the IRA guys who were involved in the seventies and eighties. One of them, Declan, filled me in on Uncle Joe," he said, pulling out a box of *Barry's Irish Tea*.

"What would he know about Uncle Joe?" I asked, wanting to hear it from an unbiased source.

"A lot. They were some kind of cousins. Aren't they all? Anyway, Declan's the one who told Uncle Joe that a splinter of the IRA – an even more radical group run by a guy named Jimmy Coonan – was setting up an arms shipment to replace the one intercepted on the *Marita Ann*."

Marita Ann? Kat asked, confused.

"A ship with seven tons of arms hidden in the caskets of dead Boston Irish being shipped back home for burial back in 1984. The Winter Hill Gang, with a complicit FBI Agent, had sent it out, not knowing there was an informant... Tea?" Sean asked as the kettle whistled.

"I will," Kat answered. "Just don't fuck it up by putting milk in it." Sean nodded, then glanced at me.

"No, thanks – but why would Declan tell Joe? If he was IRA, I mean?" I asked, trying to follow the logic.

"Because Coonan was crazy – his whole family was. His

brother Jerry blew up innocent kids because he believed that to end the conflict with the Brits – 'the more blood the better'. Declan didn't go along with killing kids, and wasn't willing to deal with the Soviets –"

"Soviets. That's where Markov comes in," Kat said, thinking out loud.

"Markov?"

"The guy whose yacht washed up on Purdy Place," I answered, not wanting to give him too many details. "– But why *were* they dealing with Soviets? And why were they coming through the States?" I asked, always confused by the convoluted politics of Ireland. Sean just shrugged, steeping his tea and breathing in the steam.

"The American sources of guns had been compromised by Uncle Joe and the Task Force. They needed a new source, but the smuggling routes from here were still more secure than from the Soviet Union. Besides, it was more lucrative to run things from here because this is where Coonan could get top dollar for what he was selling – he was paying for the arms with human traffic," Sean explained, like a history teacher lecturing on a modern slave trade.

"The kids on the plane," I said, watching Sean nod, solemnly.

"Exactly. Coonan took them from an orphanage or a mother's and babies' home in County Fermanagh or something, run by the church. Told the church he had homes for them in America."

"He paid in people?" Kat asked, horrified, reaching out for the tea Sean handed her.

"It's always been Ireland's most precious export."

"So, Declan told Joe about the kids and the Russians?"

"That's how he ended up on that case. Declan also warned him that there was somebody on this side of the pond – in law enforcement – helping Coonan and his splinter group."

"Damn," Kat said, staring at Sean with a sense of lustful adventure. "Dirty cops, trying to free slaves, gun-running... I'm like a genuine thriller-chick, caught up in some Alistair McLean novel."

"Alistair McLean didn't have unbalanced women in his books," I told her, wanting to get on with it.

"I can be the damaged type from a Travis McGee novel then –"

"Look, Sean, before she starts living out some twisted fantasy, I need to know why anyone thought there was a rat. Was there any proof of that?"

Sean sipped his tea, weighing his words. He glanced in to make sure Aidan wasn't listening, then almost whispered, "Tompkins and Germanario."

"The two cops that were murdered?"

"Exactly. Declan had told given Uncle Joe about a shipment leaving a pier in Brooklyn. Joe sent those guys to do surveillance –"

"– And somebody killed them. The only ones who would have known where they were going were cops – and some Feds associated with the task force," I finished for him.

"You really think a cop would get involved with people who

dealt in kids?" Kat asked, finding it hard to believe.

"Maybe not. Maybe they didn't know. It was a triangle trade. Trafficked kids, guns, drugs – didn't matter to the Russians. All that mattered to them was the money. Maybe the cop believed in the cause. Lots of old Irish cops did," Sean shrugged, knowing more about the 'Irish' of it all than I ever would. There was still a major loose end, though, and I couldn't figure out where it fit.

"Okay, so the plane crash was about running kids and guns for cash, facilitated by the Russians, who were in it for the money – but where does the woman who was looking for Joe come in?"

Sean shrugged, as if it made no sense to him either. "She showed up here one day, about two years ago. Asked for my father first, then Joe."

"She didn't know he was dead?" Kat asked.

"Didn't know or didn't care. Could be she was using it to find out what I knew about the plane crash. Them kids."

"She knew about that?" I asked, trying to see bow it all fit together.

"Tell you the truth, she knew so much, I thought she was either involved or a Fed, opening up the old case. That's why when I saw your dad at Aunt Nancy's funeral, I asked if he knew her."

Now I was confused. What was my father doing with the Corrigans?

"*Your* Aunt Nancy's funeral? My father went to a Corrigan funeral?"

"Yeah. And our weddings, and baptisms, and funerals... You didn't know?"

"No," was all I could say. What the fuck? "Did he know the woman? Or talk about the case?"

"Not really. He just asked questions, and then shut down, like he couldn't remember anything I asked about. I tried talking to him again at my Uncle Tommy's funeral, but he acted like I was crazy. I thought maybe it was his 'old-timer's' disease kicking in by then... How is he, by the way?"

The question was tentative, as it usually was. No one really wanted to hear about a man who had been the epitome of smart and strong being reduced to staring out the window at the rain, wondering where he was or how he got there.

"He's lucky if he can remember what year it is," I answered honestly.

"Yeah... That's rough. Sometimes memories are all you've got..." Sean's voice drifted off as he saw my face and it hit him that he was talking to me. "Damn. I'm sorry, he mentioned how fucked in the head you are. I should know better."

"Don't worry about it," I told him, turning back to the pictures. "So, this woman. You have any idea where to find her?"

"She lives right here on Staten Island. I did some checking into her. I was uh, interested in who she was, coming around, asking all these questions."

"No need for excuses, Sean. You stalked her. She's hot, right?" Kat asked, with a sour hint of jealousy in her tone.

"I didn't stalk – no. She came here first," Sean stammered. "And everyone on Staten Island knows somebody who knows somebody. I just asked around and found out she works at Saint Jude's in South Beach with at-risk teens."

"At-risk? Like trafficked?"

"Sure, I guess, but she lives right here –"

"– Don't tell me, by Wolfe's Pond?" I asked, already putting the pieces together.

"Actually, the house by Wolfe's Pond is her old place. Now she lives in a little rundown house on Sharrotts Road, right where it goes through Clay Pit Ponds. Can't miss it. Roof looks like it leaks and some of the faded cedar shake siding is missing."

"But you weren't stalking her?" Kat asked suspiciously. "So much for your long-lost love..."

"It wasn't like that. I am trying to find my *mo shonuachar—*"

"Whatever *that* is, I bet you don't need to stalk a hot hazel-eyed loon to find it."

"For the record, I don't think The Morrigan is a loon," Sean said, turning a pinker shade of pale Irish, realizing too late that he was just digging himself in deeper.

"The Morrigan?" I asked, feeling a little badly for Sean. I completely understood how he could become obsessed. Kat wasn't wrong. The woman *was* attractive.

"Sorry. It's a bit of a joke. Her name is Morrigan Kelly," Sean explained, as if that made it any more clear.

"I missed the punch line."

"The Morrigan is from Celtic mythology. Morrigan means

'Phantom Queen', or the great queen. A sort of royal spirit of nightmares and a goddess of battle."

"You're saying she's a royal bitch?" Kat asked succinctly.

"Not to her face. She goes by Rigan," he finished, and I felt my stomach roil.

Everything Sean had said was validated by that one name.

Rigan.

It couldn't be a coincidence. How many women with that name could there possibly be? What were the chances a different one called me to get me to show up at the *Chistota,* came looking for information about Uncle Joe and was most likely the woman who had gone to the High School looking for Alina and Dariya.

"Rigan is it? You know her nickname but never stalked her? I think our suspect might be lying. What do you think detective?" Kat asked with a smirk. It was clearly time to leave. Her romance had run its course.

"This was great, Sean. Thanks for the lead. Looks like I've got a woman to find."

"Don't we all..." Sean muttered, under his breath. I took Kat's arm, firmly, and gently pulled her toward the door. Sean followed us out.

"Let me know what happens."

"It's a possibility," I admitted, then grabbed for the door and stepped outside quickly, breathing in the air, thick with moisture. Kat was right behind me, quiet for once, probably reading my mood. She knew how frustrated I was. I had lived through those days when Uncle Joe was always at my house, discussing cases with my father, I had even been there the night he died – and I still knew *nothing* – about any of it.

It was all gone with my memory. All of it. My mind was as useless as my father's, and I'd have to solve this the same way I solved the mystery of my childhood – with facts. I hurried down the sidewalk and was opening the door of the Nova when I looked up to see Aidan coming down the sidewalk in his bathrobe, sandals, and black socks, glancing over his shoulder as if he was afraid that Sean would see him.

"Killian, hold on a minute," Aidan called out, a little breathless from getting out of his recliner. "Look, I heard that nonsense you were talking about in there – gun-running and triangle trade and all that horse shit. Might as well be Leprechauns at the end of the rainbow. You can't listen to Sean. He's a bit touched in the head, you know that, right?"

"I don't doubt it."

"So, then you'll drop it?"

"Hell, no," Kat told him, reacting without thinking. She shrugged when I glared at her, mouthing the word 'sorry'.

"I'm going to find those girls. Make sure they're safe. That's all I care about," I reassured him, getting into the car.

"Well, whatever you do, drop this bit Sean was telling you about. Crazy women showing up looking for dead men. It's all shite. And Sean, you know he's full of all kinds of crazy ideas from drinking the piss water they have in all them foreign countries he goes to. For your father's sake, I'm warning you – don't end up like him. Promise?"

I'd gotten in the car, out of the rain, but Aidan had crossed in front of me and come to the driver's window. I rolled it down as I shut the door.

"I'll be fine. I don't believe in anything I can't prove with facts. I know how easy it is for people to think faulty memories are things that actually happened. Trust me." I started the car, but he put his hand on the door, squatting next to me.

"Good. That's good. No sense digging up the past. Might as well let someone else find those girls, too."

"I'll rest when I'm dead. Somebody killed those kids. I can't let it go."

"Right..." his voice trailed off and he looked away, unable to look at me for some reason. When he spoke again, his voice was softer.

"...That's what Joe said the last time I saw him, too. Things were... different around here before Joe left us. You go digging around that, it's going to hurt your mother, your father, and *you*."

"I'll handle it," I said, putting the Nova in gear.

"You're not a *Corrigan*. You don't need to deal with it. Jesus, can't one of you thick-headed kids trust me for once?"

"Sure. As soon as you tell me what it is that you don't want me to find." Aidan looked up at me then, and for a second I thought he might tell me. When he smiled sadly, I knew he wouldn't.

"If I told you, that'd defeat the purpose now, wouldn't it? Let

Joe rest. Don't go off like Sean and fuck up your life chasing dreams. Trust me. Take your Little Miss Sunshine here out for some drinks and enjoy her while she's young. From the looks of her, she won't leave you wantin'."

"Excuse me?" Kat piped in from the passenger seat, finally breaking her unusual silence.

"No offense, sweetheart. It's meant as a compliment." Kat flipped him off, obviously not taking it that way. Aidan smiled. It wasn't bitter, just a Staten Island thing, a ritual establishing boundaries. I ignored both of them, pressing the point.

"Why should I drop it? Give me one good reason."

"For your mental health, how about that?" he asked, trying again.

"Too late," I told him, tired of the evasiveness. It was clear that I wasn't going to get any more out of him, so I eased up on the clutch. "Thanks for the advice."

The transmission engaged and I waved as I pulled away. Aidan was left there in the street, covered in a fine mist that had settled in his hair and on his bathrobe. I watched him in the rear-view mirror. He didn't move, just stared at me until I turned the corner.

I knew he was telling the truth. I wouldn't like what I found, but it would be mine. My life, my memory. I was going to get it back.

The bonus was that I could help Dariya and Alina in the process.

I knew where they were – with the woman who had those

familiar hazel eyes. I just had to get to her before Markov – but I was already way behind. He'd had a twenty-six-hour head start...

CHAPTER FOURTEEN

"Get out."

"Go to hell."

Kat and I were parked in front of my house on Hillside Terrace, the windshield wipers squeaking and scratching out a rhythm that was starting to make me want to rip them off. Kat wasn't helping, since she sat gripping the seat, refusing to get out of the car, acting like a five-foot nine-inch tall, pierced and tattooed toddler. We'd already been here for a full five minutes, and I was due to meet Lieutenant Burke at Rigan Kelly's place on Sharrotts Road in less than ten. I was on sick leave and I needed him as official cover to investigate my own stabbing, so I had to involve him, especially with Charlie and Tony being kept busy by Hurricane Sandy.

"Look, Kat, I have to do my job. If I want to find those girls and you want me to catch the guy that tased you, I need to follow up this lead and go get Rigan Kelly."

"It wasn't a woman who tased me. It wasn't her."

"So she knows who it was. Maybe it she can tell me if it was one of the Russians from that boat."

"He wasn't Russian. I know the sound and feel of a Russian man – how their hands move. Besides, I was assaulted inside that house. You can't expect me to go back in there alone."

"No? If you can't go in alone, does that mean you're moving out? Or do you expect me to be home with you at all times?"

"Are you volunteering?"

"Look, I'm not going to my Dad's this time. I'm not going to see some crazy conspiracy theorist. I'm going on police business to question a suspect. I can't have you coming along."

I couldn't take her with me. Not only could I not explain it to Burke, who didn't approve of me investigating in the first place, but I also couldn't predict Kat's reaction to whatever, and whoever, we might confront. If we ran into whoever assaulted her, it might get real ugly, real fast.

"So you bring me back here? Where I was tased and tied up? Where I could have been raped? When it's already getting dark out?"

"Turn on the lights."

"And when the generator runs out of gas?"

"It's safer here."

"The only way it's safer is if I have a gun. You willing to give me one of yours?"

"Fine," I said, before I'd really thought about it. I was willing to say anything just to get her out of the car. I was an idiot.

"Really?"

"Will you go?" I asked, weighing the odds that she wouldn't do anything stupid in the amount of time I would be gone. Kat hesitated, but finally nodded. That was good enough. I had less than seven minutes to meet Burke. "...Then get out. The code on the gun safe is your birthday."

"*My* birthday?" She asked, unable to suppress a grin.

"It's the one date you'd never guess because you think I don't care enough to remember it."

"You don't."

"I do when it means you can't get to my guns," I told her honestly.

"That's sweet in a demented and backward sort of way," Kat said as she leaned over and kissed me on the cheek, her mood swinging to its opposite pole as she bolted out of the car, eager to get into my guns. I called after her, regretting my decision already.

"I'll change the code as soon as I get home. They're not toys..."

Kat walked backward toward the door, grinning. "No duh. Give me some credit. You've seen me shoot. I'm army trained."

"You're paranoid and trigger happy – with a touch of PTSD. I'll be shocked if you don't shoot me when I get back."

Kat gave me her back and the finger all in one graceful motion. Too bad she was cracked. If she wasn't, she might be too beautiful to resist.

*

The city hadn't bothered with many streetlights along the section of Sharrotts Road where Rigan Kelly lived. Out of the four lights that I could see, two were out and one flickered wildly enough to cause epileptic fits, but at least they were on – that was an improvement over last night, when there was no power to any lights on the island. Now there was just enough light to see that the home Sean described was in worse shape than he'd remembered, at least on the exterior. Moss was growing on the cedar shake siding, rose bushes and lilacs grew out of control all around the yard, and the brick sidewalk in front had heaved so badly that it'd be easier to walk on the dead and waterlogged grass.

There were dozens of homes like this one on the South Shore of Staten Island, littered around the edges of the former swamps now called 'preserves': Wolfe's Pond Park, Lemon Creek, Arbutus Woods, Long Pond Park, Fairview, Bloomingdale Park – hundreds of acres of undisturbed wetlands, and all of them so close to one another that if you traveled through every one of them you'd never have to leave the woods for more than a few hundred feet. Rigan Kelly's house backed right up to Clay Pit Ponds Preserve, so the overgrown backyard dissolved into a mass of sticker bushes and low-growing scrub brush. The house was about as remote as you could get inside of New York City.

As I checked the time on my phone again, a four-door sedan came around the corner from Bloomingdale Road and pulled off the shoulder, turning its headlights off. It had to be Burke.

No one except a cop would walk the extra fifty yards in the wet and cold just to insure that he approached quietly. Even the mobbed-up guys always brought a friend when it was too dark.

As Burke approached, I rolled down my window and the stench of stale cigarettes drifted in as he leaned in, sighing that heavy west-of-Ireland sigh all the old-timers seem to have perfected.

"This better be good, Collins," Burke grumbled. "We've got other shit goin' on, if you hadn't noticed." I nodded. He wasn't wrong. Hurricane Sandy had really fucked up the island.

"The woman who took me to the hospital lives here," I told him. "Rigan Kelly, she works with at-risk kids in South Beach – including trafficking victims. I think she might be harboring the two girls." Burke stared at me for a moment, as if expecting me to go on. It was an old cop trick to see if I was holding anything back. I returned the stare and he finally nodded.

"I know the name. We send kids her way," he said, stopping to look at the old house, cowering in the dark. "So, I was right. It was no coincidence that she was out there night before last, was it? She somehow knew what was going on and was there for the kids?"

"It's possible."

"You think she's in on it? She uses her position to recruit, is part of the whole thing? Is that why *I'm* here? You can make an arrest as easy as I can."

"I have questionable standing. And you know more about what was on that boat. If I'm right, she might have the stuff I saw on the yacht inside." That got Burke's attention. He looked back at the house, knowing that if he broke this case with Markov involved, he'd get headlines – maybe even a book deal. I could see his retirement flashing in front of his beady eyes.

"What about a warrant?" he asked, suddenly invested in his own future.

"You know a judge that would approve a warrant with what I have?"

"Depends. What do you have?"

"A coincidental name. A tangential professional connection. That's it. I can't even confirm the woman I saw is the woman who lives here."

"Jesus, Collins. You brought me out here with a whole lotta nothin'?"

"It's her. Can't prove it in a court of law, but it is. Too many coincidences," I told him, not wanting to get into details about the cold case, her looking for my dead uncle, or Anthony's description of the Witch of Wolfe's Pond.

"I don't believe in those. You got anything besides coincidences?"

"Not much more than when I saw you at the hospital. The Feds claim the boat was cleaned out, remember? I can't get near that yacht. How about you, you got anything more?"

"Zilch." Burke shrugged, staring at the house. "What the Feds *should* be doing is hunting down is Josef Markov. He's running this whole thing, but everybody's assuming he'll wash up on Midland Beach in a few days. Most I can do is watch the street dealers and see if any high-grade white shows up."

"It won't if Rigan Kelly took it off the boat."

"Unless she's in it with Markov… so what's your plan?"

"We talk our way in."

"That's a crap idea. If she was in business with the Russians it's a mistake to just stroll up to the front door," Burke said with annoyance, obviously wishing that I had a better plan.

"I'm open to suggestions."

"Give me five minutes. I'll take a look. You don't hear from me, ring the bell. Just thank her for the ride to the hospital and see if you can find out what she was doing there. Maybe she'll invite you in – or give you probable cause," he finally said, moving off into the darkness.

"And if she doesn't?"

"Keep her busy as long as you can. Maybe I'll stumble across something 'in plain view.'" Burke smirked, melting into the long shadows. He was going to take a look, warrant or not, and I was going to be the distraction. I watched as he walked away, staying on the soft shoulder of the road, avoiding downed trees and storm detritus. For an old guy, he moved quickly and easily, blending into the darkness as he moved. It was only when he reached the gravel driveway that I saw him again, and then only because the flickering streetlight suddenly lit up, illuminating him for a moment before he moved beyond its glare.

I had five minutes to kill, which is nothing until you're alone on a dark street in the rain, sitting in a damp car with the engine off. Then it's mind numbing. I played solitaire on my cell phone for a couple of minutes, then got out and wandered across the street to get the lay of the land. There wasn't much to see other than a lot of downed trees, wet leaves, and some shingles that had been blown off of Rigan's house, lying in the sticker bushes. A little further up there were a few empty beer bottles and cigarette butts, as if some kids had been hanging out in a car drinking and smoking.

I looked closer at the cigarettes, noticing that they were filterless and not completely waterlogged – so they were discarded after the worst of the storm. I looked closer at the beer bottles – they were an international brand some stores had started stocking lately to cater to the blue-collar crowd that couldn't quite rise to the level of wine-snobs: *Baltika.* A Russian beer.

Shit. This wasn't good.

I tried to rationalize my apprehension away. Maybe there were Russian immigrants living in the neighborhood, or the smokers were self-conscious hipsters – but I was lying to myself. The likelihood that Russian cigarettes and beer were dumped across from Rigan Kelly's house in the last hour – by chance – was approaching nil. The knife wound in my chest started to throb. Sure, I was probably due for some pain meds, but that wasn't the only reason. I thought about numbing the pain and my nerves with more, but I was better off not being fuzzyheaded with slow reaction times.

I looked over at Rigan's house and still saw no sign of Burke. I couldn't wait. At four and a half minutes I walked up the front walk, being careful not to trip on the bricks, and climbed up the worn and crumbling stoop with one hand on my gun, scanning the night as the flickering streetlight came on.

I listened for a moment. Nothing. Peered through the side panel windows next to the door. No movement. That meant no probable cause. I rang the bell and listened as its electronic version of the William Tell Overture ended.

Then I heard movement – the light tread of feet on creaky wooden floors and the metal-on-metal sound of old hinges bearing the weight of a heavy door. Someone was inside. I was sure of it… but then the house went silent again.

I waited. After a moment there were lighter footsteps, headed for the back of the house. There wasn't much I could do except hope they ran out and right into Burke. It's not a crime to ignore your doorbell, but it should be, especially if you're leaving someone outside on a cold, wet night.

Without a warrant I was stuck. Whoever was inside was never going to answer, so I turned to go find Burke. That's when I saw her – a silhouette, half-hidden by everything that had been lifted and discarded by the winds of Sandy, standing right at the edge of the woods. The figure was slighter than a man, with longer hair and could have been a teen boy, but she didn't stand like one. I have a keen eye, and this person had curves. Hips. Serious hips. Not big, but definitely not a man's.

Whoever she was, she wasn't moving and from her position, it looked like she was watching me. I never would have been able to see her except for the fact that the flickering streetlight briefly lit up the area behind her, outlining her slender form.

Ignoring her, and keeping my eyes averted from where she stood, I moved down the walkway, running through the possibilities in my head. It could be Rigan, or Alina, the older of those two girls. From what I remembered, Dariya was smaller. Whoever it was had to have seen me knocking and had stayed hidden, not approaching or leaving, which led to one conclusion – she had something to hide.

Once off the walkway I kept going back toward my car, pretending not to see her. About halfway back to the Nova I took advantage of a downed tree, using it to obscure me from her line of sight as I ducked into the woods. During a normal fall season it would have been hard to walk silently on twigs and dried leaves, but the weather had cooperated and Sandy had left the ground cushiony and silent under my feet. I was able to circle silently around the woman. She kept her eyes on my car. When I was within ten feet, I brought my gun up, stepping slowly closer.

"Don't move," I told her calmly, but she did anyway. She was slow, and deliberate, turning to look right at me. I still couldn't see her face, but her voice I recognized.

"Pulling your little pistol on an innocent woman? Nice," she said, and for a moment I was tempted to pull the trigger.

It was Kat.

She stepped closer and a shaft of flickering light finally illuminated her face and her pale blue-green eyes. The flicker and the intensity of her stare made her look possessed. Either that, or I knew her too well and I was biased.

"Does that count as excessive force? Is that why the NYPD has such a bad rep? No manners?" Kat asked, her voice whispery-soft

"Are you nuts, Kat? I mean, not your usual bat-shit crazy type stuff, but honestly certifiable? What are you doing here?"

"That's a rhetorical question, right? 'Cause I could ask you the same thing – pointing a gun in my face just because I'm walking on public property? These woods are a nature preserve you know. Open to the public."

"You were following me."

"So you're going to shoot me?" She asked, incredulous. I so badly wanted to answer 'yes', but didn't have the time for an argument.

"How'd you get here?"

"My Vespa. I parked it out on Bloomingdale."

"I told you to stay home."

"It got dark. I *was* staying out of your way until you decided to sneak up on me and try to kill me."

"Out of my way? Did you really think I wouldn't notice you following me? You're not good at this," I told her, trying to figure out how to get rid of her. Burke was nearby and the last thing I needed was him running into Kat in the woods.

"So *you* say. I've been arrested for stalking. Twice."

"Exactly my point. You don't get arrested if you're good at it."

"Twice – *eight* years ago – before the Army trained me. There's been like fifteen times since. No one sees me coming now."

"Except me."

"Yeah. But you're like a real detective. You're better than most," Kat said, her voice going low again as she put a hand on my arm. It was warm, and soft, and in the cold damp night it felt good, but I shook it off, annoyed.

"Go home. I don't need your help."

"I can't. God says I gotta look out for the feeble-minded," she said, smiling, refusing to quit playing her games.

"I don't need help. I'm not feeble-minded," I protested, taking her firmly by the arm to lead her back out to the street. She walked with me, unresisting but still negotiating.

"Really? Tell me anything that happened to you before you were seven. Or about how it felt when you got laid for the first time."

"Fuck off. Go home. I have work to do." I left her in the street, heading back toward the house. I got five steps away and the streetlight flickered on again, causing Kat to snicker.

"If you're not feeble-minded, then why didn't you notice the motion sensor?" She asked with a mocking tone. It was her tone that made me realize she wasn't messing around.

"What motion sensor?"

"The one wired into the streetlight," she said, pointing at it. "It flickers whenever someone gets too close to that house." I looked at the streetlight and tried to recall when it had gone on or off since I got here. It could have been a coincidence, but I knew it wasn't. Kat was right.

"How'd *you* notice it?"

"I dated this mob guy up on Todt Hill once. He said no one notices a screwed-up streetlight because half of 'em are screwed up already. Great early warning system. It's like the way the Taliban uses goats – those bleating fuckers give you away every time."

At times like this Kat really pissed me off, but I didn't have a chance to be angry – whoever was inside Rigan Kelly's house had known we were coming. They knew it before I ever got to the door and before Burke went around the back. Which meant they had time to prepare. They'd already be out the back door, into the woods…

…And I hadn't heard from Burke in over ten minutes. I rushed toward the back of the house without thinking, knowing in my gut that whatever I found was going to be bad. Kat followed me.

"Stay here," I told her, without turning.

"Screw you—" she mumbled, right behind me. I moved faster, letting branches slap her as I let them go, hoping to keep her a safe distance back at the very least…

That's when I heard the scream – no, *screams* – at least two, muffled by the trees and brush and the heavy, damp air. They came from deep in the woods and I was trying to figure out from which direction when the sharp sound of three gunshots rang out – silencing the screams.

"Kat – get in the car and lock the doors!" I yelled, running headlong through sticker bushes, feeling whip-like branches stinging my cold cheeks as I lunged headfirst toward the shots.

I didn't bother to look back for Kat. I couldn't stop her if she decided to follow. She lasted two tours in Afghanistan for good reason.

My breath was coarse and coppery as my lungs spasmed from the chill in the air and arms and face were bleeding from where branches snapped, whipping wet and cold, stinging sharply. Thorns dug in and pulled loose as I ran. There was a reason these woods weren't well explored. City kids have a healthy fear of animals that lurk, urban legends, and clay pits that devour children whole, not to mention ticks and poison ivy. Why the fuck would any *Call of Duty*-playing bad ass risk getting his pristine sneakers dirty to get Lyme disease or have poison ivy complicate his acne-ravaged face?

Up ahead, I could see flashes of pale flesh as someone ran through the trees. Breathless sobs came from somewhere deeper within the woods and I slowed to try and pinpoint where they were when I heard, far-off:

"Collins! We got runners! Armed—" Burke yelled, cut off by two gunshots, a deeper, heavier sound than the sharp report of his nine-millimeter Glock.

Someone was shooting at him.

I ran, outpacing my own breath as it mingled with the thick fog. Going through my head were the horrors I'd carried with me since childhood – dreams of running through these woods, lost for days, and the stories of the people the woods had claimed, like Judy Somerville, and Holly Ann Hughes. In my mind they had all suddenly come to life, in the place I had visited in all my nightmares.

I ran straight toward the gunshots and screams anyway, wondering the whole time why I was being so stupid. Nature wires us to flee danger, and of all people I should've known better. How did I get so screwed in the head that I was running toward it?

I reached a swampy clearing just as another scream tore the night open and distracted me. I tripped, hurtling forward, catching myself as I fell over something sharp and metallic –

– Both of my wrists shot through with pain as my full weight collapsed onto them and my body sank into cold mud. Cursing under my breath, I winced in pain and opened my eyes to see that I'd tripped over some discarded bumper of an old abandoned car or – a small plane. It was half-buried under swampy mud and clay, but I recognized the broken shaft of a propeller that had been buried by the impact of a crash. Only Hurricane Sandy had been powerful enough to call up the wreckage from its grave.

If I hadn't run smack into it, I never would have seen it. Not even in broad daylight. The brush was too thick, and it was buried too deeply, half in the water and half out. Since the woods I was in were on preserved acres, no one was allowed to cut back the native plants anymore. Without the hurricane, it would have stayed buried forever – but it was here – and always had been.

I barely had time to register any of this. The screams of the young woman were now less than twenty feet away, coming from the opposite side of a small rise, covered with thick underbrush.

"No! Please. No—" she was muttering, cutting herself off with her own scream. I pulled out my gun and climbed up the small rise, quietly pushing back branches and sticker bushes, grateful that her screams had covered the sound. When I reached the top, I saw a husky Russian manhandling Alina, trying to shove dirt and leaves in her mouth to shut her up. Her shirt was torn open and he seemed to be getting a cheap thrill out of the way he touched her, but she was fighting. I should have shot him right then, but I froze for a moment, paralyzed by the nightmare of a time where I had no gun, just a tire iron…

*

…He was too focused on the girl, kicking and clawing as he pushed her flat on her back in the mud, straddling her, ripping her shirt and backhanding her across the face.

"How do you like that, little bitch? Teach you to make me run," he growled as he grabbed her by the hair and pulled her face close to his. His voice was muttered and indistinct in the rain, something about it different, maybe foreign.

"…break you in. Make you worthless," the man muttered, going on as he ripped open the young girl's shorts. That's when I saw the scar on her thigh, so similar to my own, a spiraling curve the size of a half dollar, shaped like the coils of an old car's cigarette lighter. The only difference was that hers was fresh, raised and red, as if it were brand new and barely healed…

CHAPTER FIFTEEN

…I shook off the memory of the dream. Dreams weren't going to help Alina. My gun was. I raised it and pointed it at the Russian, center-mass.

"Let her go," I said simply, allowing my Glock to say the rest. The Russian turned, putting his forearm across Alina's throat to keep her quiet as he looked up at me and smiled.

"*Nyet*. Fuck off," he said calmly. I almost pulled the trigger out of spite. I should have. Instead I did as I was trained to do.

"I'm an NYPD detective, and trust me, I'll drop you in a heartbeat."

"But not me…" I heard off to my left. I didn't move my gun, but glanced over to see another Russian holding a pistol. It was pointed right at my center mass and his hand was rock steady.

Fuck me.

"Drop the gun, Detective," he told me in an accent that grated on every nerve I had. I hesitated and he turned, reaching behind him to pull Dariya out of the shadows by her long mane of auburn hair. She was barefoot, in shorts and a T-shirt. Her face was bruised, and it was clear that he didn't catch her without a struggle. It struck me then that if her hair was just a shade lighter, she could be an older version of the girl from my dreams.

"He'll kill you if you drop it. Shoot him—" I heard a hoarse voice say from the shadows. Looking closer, behind Dariya and deeper in the shadows was Rigan, kneeling, lip bleeding, and one eye beginning to go black.

"I'll kill her if you don't. I won't ask again," the second Russian said without raising his voice, moving his gun off of me to Dariya's head.

Motherfucker.

I didn't move, talking to buy myself some time to think.

"Where's Markov?" I asked.

"He has Anton—" Rigan started to say, but was cut off as the Russian holding Dariya lashed out, kicking back, catching Rigan with the heel of his boot just above her left ear.

"Shut up," he mumbled as an afterthought.

"Will you just shoot him already?" the first Russian grunted, pulling Alina tight against him to stop her from struggling.

"Who's Anton?" I asked, my finger tightening on the trigger, trying to gauge if I could shoot them both before Dariya caught a bullet to the temple.

"The boy from the boat," Rigan said. This time the kick missed her, but that pissed off the Russian even more.

"I said shut up! Drop it now or I'll shoot the little bitch," he said, twitching the gun to one side and pulling the trigger, deafening Dariya, causing her to drop to the ground, whimpering. It wasn't worth the risk. I dropped the gun, tossing it toward the Russian with Alina, hoping that it would distract him enough to get him to stop groping her.

He didn't flinch. The second Russian grinned.

"Smart man. You just saved the little one's life. Too bad that now you'll lose your own." He pointed his gun back at me again.

All I could think was 'you gotta be fucking kidding me'. I was going to die in the same woods where I almost died all those years ago. How fucking stupid. I kept my eyes open, staring him down, mostly so I didn't piss myself. I saw his arm tense and then –

– I heard the shot, but felt nothing…

The Russian's head snapped back as a flap of skin and bone tore free from his forehead, blood spraying out onto the wet ground, all over Dariya and Rigan. It took me a full second to realize that the sound came from the wrong direction. By the time I located it, three more shots had been fired – all toward the Russian groping Alina.

It was Kat – firing at the first Russian, who used Alina as a human shield.

"Kat! Stop! You'll hit her—"

– But Kat was emptying the clip – an excellent shot, she missed Alina and clipped the Russian, but not enough to stop him. He pulled Alina back into the woods, returning fire. I raced to grab my own pistol, but by the time I looked up, the Russian and Alina were gone.

Dariya was hysterical, sobbing and trying to wipe off the blood, but Rigan was calm as she bent down to pick up the second Russian's gun.

"I'm going after them. Are you going to try to stop me?" Rigan asked.

"No. Go." I told her, somehow sure in that moment that she could handle herself and that she was a partner I could trust. Rigan didn't hesitate, just pulled Dariya up by the arm and propelled her into the woods – like a modern Diana going hunting.

I turned back to Kat, who was furious, ejecting the magazine to reload. I walked toward her slowly.

"Give me the gun, Kat." Kat looked up at me, keyed up and angry.

"I had to shoot," she muttered, turning to look at the dead Russian whose skull had been ripped open. "I'm out of practice. I was aiming for his heart," she explained, looking at the top of his head, decimated by the wound.

"Good thing. If you aimed for his head, we'd both be dead… Just give me the gun, Kat."

She did, barrel end first, like a pro. I took out another magazine in and chambered a round, then quickly fired it into the ground in order to get the gun shot residue on my hand, then I gently took her face in my hands, making her look me in the eye so that we'd be clear when we were questioned.

"Listen closely. This is important." Kat nodded. I'd have to settle for that. "The gun is registered in my name. I have the GSR on my hands."

"So do I."

"You'll get it off. I shot him. Understand?"

"But—"

"Don't argue. Just go and use the mud and water to clean your hands." Kat nodded, reluctantly, and went to the nearest water, sticking her hands in as I went on. "I'm leaving to follow them. I want you to stay here until someone comes. Don't answer any questions from anybody. Just tell them I shot the guy. You were a witness, that's all. Do you understa—"

I stopped, spinning around and lifting my gun as I heard a branch snap behind me, and turned to draw down on – Burke. He looked ragged and pale, his clothes torn and mud splashed up to his knees. As he saw my gun his hands went up.

"Goddamn, Collins. What the hell?" he asked, eyes going from me to the Russian, whose skull was in pieces like a jigsaw puzzle on the ground.

"He drew down on me. I had no choice. The other one did a runner with Rigan Kelly and the two girls. We have to go," I told him, moving in the direction they'd fled, hoping to distract him from this crime scene. No such luck.

"Where's his gun?" Burke asked, kneeling over the body. I froze, taking a beat to make sure that whatever story I was about to tell would remain consistent.

"That badass chick took it," Kat answered before I could.

Burke glanced at her, and then back at me, ignoring Kat as if she was just another piece of evidence.

"Who the fuck is she and what's she doing here?"

I shrugged, buying time to come up with a story, and then went with the first thing that I thought of. "I don't know. She's stoned or something. Heard screams and wandered in from the street."

"Dude got shot," Kat muttered, playing along.

"I see that," Burke responded, taking her in critically, suspicious.

"It was like *boom*. And then blood and... dead. Dude's dead." Kat went on with a dazed look of shock, her gaze fixed on the dead Russian. She sure seemed stoned to me.

"Christ. Like this is what we need, some trippin' stoner. We can't leave her here."

"We don't have a choice. We need to go after those girls," I told him, moving off into the woods before he could stop me. I got about ten feet in when I was suddenly blinded by a bright orange flash and was hit with horrific, blood-chilling screams –

– And I was running again, this time toward a blossom of flame and the smell of burning gasoline, wet leaves, damp wood... and human flesh. The throat that the raw screams were coming from sounded shredded, vocal cords tattered and painful. I forgot about the tree branches that almost blinded me. I forgot about the icy water that froze my legs, and the mud that gripped my boots. I ran without thought, and the heat came at me in in waves as the first vapors of gasoline burned off. Only gasoline could have burned in woods this wet, and you could feel the steamy heat of the wood it had torched on every exposed pore.

I finally stumbled into a relatively clear space, one arm shielding my face from the heat to see that brush and leaves had been piled around a lone tree. It had been doused in gasoline and its misshapen trunk looked as if it were melting in the fire.

"You're too late."

The Russian-accented voice came from beyond the flames, and I pulled my gun up, squinting, scanning for its owner.

"He told us what we needed to know," the voice spoke again and I found him –

– Josef Markov.

He was standing in the trees, ten yards beyond the fire, smiling grimly. He looked like a Brooklyn hipster that had been on a serious bender. His cheap-looking but expensive clothes were trashed, his three-hundred-dollar haircut looked greasy, and his pasty-white face with its flawless complexion was sickly yellow in the reflected light. Next to him was a shriveled up older guy with a mangy goatee. As I saw his eyes in the yellow light, I recognized him...

The last time I had seen him he had a mangy mustache and thinning hair. Now he was bald, with an overgrown gray goatee. He still had that same squinty-eyed look about him and the same bad teeth, although he'd apparently stopped looking for Swamp Pink and had taken up with the Russians.

I didn't hesitate this time. I knew what I was dealing with. I pulled the trigger – but the shot went wild as Burke slammed into me from behind and knocked my aim off. Furious, I turned the gun on him, but he just stared me down.

"Are you out of your fuckin' gourd? You kill Markov's son, the Russian Mafia will kill you and your whole family," he said, jittery. "Last time a Markov went missing we had the FBI, CIA and even the Goddamn Soviets up our ass. You do not fuck with these people."

I looked back to see if Markov was still visible. He wasn't. Neither was the Mangy Goatee Guy. I emptied my Glock in their general direction anyway. Fuck the Russian Mafia and fuck guys with goatees.

"You let him get away," I said, turning on Burke. He wasn't paying attention. He was staring at the fire as Kat arrived, breathing heavily, her eyes also transfixed by the flames.

"Kill…" she said quietly, making the sign of the cross out of some long-buried reflex. I followed her gaze, hearing something beneath the crackle of the flames, smelling something that made my stomach contract with an acidic spasm. Staring at the tree, it took me a moment to realize that the trunk wasn't misshapen…

…No. The tree was tall and straight. The thing that was misshapen was the teen boy that was bound to it, his skin already blackened and charred, his hair singed and melting, his face barely recognizable. Anton.

It was the boy from the yacht, I knew it as soon as I saw him. He was moaning in a low, keening, guttural wail because he couldn't scream any longer. The fire had dried out his throat and lungs, making him gasp desperately for the oxygen flames had stolen. As I stared, I noticed that Anton's blue eyes were open, the lids having been burned off, and that he was staring at me with a look beyond pain, and beyond hope.

Markov was right. Anton knew it. I *was* too late.

…But I couldn't accept that. I pulled off my jacket and slapped at the fire, putting out flames. I kicked at the leaves and branches at the base of the tree he was tied to, burning my hands and singing the hair on my arms. The wet ground helped to put out the worst of it, but the heat was still intense as I got close enough to cut him free. The smell almost made me step back.

The odor of his burned flesh and singed hair seeped in through my mouth. I averted my gaze, but the image of his charred body stayed with me. I looked for somewhere to grab Anton to pull him away from the ash and heat, moving in close enough that I could hear his breath, wheezing in and out. As I did, he formed barely audible words, struggling to do it in his fractured English.

"They took... Alina," he rasped. I just nodded, struggling to hold up his weight without digging into his wounds.

"Let me help," Kat said, moving in close, without hesitation. She put one of his burned arms around her shoulders, ignoring the heat and the bloody ooze that dripped onto her neck. As we carried him away from the tree, he tried to speak again.

"They wanted…" he started to say, but couldn't get a breath deep enough to finish.

"Don't talk," I told him, unable to bear the sound of his voice or the smell of his scorched lungs wafting out with each mangled word.

"It might be his only chance," Burke commented from ten feet away, keeping his mouth and nose covered. Kat and I laid Anton down on the mossy ground, and for a heartbeat I worried about infection before I came to my senses and realized no bacteria could breed fast enough to kill him. He was going to be dead before the sun came up.

Kat knelt and lifted his head, laying it gently in her lap, stroking Anton's singed hair, speaking softly.

"Just rest. It's okay. You can close your eyes and let go…"

Anton seemed to nod, but he couldn't close his eyes, so he ended up staring at Kat, unfocused for a moment. Then he took a deep, shuddering breath, grabbed her hand in his and coughed, trying to speak again.

"I …told…"

"Shhh, it's okay," Kat soothed him, trying to smile and keep a brave front for the kid as tears drifted down her cheeks. As she did, I noticed something in Anton's now opened hand – the one in Kat's. A crumpled bit of paper. I knelt next to her, putting a hand on her shoulder. She sighed, thankful for the support.

"You don't have to do this, Kat. He's already gone." Kat glared at me. Daggers. She knew that.

"…And he doesn't deserve the least bit of compassion and love before he goes?" she asked, shaming me for my aversion to his wounds.

"I... I'm... cold... But it... doesn't hurt... any... more," Anton interrupted. Kat brought him closer, holding him as he shivered.

"He's in shock. The nerve endings were burned off," Burke stated in a flat tone, just watching, seemingly unaffected.

"Shut the fuck up."

"I'm just being practical, Collins. It doesn't hurt, let him talk. In case you ain't figured it out, this looks an awful lot like that case Joe Corrigan was working when he died. You deserve to know –"

"I said shut the fuck up –" I yelled, as Kat gently stroked Anton's face where it had escaped the worst burns, whispering to him, saying things that I couldn't hear, sweet nothings that she pulled from somewhere deep inside.

"Tell... Alina... that I..."

"I will," Kat assured him, and then Anton turned to look at me, clear-eyed for a brief moment.

"You... remember ... He wants what you know."

His words knocked me off balance. "Sure, kid. Take it easy," I told him, but his eyes got more intense and his voice got louder.

"Find it..." he spat out, using his last breath before beginning to choke, the air rattling as he struggled to breathe. ...And then he gasped and caught his breath, struggling. Kat kissed him, gently, barely touching her lips to his. I swear he smiled, just a fraction, looked as if he was about to speak...

...And then he was gone. Nobody said a word for a moment. We just listened to the wind moving through the trees, causing the water to fall from their leaves like a phantom rain. Finally, Burke sighed, looking at Anton.

"Well, at least that's over. But we're still fucked," he muttered, with all the emotion coming straight from his black heart.

"No, *he's* fucked. We're still here."

"Still here with a roasted teen and a dead Russian thirty yards that way. How do we explain any of this? Neither one of us was supposed to be investigating. The Feds are gonna shit."

"Why do we need to tell the Feds? For all we know this has nothing to do with that yacht," I said. Burke shook his head, not buying it.

"You saw Markov."

"Did I?"

"And how are you going to explain that dead Russian back there? You're fucked –" Burke reminded me.

"He had a gun, if I didn't –" Kat said, starting to defend me, stopping herself before she completely fucked up our story. It didn't matter. Burke wasn't stupid. Kat caught his look and knew immediately that she'd blown the whole scam.

"You two might want to get your story straight," he advised us. "Bringing your girlfriend on cases where guys get killed is frowned upon, Collins."

"She's not my girlfriend," I told him, sounding pathetic even to myself.

"She's no random stoner either, is she?"

"Stoner, stalker – she's both. I can't be blamed for her."

"It's true," Kat chimed in, trying to help. "I was stalking him.

I was afraid to be alone." Burke just shook his head, sympathetic to my problem.

"Christ, Collins, you got issues on issues, don't you?"

"You have no idea – but I also have questions. Like how did Rigan Kelly end up with these kids and where the fuck is all the heroin that was on that yacht if the Russians are still looking for it?" I asked, turning to Burke.

"Don't look at me. Maybe the Feds have it. Maybe Rigan Kelly grabbed it when she went back for the kids. You never know with these do-gooder types. Half of them are in it for the wrong reasons. Like priest-pedophiles, power-hungry police."

"Did you get a look inside her house?" I asked.

"It was completely cleaned out."

Damn. The wound on my chest was starting to throb again. This night was turning to shit. I was out in the rain, soaking wet, with two dead bodies, two kidnapped girls, and a woman in the hands of a Russian lunatic – and I had no real leads on where any of them might be.

I hate the rain. Nothing good ever happens in it.

Finally, I looked back at Anton. "We're going to need to call Lieutenant Demetrius and a crime scene unit."

"Yes, we are," Burke agreed reluctantly. "...I got it. And don't worry, I'll cover for you – because of your old man and your uncle, but don't lie to me again."

Burke walked away, dialing his cell phone. I looked for someplace to rest, finding a mossy log not far from where Anton lay, and I sat watching the vapor drift off his cool body.

Kat came over and settled in next to me. The close warmth of her body was soothing, although I'd never tell her that.

"You all right?"

"I will be," I assured her, checking to make sure she was all right. There were tracks where her tears had run through the dirt she'd gotten on her face.

"You, know, what you did for that kid…" I shrugged, not able to compliment her the way she deserved without getting overly sentimental.

"We don't have to talk about it."

"No… But it was the right thing to do."

"I know…" her voice trailed off and Kat looked me in the eye. It was an honest moment, and not one I was comfortable with, not with her. "…I just kept looking at him and thinking about you. He had eyes like yours. Isn't that strange? I kept thinking that you might've looked like him when you were that age."

I looked away. I didn't need to identify with some dead kid in these woods. I'd almost died here myself and I didn't really want to start thinking about it again. After a moment I looked back at Anton, unable to resist, finding it hard to breathe in the thick air, dense with mist and fog and the smell of burning death. It filled my lungs and gelled there. I needed to move, but when I shifted my weight, I winced from the sharp pain caused by stretching my stitches.

"Your chest?"

"Yeah. It's just been a long day. Should've been taking painkillers."

"My grandmother used to tell me that when things were at their worst, I should look for something beautiful – that God put beauty in painful moments to remind us that we could get through them," Kat told me, getting up and reaching out for a tall, brightly pink flower perched at the end of what looked like a weed.

"I've never seen a flower like this before," she said as she reached for it.

"You shouldn't be seeing it now. It's only supposed to bloom in spring, but thanks to our freaky weather it's confused."

"What is it?"

"*Helonias Bullata* – Swamp Pink." Kat turned at that, recognizing the name from my story.

"The stuff those guys were digging for?"

"So they said."

Kat nodded, pulling at the flower, inadvertently tugging on its notoriously extensive roots as well. She stopped as it came up, still looking down at something, frozen in place.

"Kill, you might want to look at this…"

"I've seen Swamp Pink before. The roots are always like that."

"It's not the roots," she said softly, moving aside. The roots had pulled up the soil around them and had uncovered something dark and leathery, with moss growing on its surface.

I got up to look closer, pulling leaves and moss off, thinking that it might be an old discarded coat from when this area was used as an illegal dump, but then I started to recognize the shape and features of what it was. It wasn't a coat. It was too hard, and it was shaped like a rock. I had to dig my fingers into the wet clay to scrape around its edges, finally getting enough out from around it to see what it was.

When I did, the dream came back unbidden – and unwelcome.

…The man who had chased us was on top of me as something warm and wet dropped onto my cheek and I fought to get out from under him. When I did, I glanced over to see him looking back at me… with one eye. Where the other had been was the tire iron. I wiped my cheek, smearing the vitreous fluid that had flowed from his eye off of my face and looked back down at –

—A human skull, its empty eye sockets looking back at me, one with a tire iron going right through it...

…It was no coincidence that I was on this case, or that I ended up here.

CHAPTER SIXTEEN

"Great, first floods, now fire. What's next, a plague of locusts?" Lieutenant Demetrius muttered from where he stood under the warm glare of the work lights that illuminated the woods and the crime scene techs that had flooded the area. A half dozen of them were going over Anton's body and the site of the fire, and through the woods I could see more lights and could hear the other CSU team going over the scene around the Russian's body.

"You're gonna have a plague of Feds is what you're gonna have," Burke answered from where he sat comfortably on a crime scene tech's portable stool.

"Did I ask you, Burke? You think I need this shit from the two of you? In the middle of cleaning up from Frankenstorm?"

"I like 'Stormzilla' better," Kat offered, but stopped talking as Demetrius glared at her. She was sitting next to me on the decaying log, watching the crime scene unit carefully dig up the body with the tire iron through its eye.

I took it all in, fighting every instinct I had to get out of there, especially when I saw that there was still hair on the cadaver's head, matted around the skull, preserved by the clay it was buried in. It somehow made his death seem more recent and real. His leathery skin was loose around the muscle that had withered away beneath it, but the features of the face could have been those of the man from my dream. Maybe I had witnessed his murder all those years ago and had incorporated it into my dream – or maybe I even stumbled across his body in the days that I was lost in these woods.

I was trying to rationalize it, but no matter what I did, I kept seeing the arc of a tire iron in my hands, felt the jolt of it as it struck the man and the warm fluid leaking onto me as he collapsed. As I saw them brush the dirt off his body I was sure that I didn't dream I'd killed a man –

– I *remembered* that I did.

"You all right, Kill?" Kat asked, putting a comforting hand on leg. I didn't pull away this time, afraid that showing any emotion would make me look guilty.

"I'm fine."

"Liar. You look like you just woke up from one of your dreams," she said. I turned to her, wondering if somehow she knew. I couldn't remember if I'd told her about this particular dream, but when I looked in her eyes, all I saw was concern.

"Didn't we both? Wasn't this just like a bad dream?" I deflected.

"I guess. But we're not the ones buried or burned, right?"

I shrugged. It was cold way of looking at it, but she had a point.

"You getting anywhere? I ain't got all night." Demetrius grumbled at the crime scene guys, jumping up and down to stay warm as he watched them meticulously dig out the body.

"We'll have him out in the next ten."

"How long has he been there?"

"Awhile," grunted a tech, annoyed, as usual, by detectives and cops who have no respect for their science.

"That's not helpful. Can you give me a guess?" Demetrius asked, trying to be patient. The CSU tech shrugged.

"It's the conditions here. Damn thing's like a bog body."

"Bog body?" asked Demetrius, completely lost.

"Naturally mummified bodies found in bogs – like swamps – all over Europe. It has its skin and organs intact because of the highly acidic water and lack of oxygen in the soil. It's the amount of clay. If you wanted to mummify someone, the South Shore of Staten Island is a great place to bury them."

"Good to know. How old is it?"

"A guess? Somewhere between fifteen and thirty years old," the crime scene tech answered, giving in.

"So, I guess I shouldn't ask for a specific time of death?"

"This isn't a lab. The other two I can give you a time of death within minutes," the tech told Demetrius, trying to pacify him. It didn't work.

"Big deal. So can he, can't you, Killer?" He had no idea. I

could give him all three. The mummy had been there since October 23, 1985, sometime between nine P.M. and one A.M.

"I want an ID on all three bodies ASAP – and did anybody get the GSR off Detective Collins' hands?" he asked, turning back to me, looking at the bandage on my arm. "Or the blood alcohol?"

"Both. And they bagged my gun as evidence. Can I go now?" I asked, knowing the probable answer. Still, I had to try.

"In a minute. First, tell me again why you were here?"

"I wanted to thank Rigan Kelly for bringing me to the hospital."

"Right..." Demetrius nodded, playing along, not believing a word of what I'd told him when he got here. "And you brought your girlfriend with you?" he asked, letting his eyes wander over Kat.

"She's not my girlfriend. She was driving me. I was injured, remember?"

"So, she was just your driver? Why her?"

"I'm easy to use, 'cause we also live together," Kat contributed, not so helpfully.

"Nice arrangement. You told Burke she was a stalker."

"I am," Kat chimed in again, digging us in deeper. "I follow him around, but Kill doesn't want anything to do with me. Can you imagine?"

"Darlin', the crazy goes right through your eyes to your soul. I don't blame him," he told her, then turned to me. "She's a few cards short, isn't she?"

"It's not like it sounds," I told him.

"It never is."

"I rent her an apartment."

"Right. Maybe I don't want to hear anymore. It's all purely platonic, I'm sure. Let's get back to the relevant part here. You come to express your gratitude, but you call Burke to meet you? Why?" Demetrius pressed. I took my time answering, making sure that my answer would match what Burke and I had worked out before Demetrius arrived.

"I knew Burke was interested in finding those two girls, and that Rigan Kelly works with at-risk youth. I thought it might be a good idea to warn her that they might turn up."

"So it wasn't an *investigation*?"

"Not at all."

"You just stumbled across the two girls you saved from Markov's yacht, caught a Russian Mafia soldier groping one, shot him, let the other one run away with his gun, and then ran over here to find a guy you think might have been Josef Markov lighting a kid on fire. All by chance?"

"Exactly."

"You're *good*, isn't he good, Kill?" Kat said, grinning at Demetrius. She was trying to get a rise out of him, but luckily Demetrius ignored her.

"You're givin' me a fuckin' headache, Collins. You expect me to believe any of this?"

"What other explanation is there?" I asked. That stopped him. Demetrius looked back at the scorched tree, Anton's body, the mummified remains and then the lights in the distance where the Russian body was lying dead and he shrugged, completely lost.

"I wish I knew. Only in Goddamn Staten Island… Either way, you're done here. Go home. Stay there. The Feds may want to talk to you. While you're there, write me a full report on this whole mess," Demetrius said, talking as I got up and started to walk away.

"A report? Really? Is anyone going to read it in the middle of this disaster?"

"Maybe not. The Feds might decide all three of these people drowned just to avoid a diplomatic mess with the Russians. We won't know until they get here."

"Enjoy the company. I'll be home and warm and dry," I said, rubbing it in.

"If they want to talk, I'm sending them to your place – and if they want to talk to your Girl Friday, that's the same address, right?" Demetrius needled me, trying to get a reaction from me.

"She lives *upstairs*."

"She's on top, huh?"

"Funny," I muttered over my shoulder, still walking.

"Hey, Kill, I almost forgot," Demetrius called after me. "Burke tells me you know how the pieces of that plane got here." I stopped, turning back for a moment, curious as to why he cared.

"It was a case my dad worked on back in the eighties. Some

drug runners crashed here trying to smuggle some coke," I told him honestly.

"No shit…" he said, impressed.

"No shit."

"He said this is where you got lost as a kid too. This place bring back any memories?"

"No. None," I told him, turning to leave again. Kat followed me, giving me a look. She thought I was lying. I wasn't. It didn't bring back *memories*.

It brought back dreams…

*

…The wet smell of the wool blanket was comforting, in spite of the fact that the odor was a bleak reminder of the cold and damp that the blanket was warding off. As I pulled it tighter around me, I was aware that it was too dark to even see what color the blanket was, but I somehow knew that it was green. I also knew that huddled next to me under the blanket was another warm body, a girl who smelled vaguely pungent from not having washed in several days and whose skin felt so soft where it touched my own. I also knew that whoever she was, I knew her well, since she was the one I had seen running through the woods in my other dreams. The girl's relentless shivering was keeping me awake in spite of being tired, and I could feel that it was getting colder. The girl's skin was cooling off and I held her closer, but I noticed that her shivering was also slowing down – not because she was getting warmer, but because hypothermia was setting in. The fear of falling asleep, never to wake up again, motivated me.

"We need to get out of here," I told her, hearing my own childish voice. "We don't have a choice." She was about to respond when the sound of the rain on something metal began to take shape, and all of the whispered and dissonant sounds seemed to coalesce into words...

...And then they became actual words, whose accent sounded strange to my ears. I glanced out through a gap in the wall of whatever we were inside of and saw flashlights flickering between the trees. Everything they passed over was illuminated, but when they passed, a deeper darkness seemed to be left behind. Men were talking to each other out there, behind the light, their voices barely rising above the sound of the rain.

I took the girl's hand. She was still hidden in the shadows, but I pulled her out into the night, getting a quick glimpse of a face that was so familiar now. It was hard to focus on her, because in my dream I was always focused on what we'd been hiding inside of – something white and made of metal with rivets stitching it together.

The plane.

"No. We can't leave. No—" she protested, pulling back.

"We can't hide here. We have to go," I told her, grabbing her harder, needing to run before the men arrived. She finally followed, but as we emerged, a light blinded me and –

*

—I was suddenly staring into the cold white light of a uniformed cop's Maglite. We had approached Rigan Kelly's house while I was distracted and his light caught me off guard. I felt like I did in the dream – every time something became more illuminated and clear, the light would slip away and it would be left deeper in darkness.

My dreams, the ones I remembered, where all centered around these woods, and I was starting to understand why. They were reflections of some sort of reality. I had been here when it all happened. I came out here that night with Uncle Joe and the two kids my father mentioned. For whatever reason, I was with him and something happened. Something went wrong with the informant he was supposed to meet. Maybe the car crash was a cover…

"You two stop. Show me ID," the Uniform interrupted my chain of thought, flashing the Maglite in our eyes again.

"Jesus freakin' hell. Can you get that damn thing outta my eyes, you moron?" Kat asked the cop, not quite politely. I shielded my own eyes, taking in the third crime scene unit at Rigan Kelly's house.

"This is a crime scene, Miss, and unless you'd like to end up in handcuffs, you might want to leave. Now," grunted the uniform, with the tone and attitude of a guy that wore the badge with no sense of humor, little intelligence, and a self-inflated sense of his own authority. I hope I was never like that, but it didn't matter much anymore – I pulled out my gold shield, flashing it in the blinding light. My authority was more inflated than his.

"She's a material witness," I told the uniform, "…and she's

with me. So back off." I strode past the guy before he could start thinking too much. Kat followed, giving the cop a smug look.

"I appreciate you standing up for me, Kill, but he *was* kind of buff and was about to put me in handcuffs."

"Don't push your luck, Kat. Keep your mouth shut. We're going home."

"Stay dry and warm," she told the cop as we passed him, watching the ice-cold rain drip down his face with a perverse pleasure. "We're going home. Together. To bed. Where I'll keep him warm..."

Have I mentioned that Kat could be a complete bitch when she wanted to be? I waited until we were almost to the street before I confronted her. "Hand it over," I told her, putting out my hand as the streetlight started to flicker again.

"What?"

"Whatever it was that Anton handed you. I saw you take the evidence."

"Are you accusing me of a crime?" Kat asked, wide-eyed. "Are you going to strip search me?" Now she was grinning. I didn't have the patience for it.

"No. I'll have Burke do it," I told her, and when she still hesitated I pulled open her jacket and lifted her shirt – finding a torn and crumpled scrap of paper tucked in her waistband. I pulled it out, stepping away from her before she could react.

"That's the most action I've had in a week. Keep going, tiger."

I ignored her, looking at the paper. It had small, neat handwriting on one side: '*Rigan, Anton and I moved the cargo.*

Will give it to Markov when you and the kids are safe'. The rest of the note was scorched and the signature was gone, but it looked as if it could start with a 'T'.

"You're lucky I was there to help you out and grab this before Burke got it. You're clearly not on your game. This whole time somebody's been a step ahead of you, haven't they? Leading you by the nose through your own past?" Kat asked as I looked more closely at the paper.

"Thanks for pointing that out."

"I'm just wondering how they keep staying ahead of you. I mean, I don't think you're stupid, but I was only trained by the Army and not the NYPD so I'm no expert on detecting and shit."

"Clearly," I agreed, pocketing the note. "Especially since this note doesn't change anything."

"Other than proving Rigan has an accomplice. That she did go back to the boat like Burke said. Maybe she and Markov double-crossed each other and she was in on the trafficking.."

"Or she knew what he was carrying and wanted to stop him," I objected, for some reason finding it hard to see Rigan Kelly as a trafficker.

"You giving the note back to Burke?"

"No, I'm taking it and going home."

"Going *home*?" Kat asked, stopping in the middle of the street, twenty feet from my Nova. "There are killers on the loose – with those poor girls and that woman at their mercy."

I didn't want her to cause a scene out here, not with stolen evidence under my jacket, but I was tired and losing my patience. "What world do you live in? This is not a game. I need sleep. Painkillers. Dry clothes."

"You're going home. To be *dry*." She stomped her foot, ready to go all out toddler-tantrum on me. I walked away, going for the car. She wouldn't stand out in the rain for very long if I got in and ignored her.

"Yes. I am. And when I am, I'll figure out what to do next. I need to be able to think clearly, not fuck up because I'm overtired." Kat started walking again, changing tactics as I took out my keys.

"The woman was kind of hot, don't you think?"

"Not now, Kat. This isn't a night at the Four W's Bar where we both get drunk and rate the locals."

"You didn't notice what a stunning woman she was? She was the woman who saved your life down by The Annex, right? And you're not going to return the favor?"

"Will you just get in the car?"

"Yes or no? Did you notice she was smokin' hot?"

"She was hot. Yes. Fine. She saved my life. You jealous? Why do you even care?" I opened the door, hoping she would let it go once we got in. Kat followed me, unable to stop herself.

"—They're out there in the *rain*. What were their names again?"

"Dariya. Alina. Rigan… You don't need to personalize it. I know their names. I'll find them, but I need time to think." I started the Nova, putting it into gear as Kat buckled her seatbelt.

"What about the Taser King of the South Shore? The guy who attacked me – isn't he a lead? He came for some newspaper article on that plane and then here we are, right where it crashed."

"Yes. It's a lead, but it'd help if I knew more about him. You said he sounded old. Would you recognize his voice if you heard it again?" I asked, pulling out, weaving my way past police cars and crime scene unit vans.

"Doubt it. He didn't waste many words and my head was spinning after getting fifty thousand volts from his Taser. All I know is that he knew about the old case."

"Then I guess he knows more than I do."

"Apparently that's not hard," I heard from the back seat. It took me a second to realize that the voice was not Kat's –

– It was Rigan's. I started to turn, but felt cold metal against my neck.

"Don't. I don't want the cops to see you. Just drive," Rigan said quietly.

"You got away."

"They still have Alina. Dariya's here."

"Not by choice," I heard Dariya mutter in her strange accent.

"Where are we going?" Kat asked calmly, staring out at the cops without batting an eye.

"Out of here. We need to get away from the police. I don't trust them or the FBI. One or both are working with Markov," Rigan said as I turned right onto Bloomingdale Road, leaving the lights of the crime scene behind.

"How do you know?" I asked, driving into the shadows.

"Unlike you, I have a memory."

"What do you know about my memory?" I turned to confront Rigan, but felt the gun pressed into my neck again and thought better of it.

"I think she's calling you an idiot. At the moment, I agree," Kat muttered.

"You want my help, Rigan, tell me what you know that I don't."

"I know that there's no way that Markov, who's never been to Staten Island before and has no idea who I am, could have found us without help." Rigan caught my eye in the mirror, an accusation in her look. "Was it you?"

"Him? Are you out of your mind?" Kat defended me, turning on Rigan only to look down the barrel of her gun.

"Markov must have tracked the girls the same way I did," I told Rigan. "If he asked the right questions, followed them to the emergency shelters…"

"A Russian oligarch's son can't just walk around asking questions the way you did. Staten Islanders are suspicious. I'm surprised they even talked to *you*." Rigan had a point. It didn't matter how Markov found them, or who may have betrayed them. All that mattered was that we get some distance between us and the psychopaths who might burn any of us at the stake. Rigan had the same idea.

"Head for the bridge," she ordered.

"It's closed."

"Not to cops it's not. Use your badge."

"Not happening. No one's getting in or out. We can't get off and neither can Markov."

"Until they open it and he can. He has Alina. He'll take her and be gone if we don't –"

"They won't open it until they get power back – look," I said, nodding to where the bridge stood in the inky wet blackness. "No power, no bridge. We have at least until morning. We can go to my place—"

"—No," she interrupted. "They know where you live. We need somewhere Markov doesn't know about."

"Tottenville," Kat chimed in. "It's under curfew to keep out looters. Your parents—"

"—No," I said, cutting her off. Going to my parents was truly a bad idea.

"Stop being such a wuss," Kat told me, then turned to Rigan. "He's got attachment disorder or something. Family issues."

"I understand. But we need to lay low somewhere."

"Why don't you tell me what this is all about? Why did you call me to that boat? What do you know about the trafficking? The drugs? And who took the heroin as collateral for the kids?" I asked, frustrated.

"Later. Neither of them needs to hear it," Rigan said, indicating Dariya and Kat.

"I trust Kat."

"I don't. Now get to Tottenville, before I have to shoot someone," Rigan said as she pulled the gun up, pointing it at Kat.

I didn't have much choice. I made a quick U-turn on Maguire Avenue, dodging downed trees and flooded underpasses as well as barricades and power crews to head to the ass-end of the island for the second time in twenty-four hours.

CHAPTER SEVENTEEN

The seven-minute drive was tense, but I couldn't shake the thought that I was missing something, that there was something I was missing, some way Markov might have found Rigan, Alina, and Dariya. It occurred to me as I turned the corner onto my parents' street – and then only because I glanced in my rear-view mirror to make sure we weren't being followed and caught sight of Dariya in the darkness.

Dariya was a teen girl in the back seat of a dark car and there was no glow on her face from her cell phone. None. She had no electronics at all. The connected generation was completely disconnected. Apparently.

"Dariya, are you carrying anything Markov or his men gave you? Wearing anything? Anything at all?"

"Why?" asked Rigan, nervously.

"Markov isn't an idiot. He's technically savvy. His father owns part of a Russian Telecom."

"He's also former KGB who spent seven years in Lubyanka Prison after his brother – Mikhail Markov – disappeared and is now financing unrest in the Crimea and the Ukraine, dealing drugs for arms and kidnapping opponents' kids," Rigan said, lashing out. "Don't whitewash him as a businessman. He's a criminal."

"So, why's a criminal bothering with politics?"

"Money. Congress is trying to pass this Magnitsky Act thing, derailing some of the deals he's made for oil in the Arctic. Could cost him billions. Crimea has oil, though – and would make up some of the losses," she explained. "Putin and the other Oligarchs are backing him. Heroin coming in here also creates havoc – payback."

"So he has access to power and to Russian Intelligence. Which is why I need to know if you're carrying anything he gave you," I told Dariya, trying to be patient.

"Just a bracelet…" Dariya said quietly. "…It doesn't come off. One time they drugged us and I woke up with it on."

"Fuck me. That's how they found you," Kat muttered.

"How they can *still* find you," I added. "There's a GPS tracker in the bracelet."

"What's the range on the GPS?" Rigan asked, worried.

"I don't know. We need to get it off. Now. I'll need tools. Let's get inside and hope Markov's cell phones and GPS trackers are as fucked up by Sandy as everyone else's have been," I said, pulling into my parents' driveway as the motion sensor flood lights lit it up.

*

Kat was examining a bracelet that looked like it had been welded onto Dariya's wrist. She'd found tin snips, swiped from my father's tool kit and was trying hard to cut it off, distracting distract Dariya by talking incessantly –

It wasn't working.

"Are you going to cut me?" Dariya asked, gritting her teeth. She was laid out on a patio recliner in my parents' sunroom, where the sound of rain on the roof and the warmth of the space heaters made me realize that the adrenaline was wearing off and that fatigue was setting in. The power had come back on, but the lights still flickered periodically, stressing us all out. If we didn't finish this operation soon, one of us was bound to snap.

Most likely my mother.

She had let us in through the back door so we didn't wake my father, who was asleep in his bedroom on the other side of the house. I made her leave before I brought in Dariya and Rigan. Don't get me wrong, I love my mother, but she gossips like an Irish housewife, and anyone who came by asking about us would have gotten a complete eyewitness account of what we did that would be so specific it would make every prosecutor in the country drool.

"Relax, I'm good with tools," Kat told Dariya as she slid one sharp edge between the bracelet and Dariya's pristine flesh closing the snips hard. It must have pinched, because Dariya squealed and moved as a thin line of blood formed on her wrist. Before the blood even started to flow, Kat had ripped off a corner of her shirt to stop it.

"This isn't going to work. We need a bigger tool."

"Lucky I'm here then. I'll see if I can find a hacksaw," I offered.

"What do you need a hacksaw for? Haven't you done enough to that poor girl already?" My mother asked. I turned to find her brazenly coming in, focused on Dariya's cut. I shouldn't have been surprised, it was typical behavior. She never listens. Especially when it's for her own good.

"Mom, I asked you to stay out."

"That was the first red flag for me. Then I come in here to see that you brought strange women into my house, didn't introduce them to me – and you're cutting open this poor girl's arm on your father's recliner?"

"Listen, Theresa, why don't you leave the detective work to the detectives…" I began, in my father's sternest tone of voice. I knew it would send her over the edge, but I was unable to resist.

"Don't you give me that 'Theresa' bullshit that your father tries to pull. He may have lost his memory, but he's still too sharp to miss blood on his chair. Thank God this half-assed dyke knows how to dress a wound," she said, looking at Dariya's arm. This was the Theresa Collins I grew up with, and she was on a roll, turning to confront Rigan.

"Who are these people?" she started to ask, but stopped as she saw Rigan.

"My name's Rigan Kelly, Mrs. Collins," Rigan told her, saving

Mom from her momentary lapse of vicious speech.

"...Why are *you* here?" My mother spit out like an accusation. "Where do I know you from?"

"I grew up in Staten Island. South Shore. You used to be a nurse at the old Richmond Memorial Hospital, right? Pediatrics?" Rigan asked. Something about Rigan's tone put me on edge and made me suspicious. She was asking leading questions, as if trying to predetermine my mother's answer.

"...And the psych unit. You spent time there. I know your face." The distasteful look my mother had for Rigan made sense now. She had hated her time on the psych floor, having felt all the patients were either drug addicts or fakers, looking for an easy way out of work. Compassion was not one of Theresa Collins' gifts.

"As a kid," Rigan admitted. "I had a rough bit. I think you might have been my nurse at some point." My mother nodded, as if she wasn't quite sure how to respond to that. When she did, it was hesitant.

"Well, I'm glad to see you healthy. A lot of the kids I took care of offed themselves when they couldn't handle it. Or worse. Drugs. Sold themselves..." she said, as if trying to provoke a reaction, but Rigan just nodded.

"I know."

My mother stared at Rigan for a moment longer, something passing between them. I felt as if I'd missed half the conversation and they'd reached some kind of unspoken truce.

"I'll get you that hacksaw," Mom said, turning to leave. I

almost let out a sigh of relief as she left, but then heard her call from down the hall. "Killian – I'm going to need your help."

Kat grinned, enjoying the fact that my mother was as much of a pain in the ass to me as she was to everyone else.

"Mama calls. Better run," she teased. I glared at her, but turned to go. Sometimes it was easier to placate Theresa Collins. Life could be miserable if you didn't. I caught up to my mother in the garage, hacksaw already in hand, pointing it at my chest as if she meant to use it.

"You need to make them leave," she hissed at me over the sound of the rain in the damp garage. "They'll upset your father if he wakes up," she told me, glancing behind me to insure I wasn't followed. The fear of upsetting my father was the excuse for everything my mother didn't want to deal with, from the reason they never left Staten Island to why I had to buy mozzarella cheese in Brooklyn and deliver it to Tottenville. Apparently Staten Island mozzarella is too tough and might upset Big Jim Collins.

"Bullshit," I told her. "This is because you and Rigan know each other, right? What happened on the psych floor? Is she some kind of nutter?"

"Jesus, will you trust me for once? The past is done. Gone. Forget it – but nothing good can come of that woman being here. Or that girl."

"What do you think is going to happen? What do you know about them?"

"That girl has problems, doesn't she? And the other one is

part of it. She's a psych patient who went into the life and now is dragging poor foreign girls down with her."

Now it was starting to make sense. 'Poor foreign girls' was a phrase that indicated the subtle racism of the native Staten Islander. Anyone coming from off the island, except possibly transplants from Brooklyn, were 'other' – especially any girl who might have been abused in any way. They were tainted in my mother's eyes, and not to be trusted.

"That's not what's going on. Rigan's not some twisted madam selling girls to the highest bidder. She's helping them—"

"—*Rigan*, is it? You know her better than you're letting on?"

"She saved my life the other night."

"Right… Well, if she did, she had an ulterior motive. That woman is dangerous. She brought that girl here, and all the hell that will follow with her. Get them out," she said, slamming the hacksaw into my hands. I let her get to the door before I stopped her.

"What if I went and pulled medical records from the hospital to verify this story you're telling? Or better yet, what if I asked Dad?" She stiffened. I had her attention now.

"He doesn't need this, Killian. He's already too caught up in…" she started, but her voice drifted off.

"In what?"

"…In his own head, that's all."

"You were going to say the past. How does Rigan bring up the past?"

"She reminds me of bad times, that's all. I *was* her nurse.

215

Right after Joe… It was a bad time. You know that. I don't want to talk about it."

"You're being evasive."

"Goddammit, leave it alone!" she exploded at me. "You and your father, you pick at everything like a scab, making it bleed all over again. Diggin' up the past like diggin' up bodies, the both of you. Well, the bodies can't tell you nothin' you don't already know. Drop it, Kill. Get them out before your father wakes up. I'm not asking, I'm not pleading. I'm telling you," she said tersely, and then slammed through the door, leaving me alone with the sound of the rain.

Mom had made a mistake. She told me what to do, and even though I knew she was trying to protect me and that I should at least consider the fact that she might be right – I couldn't. Oppositional Defiance Disorder is real, and it can be a dangerous condition.

… But it didn't mean she was wrong. I'd find out along the way that sometimes mother does know best.

*

Kat and Rigan held Dariya's wrist, leaving white imprints of fingers and hands as Dariya whimpered, seeing the hacksaw edging closer to her pale skin, flakes of metal from the bracelet falling hotly onto it.

"Why's it taking so long? I could've cut through two of those by now." Kat criticized.

"I'm trying not to ruin the GPS as I cut through the bracelet."

"Why? You want them to be able to track it?" Rigan asked, confused.

"No. But I want to know where it came from and what system it's on. If we figure that out, maybe we can track the GPS on Alina and find her."

"Or lure them out to find us." Rigan said, impressing me with her thought process. The bracelet finally cracked in half. I grabbed it as it fell, took out the battery to disable it, and looked up at Rigan, trying to catch her off guard so I could read her reaction.

"How do you know my mother?" I asked. Her hesitation was unmistakable, but her answer seemed honest.

"We met when I was a kid. I was going through something."

"*Something*. Not on the psych ward, was it?" I asked. That stopped her. She *was* lying.

"What did she tell you?"

"Nothing. You just did."

"She *was* my nurse."

"That doesn't answer the question."

"This is getting good," Kat muttered. "Hidden secrets, psych wards, and old lies. I'm aces at this part. Practice, you know."

I ignored her, staring at Rigan, trying to read her body language.

"You know a lot more than you're saying, and I don't have time to screw around, so I'm asking you this once – why did you call *me* down to that boat? Why get me involved at all? Did you know about the old case my father worked with Joe Corrigan?"

"Yes. Obviously I know about all of that," she admitted. "I also know what the cargo was on that plane and that the only people who might be able to tell me where that cargo is would be you and your father – but since both of you are almost useless when it comes to remembering facts about the crash –"

"—Who told you that?" I asked, interrupting. I kept my issues with memory to myself and was sure that no one I knew would tell Rigan about them.

"*You* told me. …We met before, even if you don't remember," she went on, calmly, pissing me off because I didn't know if it was the truth or not.

"Now that sounds plausible," Kat interjected. I shut her up with a glare as Rigan went on.

"I tried getting in touch with your father, but his health's declined… I'm sorry, but the only reason I called you was because I needed help, and I thought maybe seeing what was going on you'd start to remember." I stared at her for a long moment, but she held my gaze. There was a lot of truth – or at least what she believed to be the truth – in what she was saying. I could see it in her eyes.

"Not a bad story – but you still haven't answered how you really know my mother, or how you knew that I might know something about that crash."

"I don't appreciate being interrogated. Or being called a liar," Rigan said as I turned to look at her again.

"And I don't appreciate being lied to." It became a standoff as I changed tactics. "Dariya. Why don't you tell me what you know about Rigan? Maybe that will help."

Dariya glanced at Rigan, looking for guidance, but Rigan didn't respond, playing her cards close to the vest.

"Did she tell you not to tell me?" I asked Dariya.

Dariya nodded, slightly, looking cornered and scared. Rigan saved her, stepping between us.

"Why don't you just tell me what you know, and I'll fill in the blanks," Rigan said evasively.

I tried to gauge Rigan's stake in this. As a professional, she was obviously interested in the girls somehow, but no one risks their lives for lost girls or get involved with cops, the Russian mob and almost thirty-year-old cases without a really good reason. Rigan had something to hide. I was sure of it.

"You want me to tell you what I know so you can make your lies fit the story? Is that it?" I asked.

"You're paranoid, are you aware of that?"

"You have no idea. Believes in nothing except 'facts', and only the ones his fragile intellect can handle," Kat chimed in. I glared at her, wishing I'd left her tied to the bed at my place.

"Don't look at me in that tone of voice," Kat snapped. "Okay, fine. You don't trust each other, so freakin' what already? Some Russian psychopath is out there collecting young girls like puppy-mill puppies and burning poor boys to death. You *get* that? If we want to nail his balls to a wall, you two are going to have to share whatever it is that you know." Kat looked between us, and Rigan nodded. Kat took that as agreement and turned on me.

"So… Who wants to go first?"

I looked away, glancing at Rigan. She knew more than I did. She could start. But Rigan didn't start. Kat stomped her foot like a toddler.

"OhmyGOD. Fine. You won't talk, I will. Let me break the ice. First, Kill knows that there was heroin on board and that Anton and someone else took it," she started.

"Kat, you have no idea who this woman—"

"Shut up, Kill. You won't talk, so I get to. He also knows that this case is somehow connected to a case his old man and his partner, Joe Corrigan, worked. It involved that plane wreck out behind your house, that there's a dead boy burned to crisp bacon out there, and that if we don't find Alina soon, she's going to be tortured to find out whatever it is that they think that boy knew. You know what they will do…" she stopped herself, unconsciously glancing at Dariya. "…Well, do I really need to say it?"

Rigan kept staring at me, and it set me on edge. It was both a challenge and oddly sympathetic. I said nothing, forcing her hand. Finally, she glanced at Kat and Dariya, then back to me.

"So… you know almost nothing." Rigan sounded disappointed in me – and *for* me. It pissed me off.

"Apparently not. Why don't you enlighten me?"

"Do you know who that boy was? Anton? The boy Josef Markov killed?"

"Besides being another kid that was kidnapped?"

"He was more than that. Anton was their friend – from birth. Their parents were friends. Supporters of Viktor Yushchenko.

After he left power they were persecuted by the pro-Russian Ukrainians and arrested. These kids were used as pawns –"

"– And then sold off to punish their parents?" I asked.

"Their parents are dead. They were sold off as a warning to others. Markov is ruthless. He's fiercely loyal to Putin and doesn't want to go back to prison after what happened last time."

"Last time?"

"His brother Mikhail went missing with a lot of money that didn't belong to him. They thought he defected or stole it or both. Threw Alik Markov in Lubyanka and tortured him, thinking he was in on it. Only the collapse of the Soviet Union saved him," Rigan explained.

"That's what Sean said too. That Markov was messed up by his brother taking off," Kat chimed in, buying into this half-assed con job.

"Who said that?" Rigan asked, worried, focused on potential witnesses.

"Sean Corrigan. The cute one who actually knows some shit," Kat told her. Rigan seemed relieved.

"Ahh, Sean. I remember. He's right. But he doesn't know as much as he thinks."

"So, what doesn't he know? I'm tired of these games. Maybe I should call Burke and have him bring you in for aiding and abetting human trafficking," I told her bluntly.

I heard Kat suck in air through her teeth, warning me that I was pushing Rigan too hard.

"Kill, you're being an asshole." Kat pointed out, trying to diffuse the situation. It didn't help. Rigan was angry.

"I'm not the one who can't remember anything before October of nineteen eighty-five. I'm not the one who thinks he's—" Rigan stopped, abruptly. She'd made a mistake. She'd just revealed that she knew a lot more about me than I did about her.

"How did you know that date? I never said anything about it." That much I was sure of.

"Yeah, I was right here. He said nada. Zilch. He's got you on that one, sweetheart," Kat added, for once on my side.

"Does it really matter how I know? He has Alina."

"She's right," Dariya finally said, softly, holding back the emotion. "You know that. Why does the rest even matter?"

"Girl's got a point. Who gives a shit about history and heroin? Markov's got her sister," Kat agreed and I was being distracted by bullshit.

"And Markov'll keep her as long as he thinks she can help him find the heroin your 'friend' took –"

"–That's not all he's after," Rigan interrupted, frustrated. "There's a reason Josef's back here, on Staten Island. This is where his Uncle went missing. His father sent him to find out what happened to Mikhail."

I heard Kat suck in her breath, as if she had just realized something crucial. "When did the uncle go missing?" Rigan looked at her, as if they were finally coming to some kind of understanding.

"Nineteen eighty-five... Apparently Alik Markov also has it on good authority that the cash his brother stole is still here. Nearby. On Staten Island. That's why he's here. Now..."

Her voice trailed off, probably because I was shaking my head as I put the pieces together. Nineteen eighty-five. The missing cargo from the plane, it made sense. "...You think Alik Markov's missing brother had something to do with that plane crash?"

"Markov thinks he did," Rigan responded, but I didn't see how that was possible. The crash was investigated. Yes, the cargo went missing, but if the task force had found Mikhail Markov, it would have been public knowledge.

"They would have found his body," I said, dismissing that theory.

"Maybe they did, Kill," Kat muttered, looking at me wide-eyed. "Maybe they found it tonight." I looked at her for a long moment, seeing the image that she was referring to in my mind –

—A human skull, its empty eye sockets looking back at me, one with a tire iron going right through it. A body that had been there since nineteen eighty-five. There since –

...*Something warm and wet dropped onto my cheek and oozed, slug-like, across it. I struggled against him, but the man wasn't moving. The mud was forgiving and let me slip to one side, wriggling out from under him. When I glanced down at him I saw nothing but his eye and the tire iron in it for a long moment, my hands balled into fists at my side, something small and hard in my right one. When I finally looked away I opened my hand, looking down at my* memento mori, *the ring that had just slid off the wet and bloody hand of the dead man below me. Mikhail Markov....*

"You said the brother was KGB as well?" I asked, grabbing my phone for an image search.

"Yes, why?" Rigan asked, even as the symbol on the ring I found appeared on my screen: A sword over a red star, a hammer and sickle worn smooth and faded underneath. The symbol of the KGB. My *memento mori* was the signet ring of a KGB officer... I stared at it as I felt Rigan staring at me.

"...Your memories have started to come back, haven't they?" She asked. "From the night Joe Corrigan died."

"No," I lied.

"Dreams then. You have dreams of that night, don't you? Of the rain? Of what happened to Joe?"

I shook my head, giving her nothing.

"He calls them night terrors. They come when it rains," Kat ratted me out.

"Did anyone ask you, Kat?" I asked, turning on her, genuinely ticked off. Kat shrugged – a half-assed apology.

"Dreams, memories, it doesn't matter. We're wasting time when these psychos have Alina," I said, seeing their faces go pale. I thought I was finally making an impact until I heard behind me –

"—Theresa... Theresa! Come quick. She found us. Bring my gun!"

I turned to find Dad with a baseball bat and wild eyes in full-on loon mode, ready to take on the world. It was going to be a rough night.

CHAPTER EIGHTEEN

The curtain tore as my father pulled it closed. He ignored it, moving to the next window, pulling the others closed. Then he checked the locks on the doors while scanning the outside of the house for potential attackers. It'd be amusing if he wasn't so palpably tense.

"Theresa! I need those Goddamn guns. Now!" He bellowed.

"Dad, it's me, Killian. There's no one out there. We're safe," I told him, even though I was unsure that we had disabled the GPS tracker quickly enough to prevent Markov from finding us.

"Safe? Would *they* be in my house if things were safe?"

He had a point. As I took a breath to figure out how to talk him off his Alzheimer's-induced ledge, my mother strode in, glaring at me as if I were ten and had just let our muddy Golden Retriever rampage through the house again.

"Jesus, Jimmy. What the hell are you doing out of bed? What

did I tell you about getting up in the middle of the night?"

"I don't remember, Theresa. I'm sick in the head. You have the guns?" He asked, pushing a chair up against the door to the backyard. Dariya stared at him, looking as if she wanted to run. Rigan looked at him with pity, and Kat was smirking at me with a look that said 'you're fucked now, aren't you, Kill'?

I was.

"Jesus, no. I'm not getting you any damn guns. You know you're not good with guns anymore," Mom told him firmly. Dad whirled on my mother with a force I hadn't seen in years – as if his addled mind brought his body back to whatever year he thought he was in.

"Pay attention, Theresa, and don't give me any crap. You see these kids?" He asked, turning and pointing at Rigan. "Take a good look. She's right here… you made me stop looking – but I never should have – she *got away*." My mother glanced at me, her expression a mix of anger and depressed defeat. After a moment, she moved toward my father, gently taking his arm.

"It's all right, Jimmy. They're not who you think they are. It's fine."

"It's not Goddamn *fine*. If she's here, they'll be back, they'll kill her for sure this time. It won't be like it was with Joe," he said, glancing out the windows again before turning to invade Rigan's space. "Tell them. You know. You *remember*." Rigan didn't back down, but had a soft look of empathy in her eyes.

"Who is it that you think I am, Mister Collins?"

My father didn't answer. He just kept looking at her as his

eyes welled with tears. It made me uncomfortable. The last time I'd seen him cry was at a dedication to fallen law enforcement officers when I was fifteen. As he heard Uncle Joe's name read, one tear fell and then no more. None fell this time, but it was a close thing. When he finally spoke, his voice was strong and sure.

"…I know who you are. You're the one we lost…" His voice drifted off as he tried to catch Rigan's eye, attempting to explain something only he understood. "…We tried. You know we tried, right? We didn't leave you. We never would have left you."

"Really? What's her name, Jimmy?" My mother asked, stepping between them. "Do you even know her name?"

My father said nothing, but I saw what the question did to him. It broke his confidence. He didn't know.

"I don't think I ever knew it. She never told us. She never spoke the whole time she was here. But you know me, don't you, girl?"

Rigan looked back up at him, composed now. "Mister Collins, I'm Morrigan Kelly. Do you recognize my name?" It was clear that he didn't, but it was also clear that Rigan hadn't answered his question. It didn't matter. He was lost to us, the confusion dragging him down.

"I don't," he said, turning to my mother, agitated and bewildered as he lost his grip on this moment in time. "Why is she here, Theresa? Did something happen?"

"Nothing, Jimmy. It's just a friend of Killian's. Come with me. We'll go back to bed." My father nodded meekly, trying to act as if he knew what was going on around him.

"Sure. Well… it was nice to meet you all. I'm sorry if I thought… Well, I… I'm sorry… Goodnight," he muttered, then turned and shuffled quickly off toward his bedroom, once again the bewildered old man I'd gotten used to over the past few years. That's when she punched me with a closed fist, knuckles digging into my shoulder. Mom could hit hard when she was angry, and at the moment she was furious.

"Jesus Christ, Killian. Didn't I warn you? Look at him. He won't sleep all night, and for weeks he's going to obsess about some old missing girl case. It's a wonder if I don't find him out searching the woods for a body that's been rotted and gone for thirty years."

"And that's my fault?"

"Get them out. You can stay tonight, but in the morning I want you all gone," she warned, walking after my father. She stopped in the doorway, turning back, unable to help herself.

"…And keep the conversation to a dull roar. There are sheets and towels in the linen closet. The spare bedroom is made up, there's the futon in your father's office, and the couch. Try not to drink all the milk."

And then she was gone.

"I don't know what your problem is with her, Kill. I love your mom," Kat said quietly. I turned on her, not finding her amusing at the moment. My glare shut her up. Then I turned to Rigan, who avoided looking at me.

"So. What the hell was that?"

"Nothing. It doesn't matter. Right now, Dariya needs sleep and I'd rather not upset your mother again," she said firmly.

"I'm not letting you off the hook."

"I promise. I'll tell you, but not now," she said, glancing toward Dariya, whose eyes were still teary. "You should get to work tracking down that GPS anyway. Does your father have a computer in his office?"

"The one I gave him last Christmas, before he took the turn."

"Good. I'll help you after everyone else is settled."

"Tonight. You'll tell me everything," I demanded, as if I had any control over her.

Rigan just nodded… and I believed her.

Before we left, I peered out around the curtains at the rain. The bridge was still dark, and I felt like I had a moment to breathe… but then something moved near the street. A man, walking in the rain, alone. It was too dark to really see, but one side of his face looked misshapen…

He was gone before I could react, so I checked my pistol and went to get the others settled.

*

Dariya looked like the child she was as she huddled under the covers in the spare bedroom in an oversized shirt of my father's that my mother had dragged out along with half a dozen other pajama options. Her back was to the headboard and both hands gripped Rigan's arm, not letting go.

"Please, Rigan. I don't want to be alone. What if they come?"

"I just need to talk to Killian. I'll be right across the hall," Rigan told her, standing up. Dariya was breathing faster, as if she was on the edge of a panic attack. Kat must have recognized it, because she stepped in, trying to help.

"I'll stay with her."

"No!" Dariya shouted, and then caught herself, trying to act like the adult she almost was. "I'm sorry, it's just, I can't. I don't know her…" Dariya's voice trailed off, embarrassed at her outburst.

She shouldn't have been. Most people think that they can handle death and violence, having seen it so many times in movies and on television. The truth is that when you see it in person, with all the added benefits of warm brain splatter and the smells of cordite and blood, you react differently. At least if you have any shred of humanity you do. It was good to see that Dariya hadn't lost that, even if she was the one who had killed four of the Russians on the *Chistota*.

"I'll stay with her until she falls asleep, then I'll be in to talk," Rigan promised. I nodded and then stepped out into the hall, followed by Kat, who closed the door behind her.

"She doesn't trust me. All I tried to do was help and now she's scared of me because of that prick I killed," she said, confused and disappointed.

"Looks that way," I told her, moving down the hall, worried that we'd wake up my parents again. Kat followed me, feeling the need to defend herself for some reason. It was probably the delayed guilt – the Catholic reflex all of us raised in that faith have – the need to confess to doing something we knew was right because some guy in a collar might judge us for it.

"I'm glad I killed him."

"I know."

"You don't hold it against me?" I turned to look at her, so she could see my eyes and know that I meant what I was about to say.

"Kat, any man that kidnaps kids or burns a boy to death – deserves to die, and die slow. You were merciful to him. I pray I find the guys he was with and I get to take my time with them." Kat smiled a genuine smile now that she felt secure I wasn't judging her.

"Amen," she said, reflexively doing the sign of the cross. "That's my prayer for the night. Give me a gun and an opportunity and I'll take out Markov too."

"No guns for you. I don't need to explain another body."

"That's not fair. You get to shoot people, but I don't?"

"I have a badge. Training."

"I have Army training *and* natural talent."

"But no badge," I reminder her, stopping in the living room. My mother had put a pillow, sheets, and blankets on the couch and I started making it up as I answered her.

"Besides, your talent is debatable, and with my badge a judge and jury will give me the benefit of the doubt. They'll hang you. You're not in the Army anymore."

"But what if I have to defend you again? I need something."

"You can have something. The couch. Good night, Kat." I

threw the pillow at her, half expecting her to beat me with it, but she'd given up. I heard her sigh and flop down on the deep cushions as I went back toward my father's office.

*

It took me twenty minutes on my dad's MacBook Pro to figure out that the GPS in the bracelet was technology issued by the Russian government. That meant it'd be untraceable without a Federal warrant and some help from the NSA.

Yeah. *Those* pricks.

They were a greedy bunch of math and computer geeks who never shared and knew jack shit about real crime – all they cared about was listening in on people's phone sex with sweaty palms and access to their webcams. I put the battery and the GPS in pieces on the desk, and went back to work on the internet, doing more research – this time trying to find Mangy Goatee Guy, who I knew had been locked up with his partner, the Toothless Giant, AKA Vincent Morocco. It didn't take long to find that Mangy Mustache Guy, otherwise known as Peter Coohill, had been paroled five years ago. That would explain why he was out and in the woods with Markov.

He'd be a bitch to track down, but his partner, Morocco – he was still locked up. Sort of. According to the New York State Department of Corrections, Morocco had been granted a conditional transfer for compassionate reasons – whatever that meant. If I could find out where he was transferred to, maybe I could get something out of him. But that would have to wait.

I wasn't going to find him tonight, and if he was upstate, I was screwed. The bridges were still closed.

I was running out of time, was too tired to do much more and needed sleep. The ticking clock in the hall wasn't helping my mood as I tried to think all of this through – tried to remember *anything*. After a while I realized that I was touching the scar on my thigh, wondering why I would have been so stupid to burn myself that way for the millionth time. I was becoming unfocused. I saved the web address and turned off the computer. I needed sleep to think straight, so I stretched out on the futon and stripped off my still-damp pants to boxers and got under the blankets. The warm, dry room felt good, and even the hum of the furnace, which made the futon vibrate slightly, was more soothing than distracting. The sound of it was steady and low...

*

...Until I heard the sound deepen and rumble, like a car downshifting. Gradually the white noise of rain intruded, keeping complex rhythm, accompanying the harmonies of the engine and wheels on wet pavement.

This time I knew, on some level, that I was back in Uncle Joe's Volkswagen Beetle, but I couldn't see anything to confirm that, since I was in complete darkness, covered by the musty wool blanket that had the vague odor of mold and motor oil.

I'd never dreamt about this specific moment before. I tried to focus, dreaming lucidly, not even sure if I was awake or asleep, focusing on the tactile parts of the dream – the rough wool against my face, the sounds of the rain, the oppressive heat in the car, and the smell of the upholstery cleaner wafting up from the car's rugs and back seat. It was claustrophobic and the blanket dampened the sound of the road and the rain, but as I listened closely, I could tell that we'd pulled off onto the gravel shoulder. The loose stones crunched under the tires and somewhere nearby, three car doors slammed.

"You kids stay under that blanket. No matter what happens. Understood?" I heard, knowing that it was Uncle Joe's voice.

"Okay…" came a soft voice from next to me. For the first time I realized that I wasn't alone. I couldn't see the girl who spoke, but I could feel the warmth of her breath under the blanket and felt the cold tension in her grip as she reached out to grab my forearm. I touched her hand with my own, listening, trying to figure out what was going on.

I heard Uncle Joe roll down the window, using the manual handle that squeaked and clunked at the top of its arc. The sounds from outside grew louder: A murmur of voices, footsteps, the creak of wet leather – and then someone was leaning in the window.

"Going kind of fast, Joe." I heard a man's deep and raspy voice say. He had a Bronx accent, the kind that sounds almost Bostonian on the vowels.

"Give me a break. Why'd you stop me?"

"Because you're on this stretch of road. Why don't you tell us why you're here so late?"

There was a micro-hesitation that, as an adult, I would recognize as an evasion before Uncle Joe answered with: "I'm headed home."

"From Jimmy Collins' house? Home's the other way, Joe."

I shifted under the blanket, trying to hear better, but as soon as I moved, the girl dug her fingers into my arm, scared that they'd notice us. I stopped for a moment, but then started moving again, more slowly this time.

"Look, Joe. Let's cut the games," a second man's voice said. I could tell that he was further away from the car, behind the first man. "...We know what you took from that plane. We want it, you have it."

"So, you're admitting guilt?"

I had the blanket up now and could peer between the seats, but all I could see was Uncle Joe's profile and the barrel of a .38 special inches away from his face – a face made to look pale and white in the flashing lights of a police car, red, blue, and white.

It was never a lightning strike that I half-remembered, it was the lights...

"Hell no – not at all," answered the man with the gun. "...But look in the mirror. You're not much better. You filed a false report about what was on that plane. You're as guilty as we are. That's why you're out here, isn't it? To collect what you hid?"

"You want it? That's easy. I'll tell you where it is."

"It's too easy. We want everything. The witnesses too. The kids. This one goes way beyond us, Joe. Corruption at the highest levels – some bullshit political game with the IRA, bent FBI Agents in

Boston and confidential informants. You gonna fuck with that?"

"They're kids," Uncle Joe answered, and I noticed his hand moving next to the seat. An inch from his fingertips, I saw his gun. He was going for it.

"They're not our kids, Joe."

"Go fuck yourself."

The barrel of the gun bounced off Uncle Joe's temple hard as the man reacted, pistol-whipping him. Uncle Joe's head snapped to one side, and I saw him wipe blood away from his eye. I almost yelled then, but held it back as the girl next to me moved closer, trying to see what was going on. She was warm to the touch, the soft skin on her thigh heating us up under the blanket where it touched mine.

"You really want to swallow a bullet for some Irish trash?"

"They're kids and you'd sell them out? Why?"

"Twenty-five grand and a recovery fee for the cash you took off that plane. You saw what these people did to Tompkins and Germanario – you think I want to end up like them? Besides, what they do with those kids once I hand them over isn't on me. Now, I'm done waiting. You got ten seconds to talk or I blow your balls off, then your kneecaps. I'll keep going until I get what I need."

I saw the man pull the hammer back on the old-style revolver and watched the cylinder spin. I held my breath and felt the girl lean forward to see what made me tense up. For a moment I saw her face, her hazel eyes, and the freckles across the bridge of her nose, all illuminated by the revolving light from the car that was somewhere out there.

When she saw the gun, she inhaled sharply. Her sharp breath wasn't loud. Not at all.

But it was enough.

I saw the gun move, the barrel swinging toward the back seat for a brief second before Uncle Joe slammed it upward with one arm while grabbing his own gun with the other, yelling – "Run!"

I hesitated. She didn't. By the time I turned to get out, she was off into the darkness, barefoot. The long grass and stickers were already whipping her lithe white legs as the door was bouncing back into my face. I dove through it, into the brightness of the flashing red, white, and blue lights as a painful, deafening sound exploded in the night air.

I knew now that it wasn't thunder.

It was a gunshot.

I never looked back to see what or who it hit. I was running as fast as I could to the false safety of the weeds, sticker bushes, and the woods beyond them. I'd just gotten caught by the stinging whip of branches pulling at me and slowing me down when there was another deafening shockwave of sound and I fell face first, feeling as if someone had just hit me behind the ear with a sledgehammer.

I was trying to get up even as I hit the ground, my legs pumping, propelling me headfirst into bushes that hooked their barbs into my face and arms. I barely felt it. The throbbing in my head and the warmth of blood running down my face was the strongest visceral pain that I had.

There was room for only one thought in my head – keep

running. Even though I was breathing so hard that just inhaling the raw, cold air made me taste the coppery sting of my own blood in my throat, I had to get away from that car. If I didn't find somewhere to hide, they'd kill me.

I scrambled forward, but the ground beneath me was waterlogged and soft, gripping my feet as I ran, tripping me with uneven roots and rocks. Something to one side of me was snapping twigs and crashing through the underbrush, so I glanced to see what it was – and that's when I saw her.

She was running in her denim shorts and t-shirt, barefoot, with mud caked on her calves, legs scratched and bleeding above the mud line as she ran flat out, long auburn hair catching on the branches, but not slowing her down. I thought for sure she would get away –

—But then she stopped between two trees, and turned back to look at me. I wanted to scream at her to keep running. They were going to catch her... but she didn't go this time, the way she had every other time I dreamt this.

Instead she spoke, looking right at me.

"I left you. I'm sorry... I've been sorry every moment since..."

I wanted to scream at her, but something was wrong with my head. I couldn't form the words to tell her to run, so I tried to move toward her, but the world shifted, tilting as –

CHAPTER NINETEEN

—I sat up, suddenly awake.

"RUUUNN…" I screamed, waking in time to hear it diminish to a throaty whisper. I tried to focus and get my bearings. That's when I saw her again. This time she wasn't between two trees, she was in the doorway of my father's study, watching me with empathic eyes.

"…I'm sorry. I saw them shoot and I just ran. I was scared," Rigan said quietly from where she stood. She was in an old dress shirt of my father's, backlit from the light in the hallway, making the fabric too sheer for my comfort. I looked away, not because I didn't enjoy the view, but because maybe she didn't know that she was backlit…

…Or maybe she did.

Either way, I wasn't going to. There was something about Rigan I didn't trust. She knew too much about me, and I knew too little about her – so I averted my eyes. No matter how much I wanted to look.

"I don't know what you're talking about."

"You know what I mean, Killian. You know who I am," she said as she came in, sitting on the edge of the futon. Her eyes were on me the whole time, and when I looked up, she was staring right into my own. I glanced away again, but her hand gently touched my chin, bringing my eyes back to hers.

"I was there. You were there. You saved me."

I sat up, sliding away from her. "It was a dream. Night terrors. Happens all the time. My subconscious makes ridiculous connections."

"That's not what happened."

"My dreams are all wrong. They're not what really happened. Joe Corrigan died in a car accident."

"He didn't. I was there. I wasn't shot like you were, so I still remember," she told me softly, as if I were mentally deficient because of a twenty-five-year-old brain trauma.

"Your scar. Behind your ear," she continued. "They shot you."

"That was from the car accident. I read the police reports," I protested, unable to separate the dreams from reality anymore.

"The accident reports that were filled out by the same police who killed your uncle and left you for dead?"

"No. That's not possible."

"You know it is—you dream about it," she said, sighing heavily. Finally, she leaned closer, her body close enough to feel its heat.

"Do you remember grabbing the tire iron, hitting the guy who was trying to rape me?"

I reacted to that, backing away again, but I was up against the wall, trying to make sense of how she could possibly know that. There was only one other person that knew the details of my dreams.

"Kat told you about that?"

"You think Kat would share anything with me? No." Rigan made a good point. Kat wasn't the type to share with a woman like Rigan.

"If not Kat, how do you know?"

"Because I *am* the girl in your dreams."

She said it without a hint of irony. That left two possible options—either she was a dangerous woman who somehow knew the content of my dreams, or she was telling the truth.

I'm a thick Mick, and I'd spent a long time believing my night terrors were just that, so I was invested. To suddenly meet a very real flesh and blood woman from my dreams was too much to take.

"They're not even really dreams, they're nightmares."

"If you want to waste time with definitions, they're actually memories."

"Memories I can prove. These I can't," I said, trying to get up and away from her. She didn't take the hint and stayed where she was. I'd have to push past her to get off the futon.

"How do you tell the difference when you don't have the facts?"

"I can't. In the absence of proof, the most logical and simplest explanation is the most likely to be true."

"So, start with some facts. When you dream, is it about me?"

Yes. I wanted to say *yes*. That was the first thought that popped into my head, that every dream I'd had for the last thirty-something years was in some way about her, the girl with freckles and green-flecked eyes. They had never been about Kat, no matter what I had once thought. I had always dreamt about Rigan, the beautiful woman who was here in a sheer shirt to save me from my nightmares and make me feel special. But why? Why her? And what did she want from me? Did she think I knew where the cargo from the plane was, the cash?

I had no idea, so I did what I always did when I had doubts. I deflected to buy myself some time.

"I dream about a girl… who might look something like you. But my dreams seem like they're about someone else's life. Nothing about them feels like they're about the life I have now."

"Of course not. I have that problem too. Before October of nineteen eighty-five, I lived a different life too."

"And what life was that?"

"I was like Dariya and Alina. I was taken from a place I called home and was supposed to be sold to the highest bidder."

"You were one of the kids my father saved from that plane?"

"Yes. Me, my little brother, a sweet boy who was my best friend, and a few others just like us. Irish orphans, the shameful reminders that even good Catholic girls had sex outside of marriage, we were raised by nuns and priests… But

243

deep down, you already know all this."

"Maybe. It still doesn't explain everything. If you were one of those kids, why was *I* with you that night? Did you hide at my parents' house? Did my father bring you home?"

"Yes, he brought me home with him... You won't believe anything I say without physical evidence, will you? How about the scar on your right thigh?" she asked, pulling aside the blankets to reveal my bare legs and my boxers. I pulled them back over me quickly as she went on. "It's from a cigarette lighter, right?"

Rigan pulled the covers away again, revealing my scar. I let her look, but when she touched it gently with two fingers, I pulled away.

"How did you know about my scar?"

"I know because I have this," she said, pulling that nearly sheer shirt up over her thighs to reveal a scar that was the twin of my own—the way it appeared in my dreams. The only difference between them was that hers was on her left thigh. It looked as if it had faded over time so that it wasn't raised and red any longer. It was now almost as pale as the rest of her creamy white skin. "They did it to both of us."

I reached out to touch it, to see if it was real, but hesitated. Rigan didn't. She pressed my hand onto her warm skin so that I could feel the tough, ridged scar as she slid closer to me, pressing the bare flesh of her left thigh to my right thigh, touching her scar to mine... I met her eyes then, and this close I could see the green and amber flecks, like moss over rich earth, amidst the blue. The pattern of her iris was unique, and I knew it by heart, as if I remembered it...

"We were friends, you and I, growing up in the care of the Church, the last of the Magdalenes. We did everything together, right up to the night they took us," she told me, staring right into my eyes. "They broke your rib when you tried to stop them from hurting me. When you tried to stop them from torturing me and burning me with the lighter... Then they burned you, just to be cruel. They tortured both of us, like they're going to be torturing Alina if we don't find her."

Her voice trailed off as the tears came, and I instinctively reached out and held her, thinking about Anton and what they'd done to him. Rigan cried into my chest, then held me tighter.

When I went to pull away she looked up at me and I felt her breath, warm, intermingling with mine... And then her lips were touching mine, soft and warm and sweet. It felt right, and comfortable, and like it was meant to be as she pushed me backward and the weight of her body pressed down firmly on me...

*

An hour later I found myself drinking the last of the milk straight out of the container, in spite of my mother's warning—and I wasn't even doing it just for spite. I was thirsty, and hungry, and exhausted in the best possible way... but still felt a deep and tender doubt in my mind about Rigan and her motives. She was the girl in my dream, but was she someone I should trust? At the moment, I had no proof, only theories. None of those theories were a good reason to sleep with Rigan in my father's office, but then again… did I really need one? It was either a reunion of sorts, with an old friend—or a mistake with a whole new level of crazy attached. I was trying to decide which one it was when I felt something behind me, a presence in the darkness, just beyond the light pouring out of the refrigerator.

"You stink," she said. I turned, startled, spilling milk down my chest.

"Kat…" I sighed as she stepped into the light, wearing nothing but a too-short t-shirt. "You scared me."

"Did I?" she asked, sniffing the air. She was staring at me in a way that made me glad her hands were visible. I had the distinct feeling she would have preferred to have a knife in at least one, if not both.

"What's wrong?"

"You tell me. Is there something really wrong with me?"

"Excuse me?"

"You made it clear that you just want to be friends. That you don't want a relationship—*any* relationship. Then this woman shows up, and hell, a few hours later you're out here stinking of sex and replenishing your lost liquids with a gallon of milk. I'm just curious as to what's wrong with me and why Princess Rigan, savior of the lost girls, is totally cool."

"Kat. You don't understand. I think I knew her before—"

"Is that the crap she sold you? She's the little girl you lost in your dreams?" she asked, and my face gave me away. "Nice romantic fairy tale. I get it."

"You don't."

"No? I've heard good sex before. That sounded exactly like good sex. Like long-lost little girl I once loved sex."

"You're jealous."

"Why the fuck shouldn't I be?" she asked, stepping closer and forcing me back against the counter, her body almost touching mine. She'd raised her voice a few decibels and didn't seem to be aware that she was about to wake everybody up. All I needed now was for Rigan to hear this—or for my mother to emerge and catch me in my boxer briefs with Kat, drinking the last of her precious milk. Nightmare, either way. I was about to slip away from Kat when she put one hand softly on my milky chest, licked that finger, then smirked and sighed, resigned.

"And at the same time… No. I'm not jealous." Her eyes met mine, pupils dilated, her look gentle, her breath warm, her voice smoky… "You should know me by now, Kill. The people I care about, I care about. I just want them to be happy, right?"

"If you say so," I told her, unsure where this was going. She leaned into me, closer, making sure I felt all of her through the thin t-shirt.

"I do. I don't know how to care about somebody and hope for anything but happiness for them," Kat said and pushed away from me with a fist to my solar plexus. "So fuck you, I'm happy for you. You needed to get laid in a bad way."

Now I was completely confused.

"So you're *not* jealous?" I asked, hoping to clarify what version of crazy Kat was manifesting at the moment. She just shrugged, retreating back into the darkness of the living room. Her voice grew softer as she walked away, forcing me to follow her if I wanted to hear what she was saying.

"Disappointed, yes. I feel something for you. A weird kind of lust I've never felt before. Maybe it's what you cisgendered straights call love. It doesn't matter," Kat told me as she sat back down on the couch with a look of acceptance that made me feel guiltier than I had in a long time.

"You're the best person I've ever known," Kat went on. "You always do the right thing. You didn't take advantage of me when you could have—and you didn't throw me out of your house when it would have been easy to do."

"I'm sorry, Kat, but I'm glad you're good with this," I told her, sitting down next to her.

"No. Be clear. I'm not 'good with this.' I'm worried. I've seen Rigan's type before. I've *been* her type. Little girl lost, who wishes that she were special and had some special person fate had set aside for her. But I got over that dream in tenth grade. The Morrigan in there is still living out some tweenie fantasy, with you cast as her long-lost prince."

"That's not what this is." It was a weak attempt at self-defense. Kat had hit upon the same doubts I had.

"No? That woman is trying to heal some deep wound, isn't she? Maybe she was an orphan. Maybe she did lose her family—but she's fucking with you because she knows you can't remember," Kat said, turning to face me, intent, her thigh pressing up against mine. "You know, when you can't heal whatever wound it is that's bleeding her dry, it's going to make it worse. Trust me, I know. Why do you think I take love where I find it? Because I learned the hard way that fairy tales and long-lost loves are just that—fairy tales."

"I didn't mean to hurt you."

"You didn't hurt me. Seriously. I know you care about me, even if you won't show it," she said, putting on hand on my thigh. "I know you think you're protecting me by not 'taking advantage' of me—but I'm not the one who needs protection. You do."

"What's that mean?"

"It means you're naïve. You slept with a stranger because you know there isn't a chance in hell it lasts, so there's no risk. You're a child when it comes to this stuff. Maybe it's because of what happened to you as a kid, or because of what you can't remember—but it's true. That woman in there has got deep dark shit going on, and when it all goes down, you'll be the one who gets hurt by it."

Kat's voice had fallen to a whisper, and her lips were inches from mine in the darkness. I could feel her warm, sweet breath mingling with my own, and I wanted to do something to make her feel better. I unconsciously leaned in—only to be slammed by both of her hands, one in the hip and one in the shoulder, knocking me off the couch and onto the floor.

"Now get the fuck off my couch and let me sleep. I don't

know why you're in here talking to half-naked *me* when you should be back in bed with the woman you just *schtupped*. It's impolite."

She was right. As usual.

"Good night, Kat."

"The fuck it is."

I went to kiss her forehead, just to show I appreciated her, but I almost got a kick in the nuts for it. I blew her a kiss instead and caught a glimpse of her grin in the dim light, and then went back to find Rigan. I should have felt great about the situation—Kat semi-approved, was still my friend, *and* there was a beautiful woman in my bed (well, on my parents' futon, but still).

I didn't feel great. Part of me wanted to go back to the couch with Kat, staying up to watch old movies, or at least play a couple of first-person shooters.

Maybe she was right. Maybe there was something wrong with me…

*

The light from the hall fell onto Rigan's face as I opened the door, but she didn't stir. She was sleeping peacefully, the sheet wrapped around her, one leg exposed—the leg with the scar. I could see it clearly, that minor imperfection on her thigh.

I moved closer, unable to resist the urge to trace the scar. Rigan stirred but didn't wake, and I wondered what she dreamt of, and whether her dreams were just memories. Watching her sleep, her chest rising and falling, I wondered how I ever could have forgotten her, and how many times I had seen her in my dreams only to forget her again in the brief interval after I awoke.

It occurred to me that if I could fall asleep next to her, maybe the dreams would come, and maybe this time I'd remember, so I laid my head on her abdomen and closed my eyes. ...I felt the soothing warmth of her skin as she breathed in and out, and I could hear her heart beating.

I lay next to her and she moved closer, the weight of one leg falling over mine. I didn't want to close my eyes. Tonight, I didn't want to dream. I just wanted to lie here and watch her.

I think I kept my eyes open for about two minutes...

CHAPTER TWENTY

If I had any dreams that night, they had fled long before I woke.

For the first time I could remember, I woke up with warm sun on my face, well rested, and feeling like I had nowhere to go. I was home, but not because I was in my parents' house, smelling bacon and eggs and something made with sweet batter. No, I was home because I didn't wake up with the feeling that I was lost, or that I was forgetting the most important things and leaving them behind in dreams. And then there was the woman in my dreams…

She was lying next to me.

I could see the shape of Rigan's body underneath the sheets, her auburn hair spilling across the pillow. I stared at it as it glistened in the early morning light. I didn't move, afraid that I'd wake her and in doing so somehow wake myself up from what still felt like a dream. I wasn't surprised that Rigan was still out and still breathing the peaceful rhythms of sleep. I'd slept hard as well. It felt for the first time in a long time like some of my demons had left during the night.

…And then I remembered what I needed to do that day, and how many hours it had been since we'd last seen Alina. I got up quickly and wrote a note to Rigan: "Went to follow up a lead. Back in two hours. We can work on the GPS then."

I pulled on some clothes, silently, listening to the low sounds of conversation and dishes rattling in the kitchen. It sounded like everyone else was awake. I'd need to be prepared for the usual harassment from my mother about being the last one up to help with breakfast. At least no one was yelling, and my mother wasn't throwing us all out the door.

Yet.

It was still early.

When I entered the kitchen, I was thrown completely off-kilter by what I saw. My father was at the table with Dariya pulled up close next to him, looking more like the child she so recently was and a lot less like a sexualized young woman who Markov had kidnapped and held captive. She was peering over Dad's shoulder as he sketched something with a pencil. My father hadn't picked up a pencil in years despite being a natural artist, and he looked as if he hadn't lost the touch. My mother was at the stove, making scrambled eggs, and Kat was buttering fresh-baked bread, piling it next to a plate full of pancakes.

The scene was almost as unreal as last night was to me. My father rarely relaxed enough to do anything other than zone out with the television or pace the living room, and my mother didn't cook. She just didn't. I remember her telling me as a child that the best thing she could do for me was to teach me how to "do it my damn self," and how she always had a list of delivery places next to the phone. Still, it wasn't just my parents that were acting out of character. Kat was smiling, helping my mother. Most of her piercings were missing, her hair was a mess and she had found old baggy sweats somewhere. It had the effect of making her look barely older than Dariya, somehow both innocent and fragile. It was all almost as disorienting as sleeping with a woman you might have known as a child, but couldn't remember except from your dreams…

As I thought about it, I realized how insane that sounded. Maybe I had slipped a gear and was losing my mind for good this time, or maybe I'd been fucked in the head for a long time and was just becoming aware of it. I couldn't quite figure out how to ask if I was always a loon or not without sounding nuts, so I asked a question that got to the heart of something else that seemed so strange this particular morning.

"You made breakfast?" I asked, and my mother turned around and smiled at me. Yeah. Something was not right. "I think I was twelve the last time you made me breakfast."

"So then you should kiss my ass and appreciate it," Mom responded, bringing me back to reality. "Your lesbian friend made fresh bread. I have to say, I didn't expect much from her, but damn, it's nice and crispy outside and soft and warm on the inside."

"All lesbians are like that, Mrs. Collins. Crispy outside and warm and soft on the inside," Kat said with a grin.

"And she's got a sense of humor, too. Who knew? She'll make some girl a nice wife someday," Mom said, and Kat was quiet, making me wonder if she had developed multiple personality disorder overnight.

"She's not a lesbian, Mom."

"No? She doesn't like girls? I thought she did."

Kat shrugged, as if it didn't really matter—which pissed me off, because any time I said something like that, Kat tore me a new one.

"I do, but I'm bi," was all Kat said.

"Like there's a difference?" Mom asked.

"There is. Depends on the night. If you want me to explain it…" Kat offered.

"Not in front of Jimmy, but I do have a couple of questions. I saw some stuff on the internet that was… interesting."

"Mom. Please," I pleaded, pretty sure she was trying to get Kat to talk about her sex life just to make me uncomfortable.

"I'm just looking out for you. If she's playing for both teams, there's still hope for you—if it doesn't work out with the psych patient."

"Her name is Rigan."

"Right. Rigan. Maybe you should go get her so you can get moving and get out of here, though I can understand how tired she might be, since you kept all of us up as well."

Damn. I felt my face flush as Kat looked away to avoid catching my eye. So that's what this was all about. Mom hated

Rigan more than Kat, so Kat was on her good side.

"Ignore her," Dad interrupted from across the room. "She just thinks you upset me."

I turned to see my father, clear-eyed, focused on me with the look he'd always had when I was a kid—seeing everything, noting every detail, and reading my body language. I used to think of that look as "detective's eyes." I hadn't seen those eyes in a long time, since he never had them when he was in the midst of an episode.

"So, you're with us this morning?" I asked carefully.

"At the moment. Being around beautiful young women makes me feel alive," he said, glancing at Dariya and getting a shy glance in response. This was good. I had questions he could only answer when he was lucid.

"We need to talk," I told him. This was going to be my one opportunity to ask my father about the old case and the plane while he was coherent.

"I'm busy with Dariya," my father said, glancing at my mother. Over the years he had taught me enough about body language to know that Mom was the real problem, and that, for some reason, he didn't want to answer questions in front of her. I didn't care. I needed to know what happened.

"Dad, there are things that make no sense about all of this." I sat at the table across from him and his face went blank, staring at me.

"Who are you again?" he finally asked.

"Don't mess with me, Dad." He looked at me again with

those detective eyes, then nodded and looked away.

"My advice? Don't ask any questions you don't want the answer to. I told you already—remember what happened last time," he warned, and then I saw his eyes flick toward my mother.

"Last time." He had said that before, talking about the Toothless Giant and Mangy Goatee Guy.

"Yeah. I remember last time. Those two guys went away after they broke your jaw—but what did they have to do with the case you were working with Uncle Joe?" I asked.

Before he could answer, my mother glared at him and interrupted. "Nothing. They had nothing to do with it. And I'm tired of crazy conspiracy theories, understand? It's in the past. Leave it there."

"Doesn't matter, really, does it?" my father asked me, shrugging. "They were tied into local organized crime. The big guy, Morocco, he was sentenced on the three-strikes law back in eighty-six for dealing steroids, cocaine, and heroin. He was also suspected of being a rapist, arsonist, and all-around nice guy. The little guy got out, I think. So-called good behavior. But I heard the giant was dying last time I went to a parole hearing—bastards granted a conditional transfer for compassionate reasons."

"I saw that when I researched him last night. I'm going to the precinct this morning to find out where they sent him."

"Don't need to go to the precinct. I know where they sent him. Corrections notified me since I was a witness at his trial.

He's in hospice—on a secure ward up at North Shore Medical, right here on Staten Island. So he could be close to his family. Ask me, they should've let him die in prison."

I agreed, but Morocco still being alive and on the island might just be the break I needed. Grabbing my keys off the counter, I got up to go, not even bothering to make an excuse as I made sure I had my gun and jacket, dialing my cell phone.

"What are you doing?" my father called after me.

"Following a lead," I told him as I bolted for the door before anyone could stop me. Time was not on Alina's side. If Morocco knew anything that would help—I'd get it out of him. As I walked out, I got the precinct on the phone.

"This is Detective Killian Collins. I need status on the bridges and maritime traffic," I told the sergeant who answered. Thankfully he was loud enough in his response, telling me that I had at least another four hours.

"And you're going to leave the psych patient, the lost girl and the lesbian here? What am I supposed to do with them?" Mom yelled, once again making it all about her.

"Pretend they're actual people who need your help." I let the front door slam behind me, hoping it pissed off my mother as much as it usually did.

I was already in the car when Kat came out the front door, carrying her clothes under one arm, running barefoot down the driveway. She bolted for the passenger door, pulling it open as I put the car in reverse.

"What are you doing?" I asked, afraid of the answer.

"Coming with you," she said. "You think I'm gonna stay with your bat-shit crazy mother and all that insanity? Besides, you're in no emotional state to go it alone right now."

She wasn't wrong.

"What about Rigan and Dariya?" I asked, trying to deflect her attention from my mental state.

"Rigan's on her own, and Dariya, well, your dad's half in love with her. She'll be fine. Where are we going?"

"To visit a giant. Get some information out of him."

"Great… Exciting. Are we gonna beat a confession out of him? Work him over? You know, I could—"

"Help if you had a gun? Yeah, I know."

*

Once on the secure ward at North Shore Medical, a male orderly escorted Kate and me to the visiting room, passing windows covered by metal grates and alarm wire on the way. Through them I could see the Verrazano Bridge, still dark and shadowy in the mist—and beyond that—the skyline of Manhattan. Everything below 23rd Street was still dark. It looked like a dead city from one of those teenage dystopian movies.

Fuckin' Sandy.

When we reached the last set of secure doors at the visitors waiting room, I turned to Kat and tried to be firm. "Wait here. I'll be back in less than an hour."

"The fuck you say," Kat answered. I didn't want to compromise with her this time, but I saw the guard look at her as he heard her tone. It was the same one used by every person who ever resisted arrest and it said, "I'm about to fuck up your day if you try it."

I didn't need Kat distracting Morocco the Toothless Giant. He was on the verge of death, had been in prison for years and hadn't had any contact with a woman since being locked up. The sight of her in yoga pants might send him into cardiac arrest—hell, it caused me to have health issues if I didn't purposefully focus on other things. I tried to explain that to Kat.

It didn't work. Three minutes later we walked into the visiting room together, with Kat's shirt pulled as far down over her ass as it would go without exposing her breasts. Lucky for me, the whole place was less than romantic. We had to sit on stiff chairs in the midst of sick or dying criminals who apparently weren't quite up to showering. The whole place had the smell of death disguised by antiseptic, ammonia, and Febreze. Sliding into a chair with uneven legs and a cracked seat, I took in the room, looking for all the possible ways this could go wrong. That's when I saw him coming through the gate.

He'd shrunk.

The Toothless Giant that had stood six-foot-six now looked to be about my height, if not shorter, and at least thirty pounds lighter. The corrections officer assigned to the ward led Vinny Morocco over, and he smiled as he saw Kat. His teeth had gotten worse, and the muscle tone that he'd used to punch the van window and break my father's jaw had wasted away to loose skin, bones, and what seemed like a few random tendons that held them together. I stood when Morocco got close, getting between him and Kat.

"You remember me?" I asked.

"You look like a cop. You arrest me for something?" he asked, peering around me to look at Kat.

"I caught you digging for Swamp Pink once. I'm Detective Killian Collins."

Morocco sat down hard in the plastic chair, trying to put it all together. When he did, he smiled again. "Holy-mother-fucking-shit. It *is* you. I see it now. Fuck. Never expected you. Last time I saw you, you was a little punk ass."

"And last time I saw you, you were a giant," I reminded him.

"Shit happens. Got a dirty needle in the ass at some point. Got the AIDS," he said matter-of-factly, then turned to Kat. "Condoms work great, though, no worries."

"I'm a lesbian," Kat said with a smile to shut him down. It didn't seem to deter Morocco. He kept grinning.

"You got AIDS while you were in prison?" I asked.

"Nah, before I met you even. When I was juicin' with the 'roids… But havin' the AIDS saved me from gettin' worse stuck in me in the joint. The meat syringe, you know?" he asked, winking at Kat.

"I got it," Kat told him. "We're here to ask you some questions, not hear about your sex life."

"Questions? Why don't you ask this guy why he took a wrench to my head," Morocco snapped, with just a hint of bitterness.

"It was a ratchet."

"Felt like a wrench."

"Well, either way, it didn't do much. You kept coming."

"Yeah. Barely felt it. I was stoned to the gills."

"Look, Vin, can we talk about something else?" Kat asked sweetly. "All this talk about AIDS is ruining my fantasy of you."

Morocco laughed out loud, getting stares from the C.O.'s and prisoner/patients. "Sorry. Yeah. I get it. Your girlfriend here is right. I talk too much about the AIDS and takin' it up the ass. My mom says the same thing."

"Your mom?" I asked, trying to reconcile the shrunken man in front of me with not only the giant I remembered, but also with a boy who once had a mother. If there ever was a motherless prick, this guy was it.

"Sure, kid, everybody gots a mom. Mine thinks I could use a little human contact. A hug, even if it is from some moolie with a pot sticker. …Like she ever hugged me when I was a kid."

"His mom's kinda cold too," Kat chimed in, leaning forward to give him a glimpse of cleavage.

"A heartless mother explains a lot. That how you ended up a cop? All discipline, no love," Morocco asked, his eyes never leaving Kat's chest.

"I'm looking for Pete, your old partner," I told him, changing the subject. "I saw him, and I think he can help me find a girl who's in danger."

"Sounds exciting. She a hot little number like this one?" he asked, but I just went on, ignoring the comment:

"He was in the same woods where you two were digging for Swamp Pink—up by Clay Pit Ponds," I told him, trying to goad him into revealing his connection to that place and expecting him to maintain the decades-old lie.

Instead Morocco laughed so hard that he started to wheeze. "Swamp Pink? Yeah... Right. Only the pink was green," he gasped through laughter.

"Cash? From the IRA gun-running?" Kat asked, distracting Morocco from the point—finding Pete and Alina.

But Morocco stopped laughing. "...Yeah. Somethin' like that. A lotta fuckin' money anyway. I don't know. They hired us to look and dig. Said it was out there in some kind of box, but if we came across any bodies, we were supposed to let 'em know that too. Some major player had a brother go missin' out there. I thought it was crazy, but they was payin'—just a straight job until we seen you spyin' and chased you down. When Pete told the boss what you looked like and that about scar of yours, he practically lost his mind."

"My scar? What about my scar?"

"And who was this boss?" Kat asked, keeping the interview focused. I was letting my personal involvement distract me.

Morocco leaned back and folded his arms, looking at Kat, not me. He had information that we wanted, and that meant he had leverage.

"I ain't no rat, and I'm not stupid, so forget sellin' the boss out. At least not without a deal on the table," Morocco said, smirking.

"Fine. Tell me what the deal was with my scar and then we can get back to the boss."

"The scar? Don't really know. He just seemed to know who you were 'cause of it. Said we should bring you back to him Æcause we needed you or the girl to find what was missing."

"What girl?" Kat asked, suddenly more interested

"How the fuck would I know? She went missing like six years before. Nobody knew where she went. She ran away."

"Ran away from who?" I asked, trying to get him to focus.

"The *boss*. Ain't you listenin'? He'd been buyin' and sellin' kids for years. Used to do it through bogus church adoptions, had a bonanza with all them Amerasian kids after Vietnam, and then all the Russian kids after the Soviet Union went all *fakakta*. He was a coyote before coyotes were cool."

"If your boss was selling kids, where did the cash and guns come in?"

"Kids was the boss's regular trade and I guess somebody along the line was short on money—so they were using the kids as cash to get themselves even. Paying for guns with people. They brought him in as a consultant like, to get top dollar and say what they were worth. They needed a pro."

"Why?"

"How do I know? Someone on the inside knew the boss had a way of breaking kids. Getting them to talk and cooperate, you know?"

"'Someone on the inside?' Prison?" Kat asked, trying to follow his train of thought.

I knew what he meant and wasn't really surprised. I remembered enough of my dream that I'd started putting pieces together. Someone had killed Tompkins and Germanario. Someone was helping the IRA get guns.

"He doesn't mean inside prison. He means inside the establishment. Law enforcement," I explained to Kat.

"Exactly. This guy came to the boss with a deal—break the kids, smuggle the guns," Morocco confirmed.

"Did he break the kids?" I asked, wondering how far this went.

"I have no fuckin' clue. I wasn't there at the time. But I bet he did. All kids get turned out the same, and all kids break at some point," he said.

"He 'broke' the kids? You're proud that your boss 'turned out' kids?" Kat asked, thankfully restraining herself enough that she didn't launch across the table at Morocco.

"So, how did you 'break in' these kids?" I asked, trying to silence Kat with a look.

"Same way we usually did. First you make 'em feel like they're worthless and all alone in the world. Parents, family, teachers—all gone. It's easy really. You just gotta destroy everything they love. Everything that makes 'em who they are. Then you build 'em back up. We thought this time'd be easier, 'cause all we needed was information. Shoulda been easy. There's a method. Take away sleep, take away food. Do whatever you want to their bodies. The worse and more degrading the better, if you know what I mean."

"I'm afraid I might."

"It can be fun, but it's real work, you know? It usually pays off in the end, 'cause when they're all broke down and you give them anything, and I mean anything—a slice of bread, a touch without pain—you're like a savior. You can starve 'em for a week and then buy them a slice of pizza and you're an angel. Rape them five times and then let them sleep eight hours in a warm, dry bed and you're their favorite person. It's like Sweden syndrome."

"Stockholm. It's the Stockholm syndrome," I muttered.

"Norway, Sweden, what's the difference? Whatever. It works. It's why prostitutes always go back to their pimps and abused women go back to their men. They want the only kindness they've ever had. Even if it's fucked up and vicious, it's all they know. Never fails, always sticks. They get to like it."

"No. They don't," Kat snapped.

"What would you know? You see these kids all grown up, they're all hooking or stripping, still using the same tricks on other people. Sex as a weapon. They fuck anyone just to get something out of 'em. If you was abused, you'd be some kinda nympho too. If it's your stock in trade, you use it… But them kids were just gone after that plane went down. Like 'poof'—in the wind. The cash too. That's why we was still looking years later."

"So, you never found the cash—or the kids?"

"Nah. Too bad. I heard it was like almost ten million."

"And why didn't your boss keep comin' after me?" I asked. If

I was so important, why was I left alone all these years?

"You? Boss's inside guy said you was half a retard. Hit in the head. Had no memory of nothin'. Your dad bein' a cop, who needs the shit we'd get for kidnapping a moron?"

"Thanks for that," I muttered, unsure if I was supposed to be glad that I was some kind of a retard.

"Yeah, no worries. Probably saved your life. But now it's your turn to save mine, or what I got left of one. Can you get me a deal? I'll give you the boss's name if you get me off this ward so I can go home to die. I'm not really a threat to nobody no more, and it's awful hard on my moms comin' in this place."

"I'll need something I can work with if I bring in the U.S. Attorney. Dates, times, places. I'm on a clock here, Morocco. The guy I'm looking for can take off as soon as the bridges open up again."

"Not fuckin' likely. If he wants that cash, he ain't gonna leave without it. You tell the U.S. attorney-guy that I'll give him whatever he needs, but here's a tidbit to tease you. After 9/11, the boss gave up on flyin' stuff in—we bring it all in by boat now. Right through the graveyard. Never stay long, just take up residence on the day. Check that out, that'll show him what I know," Morocco offered. "I just want to go be with my moms. I'm dyin' in here."

"I'll see what I can do. If you want to help it move faster, call me with something more." I got up to go and was halfway across the room when I thought of another question, calling back to Morocco.

"Morocco, what would your boss have done if I ever remembered?"

Morocco shrugged, as if it was obvious. "Whatever he had to. He had a guy keepin' tabs on you. But it never happened. You stayed fucked in the head."

I heard Kat snicker. Lucky me, I was still fucked in the head.

CHAPTER TWENTY-ONE

Kat and I were walking to my car when I reached my connection at the United States Attorney's Office, Tommy O'Connell. Tommy grew up next door to my buddy Charlie Pederson and still hung out at The Annex with us, at least whenever his wife was out of town. He was a Staten Island guy at heart, even though the wife had made him move to Williamsburg a few years back. Tommy had hooks in on the federal side because his ambitious aunt with the breast implants and a degree in modern dance was the third trophy wife of a federal judge. If anyone could help me get some kind of deal for Morocco, Tommy was the guy.

"It's a kidnapping case, Tommy, RICO Act stuff. You want to make a name for yourself, this is the case to do it on. Tt's an ongoing enterprise going back at least to nineteen eighty-five," I told him. "I have a confidential informant willing to talk, but he wants a deal. He's dying of AIDS anyway."

"I'll talk to the boss. And hey, Kill—is it true what I hear about The Annex?"

"It's gone, Tommy."

"Fuck me… We gotta find a new place. I can't drink with all these douchebags in Brooklyn," he said, with genuine sadness.

"I hear that. We'll find someplace," I assured him and hung up without saying good-bye. We never did. We knew when a conversation was over.

"Jesus and ever lovin' Mary, what the fuck?" Kat asked, suddenly taking off at a run toward my car.

I looked up and saw what she did—four teens with gas cans, siphoning gas from my Nova and the Hummer next to it. They looked up as they heard Kate and ran like hell. I angled down the slight slope of the parking lot to cut them off, but they must have been the track team from nearby Curtis High School. Those fuckers flew, darting in and out between parked cars, gaining ground on me until I finally cornered one as he ran smack into a chain-link fence. As I went to grab him he turned and threw a can of gas at me, spraying the cars around us—

I ducked to avoid it and by the time I was moving again the little fuck was over the fence and all the gas was on the ground, washing away in the rain. A half second later Kate ran up, looking at the empty gas can lying on the ground.

"You lost him?"

"What's it look like?"

"Like you're slow as shit."

"And you? I don't see any gas in your hands," I shot back.

Kat just shrugged. "They had a car waiting. Kid in the driver's seat pointed a gun at me. I let them go."

"Good choice," I told her, and I meant it. With gas stations flooded, closed, or just plain out of gas, there was a black market to keep generators running. The gangs on the North Shore had a long history of knowing how to make money off the suffering of others. Leave it to Staten Island punks to steal from the most vulnerable—the people visiting a hospital. I started walking back to my car and Kat followed, her adrenaline surge slowly turning to anger.

"You know, I coulda stopped the little pricks if . . ."

"You had a gun. I know."

"And now we're screwed. There's no car service with Sandy, no buses. The train tracks are flooded. We're stuck... Unless..." Kat thought out loud -- then held out a hand for my phone as we reached the Nova.

"Who are you going to call?"

"My new best friend. Your *mother*. And I don't mean that colloquially."

"You're not calling my mother. I'd rather walk," I said, getting in the car.

"In the rain?" Kat said, smirking at me. I turned the key in the ignition. It was dead. They'd gotten all my gas.

I didn't let Kat make the call. I made it, and then got in the car to keep the damp and chill away while we waited. I needed the time to think anyway. To put the pieces together with all the new information Morocco had given me. Did Markov actually believe his brother and the cash were still here? That either Rigan or I might know where either one was?

Even if he did, the cash had been in the plane, lost in Clay Pit Ponds, and could have either rotted away or been stolen by someone else by now. Or, worse, Uncle Joe could have hidden it before he died and the location died with him. I still felt like I was missing something. Why was Josef Markov here *now*, so many years later? What prompted him to come to the States for his uncle and the cash after all this time? And what did Morocco mean when he casually mentioned going "right through the graveyard"? I felt like I should have known what he meant by that, but it was another fact lodged somewhere in a memory I had no access to.

There was nothing I could do, because right now I was stuck—with the sound of rain on the metal roof of the Nova growing louder once again. It was a soothing sound at this point, somehow, and helped me focus. I focused so deeply that I'm not even sure I was still conscious as the case, and my nightmares, slowly started to merge in a limbo of what might have been a waking dream. Or maybe I drifted off. In my defense, it had been an exhausting couple of days.

*

The box was heavy and awkward, the cold metal constantly slipping out of my grasp in the rain. I knew I needed to hide it before they caught me, but I had nothing to dig with to bury it, and there was nowhere that I could put it down without it being obvious. I was stumbling and staggering toward a nearby tree line that was full of firs and oaks—a place that should be perfect for hiding. That's when I saw the flashlights illuminating the night again.

I started moving faster, branches slapping my face, sticker bushes and burrs tearing my legs. I was panicked and running out of breath—and in that way of dreams, I stumbled out of the woods I had just entered into someplace much farther away in reality—to the shore of the Arthur Kill, a tidal strait separating Staten Island from New Jersey, where cattails and sharp-edged bladed grass suddenly surrounded me. The ground was no longer solid, but amorphous under my feet. Ahead of me I could see the splotchy reflections of rain hitting the oily and polluted surface of the water. I was cold and soaked to the bone, carrying the box that had somehow grown heavier. I started moving slowly, trying not to rustle the cattails.

In another five feet I was in water up to my shins and able to see through the cattails to what lay beyond them—a hulking, rusting fleet of abandoned and decaying ships—the Arthur Kill boat graveyard. Everything from splintered and sinking tugboats covered in algae to oxidized and rusting trawlers were creaking and groaning with the tides, left here to be reclaimed by a salvage company that never seemed to reclaim anything.

Maybe I could hide here, on one of these boats. Or maybe this was my way out, if I could find anything that could float. I could go through the graveyard. I started wading deeper into the water when something behind me moved the cattails, rustling them as if they were trampling over them, coming right toward me. I tried to run, but the muck and sludge that had settled at the edge of the Arthur Kill sucked my feet in and I tripped, falling face first.

I inhaled a mouthful of oily and polluted water, my eyes stinging as the viscous liquid stuck to them. I wiped them, only making my vision blurrier as something in the mud moved, squirming underneath me. It felt like a muscular snake, five-foot long and six inches in diameter, with open sores on its slimy skin.

It was a conger eel, poisoned by the pollution in the Arthur Kill, and as I saw its flattened head and beady eyes rise out of the water with thin, razor-sharp teeth gnashing at my face, I screamed—

*

—And I woke up with my throat ripped raw. I stopped screaming as soon as I was fully conscious, only to scream again as I looked out the driver's side window.

My mother was tapping on it, her gray hair plastered down by the rain. I stopped as I recognized her and looked over for Kat, but she was gone.

"Where is Kat? When did you get here?" I asked.

"She's already in your father's car. She was standing in the rain when I got here. Said you were snoring—but she had your gun and was watching every car that came by like it was full of hit men. You ask me, that girl's got some anxiety issues."

"I figured out where Markov is," I told her as I grabbed my stuff and opened the door. I was almost positive that I'd seen the answer in my dream, or memory, or whatever the hell I saw when I slept.

"You have an address? I have your father's car. I don't like to drive mine out this end of the island. Can't trust the lowlifes around here. I got a radio stolen from my old Toyota in 1982 right on Targee."

"Jesus, do you let anything go?"

"No. This is proof. They stole your gas. Let's get moving. I hate this part of Staten Island, and since I have your father's car, I can get directions to wherever you want. Deliver you straight to the Red Mafia. He's got his bitch-in-a-box that can tell us where to go."

"It's a GPS, Mom. And I don't exactly have an address," I admitted, seeing Kat already in the back seat of my father's old Honda.

"So, you *don't* know?" Mom asked, with an element of derision in her tone that reminded me of the days when she tried to teach me the nine times tables. The nines still screw me up.

"I know exactly where it is. I'll drive," I told her, trying to grab the keys.

She snatched them out of my reach. "You can't drive. You're in no shape. When's the last time you slept?"

"Just now. Maybe. And it doesn't matter. We need to move fast and you refuse to speed," I protested. It was a weak excuse, since my mother actually had a lead foot. When I was a kid, she had a second job driving an ambulance, and my father had taught her to drive—the man who had taught chase driving for the NYPD. She could drive fast. She just wouldn't.

"I told you. I have your father's car," she said, as if that would explain why she could speed this one time. It did, in a way. My father was enamored with gadgets, including radar detectors, police band radios, and a GPS system that tracked traffic, radar traps, and red-light cameras. To back that up, he had cell phone apps that did the same thing. "Safety in redundancy," he always said.

*

Ten minutes later we were taking the ramp from the Staten Island Expressway onto the West Shore Expressway at seventy. Mom was driving; Kat was up front in the suicide seat, disgusted by the smell in the car. Apparently, Mom had chain-smoked her way across the island to get us, even though she refrained from lighting up on the way home. The same cigarette she had put in her mouth in the parking lot still dangled from her lips.

Still, the car smelled like an ashtray and Kat kept cracking the window to breathe. It became a battle of wills as my mother rolled it shut after a few seconds, and then Kat cracked it open again. After about five go-rounds of this passive-aggressive window rolling, my mother put the window lock on.

"You know what you did, right? By dragging up all this nonsense?" she started lecturing us, her captive audience.

"I didn't exactly 'drag up this nonsense,' Mom. Hurricane Sandy blew up that yacht on shore with kids dead in the hold."

"You upset your father."

"When? Today? Or twenty years ago? Does he know the difference?"

"You find this funny?"

"He doesn't find it funny. Do you, Kill?" Kat interrupted, noticing that when my mother spoke to me, she glared at me in the rearview and paid no attention to the road ahead. Kat wanted to end the conversation, for safety's sake.

"Call him Killian, not 'Kill'—and you're the one that got me going with all this obsessive rolling down of the window for fresh air. Open windows make a noise like torture and lets in all the exhaust."

"Can we drop it, Mom?"

"No. The crazy bastard started pulling the whole house apart after you left. Went in the garage and tossed boxes all over, looking for something. He wouldn't stop. Went and found his old snub-nose back-up revolver and started to load it, the jackass."

"You left him alone when he was like that?"

"Do I look like an *amadon*? I put an Ambien in his orange juice before I left, and that little slip of a strange thing is with him. Maybe the old mare you rode to exhaustion is even up to help by now."

"Rigan was still asleep and you left that girl in charge of an old man with dementia and a revolver?"

"Calm down. She adores the loon. He'll sleep it off, and she'll take care of him if he wakes up," my mother answered calmly, as if this was a routine procedure.

"You slipped Dad Ambien?"

"I was a nurse for almost forty years. He'll be fine. I just couldn't have him calling any more dead people."

"Calling dead people?" Kat asked, fascinated.

"He does it when he's tense. Calls the cops he used to work with," I explained.

"He upsets the widows something terrible is what he does. Even worse, he gets emotional when the old ladies tell him his friends are gone. Goes to pieces like it's the first time he heard about it."

"Why was he calling dead cops, Mom? Was it the plane?"

"How would I know? He was just ranting about a conspiracy. He thought someone was knocking off his old friends and had them all on a hit list. Even caught him trying to call your Uncle Joe a couple of times."

"Were his friends murdered?" Kat asked, horrified.

"Hell, no. Vinny Gatto died screwing his granddaughter's babysitter. Dave Coonan ate his own gun after his kid OD'd, and Bobby Michaels went out like Elvis, on the shitter," Mom related matter-of-factly.

"Lovely, Mom."

"They were cops. It's to be expected."

"What did Dad say about this so-called conspiracy that you didn't snoop into?"

"He was just rambling, and *don't* ask him about it. He's been enough trouble lately. Had all his old charcoal pencils out today, making crazy drawings and sketches."

Sketches and drawings. My father had done that ever since I was a kid. He claimed drawing helped him think in another dimension.

"What were the drawings of?"

"Trees. Streams. That damn piece of junk ring you kept."

My memento mori. My father knew more than he was saying, and I'd need to find out what it was while he was in the present and in his right mind.

"Yes, but thank God, he chilled out and went back to sketching ships and river scenes."

"Ships? Or *shipwrecks*?"

"How do I know? It was a crappy sketch."

That was all I needed to know. My hunch about where Markov was had to be right. Markov was using the "graveyard"—the Arthur Kill boat graveyard.

The boat graveyard was actually a salvage yard for wrecks going as far back as the turn of the last century. If Markov wanted to, he could anchor his yacht offshore and use the life rafts to ferry kids and drugs on shore without any prying eyes at some marina seeing them. Because I knew the neighborhood, I knew that Markov would have to transfer the kids to a truck or some other means of transport nearby and couldn't risk moving too far from the graveyard without getting noticed. That meant he'd have a base of operations...

Which is where something else Morocco had said started to make sense—that Markov took up residence on "the day."

I knew he didn't mean that Markov stayed in Staten Island—he meant something different entirely, something I knew only because I remembered specific details about the graveyard.

Maybe my memory was getting better.

"Drive faster, Ma. We need to get back before the Ambien wears off and Dad figures out where Markov is by himself."

"You know where Markov is?" Kat asked.

"Yes. Maybe," I told her, knowing that the bridges would be open again in the next few hours. I dialed my cell, hoping to stop my father from doing something that he thought he could still do because he was living thirty years in the past. The phone just rang off the hook.

That was bad news. As a former cop, my father answered every call as if it were a nine-one-one call. He refused to screen them because someday he might miss a call that was life or death.

"Don't you dare call your father, Kill. If he wakes up, there's no telling what he'll do. We'll be home in ten minutes at most."

"He's not answering."

"Maybe I gave him more Ambien than I thought," Mom said, trying to reassure me, but I noticed that her speed had gone up as she reached over the back seat and in one swift motion snatched my cell phone.

Never underestimate your mother when she's angry, kids.

"You can have it back when we get home," she told me, sliding it under her thigh in case I tried to take it back.

"Mom, I need to call the precinct. I need to know when

they'll be opening the bridges and the Arthur Kill to boats."

"They announced it on the radio. The bridges open at eight tonight. You can have your phone when we get home."

"This is ridiculous," I told her, reaching for it. She slapped my hand, pissing me off. I had a little less than three hours to find Markov before he could move.

"No. What's ridiculous is that I can't have a cigarette because of Miss I Can Pierce Holes in My Body But God Forbid My Lungs Have to Deal with a Little Smoke—and you expect me to be rational. Get over it."

Mom put her foot to the floor and Kat inhaled aggressively, as if she was taking what might be her last smoke-filled breath. All I could do was hope that my mother's reaction times were still as good while she was driving as they were reaching back to grab my cell phone.

I wanted her to slow down, but instinct told me that no matter how fast she was going, it wasn't fast enough.

*

The tires squealed as we rounded the corner, and I could see my parents' house with the garage door and front door wide open. Something was wrong.

"Did you leave the garage open, Ma?"

"I don't live in a damn barn. It lets out all the heat I pay good money for. Damn Ambien—never works the same way twice."

"So, you drug him often?" Kat asked, starting to relax as Mom slammed on the brakes, sliding to a stop.

"I deserve a life, dammit," Mom said, trying to convince herself more than either of us.

I didn't wait for the car to stop completely. I was out the door and running over the lawn even as Mom slowed. When I got to the open front door, I saw that its frame was splintered. Glancing left and right, I pulled my gun and went through, looking for anyone who might be inside.

The house was torn apart, bookshelves emptied, couch cushions sliced open, tables overturned—just like my place had been. I heard water running in the master bathroom and ran through the bedroom, barely slowing to make sure the room was clear before trying to push open the door.

It was stuck. Something heavy and unmoving was in the way. I shoved harder, looking through the crack, but all I could see was part of the shower curtain, the white enamel of the bathtub...

...And the swirling red tendrils of blood in the flowing water at the bottom of it. My father was the heavy and unmoving object blocking the door.

...And it was his blood in the water.

CHAPTER TWENTY-TWO

"Dad! Dad!" I yelled, pushing on the door. I was about to smash through it and take the damn thing off the hinges when it suddenly gave way and I stumbled in to see my father's head hanging over the side of the tub. As I knelt to grab him, he turned.

"Jesus Christ, calm yourself, Killian," he said, lifting his head up. "I'm fine. Just cut my head on the faucet when they pushed me under. Scalp wounds bleed like fuck." He grabbed a towel on the rack nearby and pressed it to his forehead just below the hairline.

"Jimmy, there's no need for cursing," Mom admonished him, appearing in the doorway with Kat, "...and you're ruining the good towels."

"Christ, Theresa. Can you show me some sympathy before

you light into me? We've all heard 'fuck' before."

"I meant the 'Jesus Christ' bit."

"I was fucking praying, okay?" he lashed back at her as Kat slid between all of us, taking charge of the head wound.

"Put pressure on that," she told him, her body taking up what was left of the space in the small bathroom, making it unbearably close. "It doesn't look deep. It should stop bleeding in a few minutes. Do you have any antibiotic gels?"

"There you go, see? *She's* nice," Dad said. My mother ignored the insult and pulled the towel away from him, handing him one of the frayed and faded ones from under the sink, as well as an antibiotic. I was glad Mom and Kat had it under control, but all three of them were so focused on the blood, they were missing something else.

"Where's Rigan and Dariya?" I asked.

My father looked up at me from under the bloody towel, hesitant. "Gone," he muttered from under the towel.

"Gone where?"

"Rigan tore out of here the minute your mother left."

"With Dariya?"

"No," he muttered, like an admission of guilt. "Dariya left with the Eastern European trash that smashed my head in."

"Damn," Kat muttered, almost under her breath as she looked at me, "that sucks. You just keep losing people, don't you?"

"Not now, Kat," I warned her, then turned back to my father. "What happened, exactly?"

I needed him to be clear before he drifted off into an episode. If whoever had done this to my father had taken Dariya, we were running out of time—by my calculations about two hours and twenty minutes.

"I was in my chair drifting off when I heard someone at the door. I thought it was Rigan coming back—until that asshole nearly tore the door off the frame and Dariya started throwing a bloody fit. Then suddenly some guy was bellowing at me in some commie language. Took me a minute to realize it wasn't a dream."

"How many were there? What did they look like?" I asked, interrogating out of habit.

"Jesus, Killian. Fucked if I know. It's not like I've got the Russian Mafiya playing cards—but half of the one guy's finger is on the kitchen floor if you want to get a print."

"Please tell me that's a joke," Mom said, looking down the hall toward the kitchen, disgusted.

"I'll clean it up, Theresa, Jesus… that girl had the stones to bite the damn thing off. That little bit of a thing is one tough motherfu—"

"Jimmy," Mom snapped, cutting him off.

They started fighting as I stepped out of the bathroom and went toward the kitchen. It was a mess, what with the blood on the floor… and a small, very hairy finger. I stared at it as I heard my parents still arguing in the bathroom.

"Don't goddamn 'Jimmy' me, Theresa. Maybe if I wasn't so fuzzy-headed I would have had a better shot at dealing with them," he told her. "I know what it feels like to be drugged."

"You were getting paranoid. I had to do something," she pleaded, turning toward me as I returned to the bathroom so she could throw me under the bus. "This idiot ran out of gas. I had to go get him."

"Ran out of *gas*? What kind of mental midget did I raise?" Dad asked.

"The gas was stolen. Siphoned right out of my car. Please, Dad—focus. What did they want?"

"Doesn't matter. I told 'em jack-shit. Assholes thought it was the old-timer's kickin' in. They woulda killed me but they didn't bother 'cause they thought I was 'half-a-retard'," he muttered, wincing as he put the towel back to his cut, putting pressure on it.

"Wait. They called you a 'half-a-retard' or is that your phrase?"

"What kinda mental midget calls himself 'half-a-retard'?" Dad asked, making a good point.

"So it was the same guys…" I said as I turned to look at Kat. She nodded, worried.

"How do you know that?" asked Dad, getting up off the floor, more focused and interested than I'd seen him in a long time.

"They called Killian half-a-retard too," Kat explained.

"Well, after he ran out of gas…" muttered Mommy dearest. Dad glared at her and she stopped talking. I just ignored her.

"How'd they even find Dariya all the way out here on the

ass-end of the island?" Kat asked, getting to the heart of the issue.

"Dad. Mom said that you called people—and Morocco said they had people watching me all these years. Who did you call?" I asked, but his eyes slid away from mine. He didn't know, and he was ashamed of it—or he was playing me again. It was so hard to tell with him.

"I… don't know. Maybe if your mother hadn't drugged me —"

"Again with this?"

"*Enough*. Dad, if this was twenty-five years ago, who would you call?"

He shrugged, thinking about it. "Everyone in the unit. I have the old list in my desk, in the office. The damn Russians went in there too."

I started moving that way before he even finished. He called out after me:

"Whatever they found, they said something about knowing right where to find the bitch. That's when they left to catch up to Rigan."

Fuck me. That meant they knew where to go, and that they had found some clue in the office. I made it down the hall and slammed through the door… and lost all hope. The drawers had been pulled out of the desk, the couch sliced open, and books torn off the shelves. Papers were strewn everywhere. I stared at them all as the rest of them came in behind me, taking in the mess.

"The guys who were here, tell me the specific questions they asked."

"He doesn't recall," Mom interrupted.

"Stay out of this, Theresa," Dad told her, maintaining eye contact with me. "There's no point in hiding whatever I can remember anymore. He's got to know."

"Know what?" I asked, but Dad was already moving, reaching for an electric outlet next to the recliner. It had nothing plugged into it and he pulled the whole thing out of the wall—no wires attached. His hand went into the empty cavity and pulled out two manila envelopes.

"So that's why you never fixed that damn outlet," Mom muttered under her breath.

"Everything I can tell you is in those," he said, handing me the envelopes.

"Can tell me, or will tell me?"

"Whatever's on that paper is better than what's in my head at this point. More reliable, anyway. Take what you can get, Killian," he warned as I opened the first envelope. "Those are the crime scene Polaroids."

I knew what crime scene photos looked like. They were never pretty.

"Dead kids?" I asked, just to clarify. He nodded, solemn and fully aware for once. I hesitated, and then opened the envelope anyway. The dead kids were there, some of them thrown from the plane, limbs torn from their bodies, deep lacerations from aircraft aluminum and glass leaving them bloody. The pilot and another man lay dead in the cockpit.

The next photos were close-ups of the kids. Rigan wasn't in them—because she had survived, obviously. I kept going, looking at the close-ups. I took it all in, knowing there was a lot of the story left untold in these pictures. I turned back to my father, who was still in the present.

"Where was Rigan when these were taken?"

"We found her right after that. But look closer. Tell me what you see in the lower right corner of the photo, inside the fuselage," he said, nodding toward the photos of the fuselage. It was in the shadows of the photo, but I knew what it was as soon as I saw it:

A metal box, half hidden by an oilskin, about two foot square.

"The cash was in that box, wasn't it? It wasn't lost."

It had been there. Markov and Morocco and all the rest weren't wrong. Uncle Joe had seen what they said he did, and he died knowing where it was.

"It wasn't lost then, and look at the size of the box. I did the calculations. If it was filled with hundred-dollar bills, there could be close to ten million in that box," Dad muttered. "We had it all right there until Joe moved it. When we got there that night we expected to find drugs, even money, but not kids. Joe didn't seem surprised, but he was worried that someone in the unit might be corrupt and could show up any minute, so he had me get the kids somewhere safe, and he stashed the cash, figuring we could use it to lure out whoever was dirty."

All the complications in my life suddenly started to make sense.

This is why Mangy Mustache and the Toothless Giant had come after me, and why Markov and his guys thought Rigan and I knew where everything was. That's what Morocco meant when he said they had guys watching me. They all thought that I remembered where Joe Corrigan had hidden their money.

"Uncle Joe hid it? You need to tell me where it is. Now. We can tell Markov and trade that for the girls."

My father shrugged hopelessly. "I can only tell you where it *was*. Joe told me what he did with it and was going to move it the night he was killed, but no one knows if he ever got there. He's dead, and you don't remember. For all I know, you could have helped him move it. You were alone in those woods for three days, Killian," Dad said gently. "If Joe had shown it to you, you would've had time to hide it."

"Me?" I asked, concerned that all of this was my fault somehow.

"You had the memento mori when you came back," Mom pointed out helpfully. "If you could remember where you put anything, things would have been a lot simpler."

I turned on my father, wondering now how much he'd really known. "Do you know what that ring really was?"

"You mean, did I know Mikhail Markov went missing?" he asked sadly. "Bodies don't bury themselves, son."

No shit. So my father covered up Markov's murder and knew that the location of all that money could be in my fucked-up head all these years—and all I had were glimpses, in dreams—in dreams…

"What if I know where the cash is now?" I asked.

"What do you think you know?" my father asked cagily.

"Actually? Nothing. But Markov doesn't know that. If I can get him to believe that I know where the money is…" I let my voice drift off. A plan was forming.

"You can bluff him and tell him you'll trade it for Alina," Dad finished, getting it.

"And now Dariya too."

"And when you don't give it to him?" Mom asked, the ever-practical pessimist.

"He'll kill you," finished Kat. They were both so helpful.

"Maybe. One step at a time. First, I have to get to Rigan before he does. Then I need to set up a trade for the two girls," I told them, going for the desk drawer to get the GPS tracker that I could use to lure Markov in, but the GPS tracker in the bracelet and its battery were both missing. On the desk was a note: "*I can't risk losing you. I'm sorry. Rigan.*"

I glanced at the desk, the broken lock, and the files all over the floor and had an idea of what she might be planning.

"Dad, did the Russians break into this desk—or was it Rigan?"

"Does it matter?" he asked, avoiding the question.

"*Yes.* What did she find?" I reached down to pick up the files. Two were empty. I pulled them out, and one lone paper that was stuck to the back of a file folder floated to the floor. I saw nothing on it except my parent's signatures, the signature of a priest, and the raised seal of Saint Joseph's Catholic Church, our local parish when I was a kid.

That was it. There was no indication what the paper was the signature page to, but the end of the last sentence on the previous page had carried over onto this one and read "...*to be located in Zone C, Section 43, Pt. 541.*" It was also dated July 17, 1985. Three months before the accident that took my memory. I could see the pressure marks of a pen on the paper, where someone had written an address on the page that was once above it: "*926 Clove Road.*"

"I need your keys."

"What's going on?" Kat asked.

"Rigan found something in my father's desk and took off. She's going to try and find Alina on her own—and whatever it was she found, the guys who took Dariya found it too. They're going after her."

"Damn, that bitch is crazy," Kat muttered. I glared at her.

"Don't look at her with that tone of voice. Rigan's unbalanced," my mother said, defending Kat, looking for a fight.

"Theresa, stop. We should have told him a long time ago."

My mother stopped. Kat stopped.

"Told me what?" I asked, trying to make sense of the non sequitur.

"The kids in the plane, the ones didn't make it," he admitted. "It wasn't pretty... we buried all of them."

"Before or after Joe died?" I asked, knowing it was important.

"Before. There was no family. We had them buried the day he died. Why?"

"Did he make any arrangements?"

"The caskets… That's what Rigan was on about. Shit," he muttered, putting it together the same way Rigan had. Too late. "We buried them at Saint Peter's."

Saint Peter's Cemetery in Staten Island was on Clove Road. 962 Clove Road. That's why the address looked familiar. It was the cemetery where we used to drink and party in high school, because the cops never bothered the dead and the headstones made perfect backrests when you were too drunk to sit up on your own. I grabbed my father's car keys from my mother and headed for the door.

"What are you doing?" my father called after me.

"Finding Rigan," I told him, never slowing down. "And maybe that money."

I was already in the car when Kat came out the front door. I didn't even try to stop her this time, but I also didn't slow down. The car was already moving as she got in at a run, slamming the door as I hit twenty miles an hour.

"I can't protect you—and ask me for a gun and I'll shoot you myself," I told her. For once Kat didn't push it. She just glared at me as I rounded the corner, already doing forty.

CHAPTER TWENTY-THREE

Kat and I drove in silence for quite a while, staring out at water and food trucks making emergency deliveries to the shelters on the island and watching old Italian men shovel the dirt and clay out of the street to keep the storm drains clear.

We were already on the expressway when I felt her hand patting my thigh. "It's okay, you know," she said softly.

"What's okay?"

"Having someone use you. Lie to you. Make you feel special just to trick you. Rigan fucked you for her own gain. It happens."

"That's not what happened."

"Right."

"Look, Kat. I can spot a liar. She really cared about me, even if—"

"Jesus Christ, do you hear yourself? You're such a girl. No

one can spot a liar when they're psychotic. Psychos believe their own lies."

"That's assuming she's psychotic. She didn't seem it."

"Neither did Ted Bundy to all those dead girls. That's how he got to be Ted Bundy. You know psychos are the exception. They don't have tells because they really believe the bullshit they're slinging."

I didn't say anything. Mostly because Kat was right. Still, it *felt* like Rigan was being honest.

"So, who were you in her little fantasy? Some long-lost love, destined to be with her from the dawn of time?" Crap. She hit it so close to home.

"Something like that," I admitted as I pulled to the curb in front of the rectory that held the records to Saint Peter's Cemetery. I got out before she could lecture me. Two minutes and no words later, we were knocking on the door, but no one answered. After waiting an appropriate length of time, I knocked again, harder, glancing across the driveway to the old brick church, noticing that the basement was a hive of activity. It was obviously a makeshift shelter for those without power after the storm. I was about to go look for the priest over there when the door finally opened and Father Tim Finnerty smiled at me as if I was the prodigal child himself. He had to be almost eighty, but in my mind looked the same as he did when I was a kid, prematurely white-haired, with the papery skin of a man who secretly used too much moisturizer, never went out in the sun, and avoided sweating.

"Killian. Didn't expect to see you here," Father Finnerty said as he looked down at me from inside the doorway. I already felt guilty. They must give lessons in guilt induction before you're allowed to wear that collar. Father Finnerty had a flair for it and did it with a slight tone of disappointed indulgence.

"It's been awhile, I know," I admitted. "'*Mea culpa, mea culpa, mea maxima culpa,*'" I admitted through gritted teeth. It gets them to stop every time.

"And Katherine. How is Mrs. Ryan?" he asked, turning his attention on Kat—but how did they know each other?

"She's still in the sauce, but she promised me that she'd come to Mass this Sunday," Kat answered casually, as if these two spoke often.

"Mrs. Ryan? How do you two know each other?"

"Mrs. Ryan is one of the seniors Katherine cares for. That's a fine girl you have there, Killian. A real blessing. All the seniors love her."

"She's not my girl, Father."

"That's a shame. We do so many fewer weddings in the church these days."

I started talking before he could go on. All I needed was to have him get Kat started. "I have a few questions, Father—and we're in a bit of a rush."

"Right. You didn't show up for spiritual advice, did you? You never were interested in finding out about your own soul," he said, distracted by a mud-encrusted box truck that was backing up toward the church. "Just give me a second.

We're trying to collect food and blankets for the families that lost their homes, and it looks as if Juan Carlos is back with another load," Father Finnerty said as he started across the driveway to meet the truck and the four or five Hispanic men who had emerged from the church basement. I turned to look at Kat, who was watching the muscular young men take boxes off the truck.

"I don't have time for this. If they find Rigan and the cash, they'll kill her and the girls. We need to just go look," I said, starting toward the cemetery.

"You're pretty stupid for a smart guy, you know that? That cemetery is fifty acres. You won't find shit," she said calmly, pissing me off. "Wait ten seconds and save ten minutes." She was right. I stopped. Not happy about it, frustrated with her.

"Fine. While I wait, what's this about volunteer work?"

She shrugged without looking at me. "It was court-ordered. It's all good."

"You were arrested for something I don't know about?"

"Will you relax? It was a misunderstanding. I copped a plea to keep it from getting sticky, that's all."

"Copped a plea to what?" I asked. I knew she was trying to avoid telling me, but now that she could see I wasn't going to let it go, Kat got defensive.

"This dirty old bastard was harassing some poor high school girl at the train station."

"And?"

"And I might have hip-checked him."

"You don't get community service for a hip check. Not in Staten Island."

"He lost his balance. Ended up falling on the tracks…" Her voice trailed off and I stared at her, waiting for the rest. "All right, fine. He was also a lawyer. And old, and he fractured his hip, but the train was still like a mile away. It wasn't like I meant to throw him in front of it."

"So now you have to do community service with old people."

"Exactly. No biggie," she said, downplaying it. I kept looking at her, wondering how everyone could possibly look at her and keep seeing a girl I should be lucky to have. "Don't look at me like that, all right?" Kat went on. "The guy's old enough to fracture a hip, he shouldn't be sexually harassing young girls. He called her a little slut."

"Was she?"

"All she did was kiss her girlfriend good-bye. Then ye olde douchebag tells her she needs to get straight, learn what it's like to get a good schtupping from a real man. That's when he smacked her ass."

"What's with the schtupping? That's the second time in the last twenty-four hours."

"It's a good word, isn't it? I love Yiddish. Everything sounds exactly like it means—putz, schmuck, mensch, schlock—what's that called? An onomatopoeia?"

"How do you know these things?" I asked, trying to reconcile Kat's personality with all this random knowledge.

"I'm an autodidact," Kat said, and must have seen my blank stare. "Look it up."

I ignored her, still trying to figure out what had happened and why. "Was the guy you assaulted drunk?"

"Maybe. But I was just standing my ground."

"You can't claim that. He wasn't assaulting you."

"Okay, I was standing that girl's ground *for* her. I was a ground holder by proxy. What's the diff? He deserved it."

"And she did confess," chimed in Father Finnerty as he made his way back from the truck. "She even called an ambulance for him."

"I'm almost a saint," Kat grinned.

"Well, anyone can be redeemed. Even you, Killian," Father Finnerty rubbed it in. "You had questions?"

"Yes, and I need them fast. Do you recognize this?" I handed him the sheet of paper from my father's office and the priest glanced at Kat, as if looking for a hint as to what this was about. The paper had clearly struck a chord with him, even though he played it off in a millisecond.

"This is the location of a gravesite, in the cemetery, straight up the entrance road three hundred yards, a left on the second cross road and down the hill. It's the one your parents bought in nineteen eighty-five if I'm not mistaken... Look, Killian, why don't we go inside, where it's warm and dry? I remember things better when I'm not distracted by the dampness in my bones."

Father Finnerty opened the door and stepped inside, into the past, before I could stop him. The rectory smelled the same as it did when I was a child, a mixture of sharp, stale odors that included vague hints of mothballs, incense, and bacon, with a tinge of lemon-scented cleaning solutions and alcohol. The furniture looked like it was from the sixties and, in my admittedly poor memory, seemed to have been in the same positions since the Reagan administration.

"Father, right now I only care about that gravesite. Don't mess with me or give me the runaround," I said, in full-on interrogation mode. I had good reason. Time was against us. If Rigan turned on that GPS tracker, or found the cash, we might already be too late.

"For chrissakes, Kill—sorry, Father, didn't mean to take the Lord's name in vain—just ask the questions," Kat said, coming to his defense.

"It's okay, Katherine. I know what he wants," Father Finnerty reluctantly admitted.

"You do?"

"Yes. She was already here. Rigan Kelly. She was also asking about the gravesite. The family plot. I didn't tell her anything. It wasn't her family's plot. I didn't think she had a right to ask, even if she did think something was hidden in those graves. I'm not sure she's completely sane."

"You're not the only one. If you knew what she did last night…" Kat muttered.

I ignored her. "You need to show us the plot." I told Father Finnerty, taking him by the arm to escort him toward the door.

He pulled back. "You don't want to go out there, Killian."

"Why not?"

"There's nothing there for you to see." The priest looked down, folding his hands in an unconscious imitation of prayer.

"Except the kids from the plane?"

"You know about the plane crash?" he asked, shocked. As I nodded, he went on. "Your father wanted them to have a proper burial. They had no family, the city wouldn't pay, and no one was claiming them... It seemed like the right thing to do."

"You said *four* graves. Weren't there more kids on the plane?"

"Some survived. We... well, I guess, I got them baptismal certificates. In the names of other children who had died."

"You did what?"

"It was easier in nineteen eighty-five than it is now. I had to. There were men looking for them. Men with a grudge. We did what we had to do—to protect the other five. You have to understand, we just wanted the ones that lived to have a chance at life. They were being hunted down."

"Damn, Padre. That's all kinds of illegal," Kat muttered, disappointed in him.

"It was for the right reasons. We found them families."

"Did you actually see the kids in the coffins? Or could they be filled with something else?"

"You think that's what your father did? He's a better man than that. He never did anything except try to protect those kids."

"Maybe he hid it to protect them, or maybe Joe Corrigan did, who knows? But we need to get to that gravesite. Now.

Rigan's out there. My bet is she thinks the money is in the grave and she's going to turn on that GPS to call in Markov and trade it for Alina," I told them both as I headed for the front door.

"That's idiotic. They could just shoot her."

"Exactly my point," I said as I walked out. The only thing that would slow Rigan down was digging up the bodies, but all she'd need to do it would be a backhoe.

I hoped we were in time.

*

The backhoe was already at the gravesite. Someone had the same idea I did. I saw it as I sped up the narrow road that circled through the granite headstones, but it wasn't moving. It looked like it had sunk a foot or two into the muck and mud left after the storm.

"We're too late," Kat said, giving voice to what I was thinking. She had joined me, but Father Finnerty stayed behind, trying to convince us both not to head down this particular highway to hell. He had stood on the stoop of the rectory shouting after us that disturbing the dead was its own curse and that he wasn't responsible for what we'd find.

Screw him. Besides, as a former and recovering Catholic, I knew that even if I completely screwed this up, I could always confess my sins later and he'd have to forgive me. Right now my major concern was that the backhoe was where the gravesite should be and that the engine was running, but the operator wasn't.

He was dead.

The evidence I saw added up pretty neatly—the windshield of the backhoe's cab was splintered and sprayed with something red, the Hispanic operator was slumped over with a dark hole in his temple, and Rigan had her back to the treads of the backhoe, facing down a weaselly-looking bald guy with a mangy goatee, bad teeth, and a nine-millimeter pistol pointed at her chest. Two other pasty-looking, acne-scarred assholes were standing in the open graves. Russians.

I took in the rest of the scene as I sped closer. Two cars were parked ten feet away from the backhoe. The first was my mother's Toyota Camry, and the second was a black Cadillac Escalade. Damn. Why is it always a black Escalade?

"Take the wheel and steer straight at the Escalade," I told Kat, reaching for my gun. If I could get close enough to get a shot off at Mangy Goatee Guy, I could keep him from getting Rigan to his car at the very least. Then I could deal with the other two.

"What are you doing?" Kat asked as I rolled down the window. I had started to lean out the window when the sound of my car alerted Mangy Goatee Guy and he beat me to the punch. I saw his hand kick back and the briefest of muzzle flashes, hearing the shot a half-second later. He missed. I got a shot off back at him, but Kat was having a hard time steering with her left hand, especially since the stress had made me tense up, forcing my foot down on the gas pedal. Mangy Goatee Guy stayed cool, leveled his pistol—

—And fired again, shattering my windshield in a spider web pattern.

That pissed me off, since I knew exactly how much overtime it was going to cost to replace the windshield. I let go two more rounds in anger. Unfortunately, Kat also let go of the wheel when the window shattered, screaming and taking cover under the dashboard. That left the car to find its own way through the graveyard at sixty miles an hour.

Just about then the Russians opened fire and it all went to shit. Bullets punched holes through the car like it was a tin can, and for all Kat's Army experience, her driving didn't improve under fire.

It was a clusterfuck.

The first set of gravestones we hit only slowed us down, ripping up the undercarriage. The second set stopped us dead—not dead-dead but completely messed up. My ribs slammed against the doorframe and my head bounced off the windshield. Kat slammed into the dashboard, rolling off the seat and taking most of the impact to her shoulder.

Dizzy, with my head throbbing and my arm numb from where it had gotten pinched between my body weight and the car, I tried to climb out the window but couldn't move. Then I realized that I still had my seatbelt on. I unbuckled and glanced at Kat, hoping that she was all right.

"You okay?"

"I've had worse rides at Six Flags."

"Good, then let's go. Get out your door and stay low, behind the headstones."

"You don't happen to have an extra gun, do—"

"Just get out and go. Run and keep running," I ordered, opening my door. I took my own advice and stayed low. Good thing, since the second the door opened, a headstone in front of me splintered and threw up dust as a nine-millimeter round hit it.

"Killian, don't! He doesn't –" I heard Rigan scream, getting cut off by a second round hitting a gravestone nearby.

I dropped and rolled, looking for a way to flank Mangy Goatee and the Russians, but by the time I got some cover, I heard the Escalade start. They were in the car. I knew that I'd only have one chance, but as I stood to take it, I saw Rigan in the car with him—and Dariya in the back seat. At this distance I was just as likely to hit Rigan or Dariya as I was to hit Mangy Goatee or his friends.

I held my fire and wiped the warm, dripping blood from my eyebrow as the Escalade drove over the grassy hill.

"Shoulda taken the shot," Kat said from right behind me.

"I might have hit Rigan."

"And your point is?"

"I thought I told you to run."

"What? And leave you by yourself? Besides, I don't like being alone in cemeteries. It's creepy."

"You'd rather be shot at?" I asked, walking toward my mother's car—the one Rigan had arrived in, past the graves.

"I didn't say it was logical. Aren't you going after them?"

"I'm going to try, but my father's car isn't going anywhere after you drove it through a ton of granite—"

"After *I* drove it? You were in the driver's seat."

"We can take my mother's car."

"We'll never be able to catch them."

"Don't need to," I shrugged. "I know where they're going."

I reached the open graves and saw that the edges of the hole were water-soaked and had collapsed several times before it was big enough to get access to the caskets. I had to be careful as I approached, peering in, seeing that the four caskets were all open. In each was a cadaver, neatly dressed in early eighties era clothing, all well preserved. Against their translucent skin their auburn hair was vivid and bright. It almost made me understand the Greek belief that redheads became vampires after death. All four looked as if they might open their eyes and climb out.

"Kat, if the backhoe driver's got a pulse, call an ambulance," I told her as I jumped down into the grave.

"Screw that. If he's got a pulse, he's the living dead. Dude's got a bullet in his temple. And what the fuck do you think you're doin'?"

"Looking for any sign that there was anything else in here with them," I told her, trying not to breathe in the smell coming off the bodies as I lifted their limbs. They were all familiar to me, so it was a little harder to deal with. These were the dead kids in the crime scene photos my father had shown me. Kat circled the rim of the grave as I did, glancing from me to the horizon, making sure Mangy Goatee didn't come back. I could tell that she was getting paranoid, so I hurried—but there was nothing there. No cash. No hidden evidence. The next two bodies were the same, but the fourth body, a boy of about seven, was different. Not that he had any evidence on him, but he also didn't look like he'd been through a plane crash. He was emaciated, his hair thin—as if he'd been gravely ill before he died. He also didn't look familiar. He wasn't in the crime scene photos my father had, for whatever reason.

"Jesus Christ, Kill. We've gotta go."

"They're just bodies," I said, looking up at her.

"No, they're not. Please, now. I'm having freakin' palpitations up here.

Come on. Let's go. There's nothing but death here."

"Just let me finish," I told her. "Why are you suddenly so freaked out?"

"Why? *Why*? You don't feel the bad juju here? You're disturbing dead kids."

"I'm looking for evidence."

"Don't fuck with me, Kill. You don't mess with shit like this. They'll haunt us. We're leaving," she said, insisting as she pulled me away from the graves and the gravestones, suddenly pale.

"I thought you don't believe in ghosts."

"Yeah, well, there's a lot of stuff I never believed in until I saw it," she told me, striding quickly toward my mother's Camry, pulling me behind her. "You said you knew how to find them, so let's go."

"I *think* I know."

"Think or know, Kill? It can't be both. We've got like an hour and a half until the bridges open," she told me as she opened the doors to the Camry.

"An hour and twenty-six," I told her, looking at my watch as she immediately slammed the Camry door, not getting in.

"That car smells like a goddamn ashtray. I can't ride in that. I won't get the smell out of my hair for a week."

"Well, the other car's perched on 'Michael Sherman 1910-1987' and has a shattered windshield. It's not going anywhere."

"It can. Give me two minutes and we'll be on the road."

"And the windshield? You expect me to peer between the cracks?"

"Like you ever really look where you're goin' anyway."

"Just get in the Camry, Kat," I ordered. "Get in the Camry."

"You don't even know where you're going."

"Yes, I do."

"You know where Markov is?" asked Kat, with attitude.

"Yeah, Morocco said that Markov was coming into Staten Island 'right through the graveyard' and that he 'never stayed long, just took up residence on the day.'"

"And that means exactly nothing to me," Kat pouted, petulant.

"It does to me. There's a boat graveyard on Arthur Kill Road. That's the only kind of graveyard you can come through to get onto Staten Island," I assured her. "We know he was arriving on a yacht. If he anchored, then used lifeboats to come in close, no one would ever know. Planes are too easy to spot now, but ships coming into port... They could off-load right there."

"Sounds like a stretch to me…" Kat muttered, still unsure.

"Maybe, but Morocco also said 'on the day'—and an old freighter abandoned there is called the *Eldia*. I think Morocco assumed it was in Spanish and translated it as *El Dia—The Day*." I pulled open the driver's door, got in, and turned the key that Rigan had left in the ignition. Stale, smoke-scented air blasted out of the vents into my face, and my mother's Barry Manilow drifted out of the speakers, a dirge about friends being hard to find.

Hate was too kind a word for what I felt about that particular song. Kat smirked at me. "I'm not getting in that car."

"Well, we're *not* taking my father's Accord, since it's currently perched on top of Mr. Sherman," I said, ending the conversation. Kat just smiled at me.

*

The windshield of my father's car wasn't as badly shattered as I thought, and I could see through a three-inch by three-inch undamaged spot if I hunched over just the slightest bit in the driver's seat. Kat had somehow managed to rock the car back and forth enough to get it off Michael Sherman's headstone— only pulling off the muffler a little bit. Including the thirty seconds it took to curse her for the damage, we were back on the road in about two minutes. It was a compromise, and to be honest, driving the Accord wasn't so bad once the loose pieces of glass stopped falling in on us.

I didn't have time to argue with Kat anyway, since now

Markov had Alina, Dariya *and* Rigan. It was slow going as I drove, looking through the cracked windshield. Rain and spray from the standing water in the street was coming through the cracks, and periodically branches of downed trees, camouflaged by the damage, would slap the windshield, scaring the shit out of both Kat and me. She was quiet on the drive over, which was both a relief and a worry.

"Give it up. What's bothering you? The bodies?" I finally asked.

Kat shrugged, looking out the window. "They were just kids... And did you notice anything strange about one of them?"

"Like what?"

Kat turned to look back out the window, shaking her head. "Nothing. It just creeped me out. Like seeing a ghost, you know? Like they were peaceful and happy and then Rigan came along and dragged it all back up again," Kat muttered.

"Dragged what back up again?" I asked as my phone rang— Burke. There was only one reason for him to be calling. The dead guy in the backhoe. It had taken him about twice as long as I had expected, but Hurricane Sandy had probably slowed everyone's reactions down.

"Collins," I answered, trying to sound cheerful.

"Where the hell are you?" Burke growled.

"Is that Burke? Put him on speaker." I slapped away Kat's hand as she reached for the phone, causing the car to swerve.

"Just out for a drive," I told him, waiting to see what he knew before incriminating myself.

"Cut the crap, Collins. You know I got a call from Demetrius," Burke told me, getting to the point. There was no avoiding the lecture now. Kat leaned across the seat, trying to listen in.

"So, you're not calling me because you got a lead on Markov?"

"I'm covering your ass out of respect, but you're leaving me hanging here. I got an ashtray that doubles as a car in front of me, parked in Saint Peter's Cemetery. It's registered to your mother—and I got a gravedigger that looks like he dug his own grave," Burke went on. "The other diggers here said your mystery lady paid the guy a pretty penny to bring up the bodies."

"From the looks of his head, he's not gonna get to spend that cash."

"So you admit that you were here?" he asked, building a case against me already.

"I'm taking the fifth for now. I'll have a better idea what's going on soon. I need to go visit an old friend first. I'll call you in an hour. If I am unable, my tenant will call you and tell you where I am."

"Your tenant, huh? How many lies are you going to tell me today?"

"Just buy me some time with Demetrius."

"You've got an hour. Soon after that the bridges will be open and this whole thing will go to shit. I'll telling him you admitted to shooting the guy in the backhoe and I'm putting out a BOLO on you, and I will find you. If you fuck up my case up for me, I'll be pissed—" he warned me. I hung up on him.

"You hung up?" Kat asked. "Was that a wise decision?"

"Maybe not. But what's the worst that could happen?" I asked, heading for another kind of cemetery—one filled with the wrecks of decaying boats.

"I'm not seeing your plan here," Kat said. "How am I going to fill him in if I'm with you?"

"You're not going to be with me. I need you to be backup—the cavalry if I get jammed up. You need to be ready to call Burke and the whole goddamn NYPD if this goes wrong."

"But—" she started to argue.

I stopped her, putting a gentle hand on her thigh before it became another argument. "Kat, I'm asking because I trust you. I really need you for this."

"For what exactly? What's the plan?"

"Well, first, we might need another car."

"You plan on wrecking this one? Not that I'd miss it."

"No. But if you're going to follow me, you can't be in the same car I am, can you?" I asked, and saw her eyes light up. Kat was excited to be involved.

"Father Finley drives a BMW," Kat said, almost too quickly.

"He'd lend you his car?" I asked, wondering what kind of priest drives a BMW.

"He has before."

"Does he know he has? Or did you 'borrow' it?" I asked, already knowing the answer even before Kat grinned.

"It's fine," she reassured me. "He barely even uses it. It has like seven hundred miles on it. I'll get it and follow you. I just have one question—"

"Yes. I'll give you a gun," I answered, tired of her asking already.

CHAPTER
TWENTY-FOUR

The Arthur Kill boat graveyard is more like an auto salvage yard than anything else. It's surrounded by a crappy chain-link fence with hand-lettered warning signs to keep out and has random, unidentifiable pieces of steel and metal piled up in what someone, somewhere, must recognize as a Picasso-esque vision of order. At one point, over four hundred ships lay rotting here. In the past few years, a lot of them had been salvaged for scrap metal and parts, but the place was no less creepy for being less crowded.

In order to enter the graveyard stealthily, I'd parked on the side of Arthur Kill Road and walked through the misty night, passing through a centuries-old roadside cemetery with its grave markers nearly worn clean from hundreds of years of rain and weather. The garbage-strewn path that led toward the rusting fence and sheet metal walls that surrounded the yard was full of mud that sucked my feet in, and the wet grass soaked my pants to the knee before I got close enough to see the floodlights that lit the water's edge.

The darkly reflective surface of the flat, calm Arthur Kill appeared suddenly as I got close enough to see it, but the marshy smell of its tainted water had reached my nostrils several minutes before. It gave off a rotten odor, and I wondered if the Dutch subconsciously adopted the word "*kill*" from English because the stagnant water smelled like death. I could just see the *New York Post* tomorrow with my picture on the cover, a morgue shot, and a cheesy headline: "Great Kills" and a story about murdered women and a dead homicide detective washed up on the edge of the "kill."

The hulking shadows of the abandoned and rotting ships came into view beyond the fence. The gentle lapping of waves against their sides gave the graveyard a sonic shape and size, drowning out the rustling of swamp reeds and far-off traffic on the West Shore Expressway. Once I was inside the yard, I headed straight across to the water. I was looking for something that would float well enough to get me out to the *Eldia,* which I could see anchored a hundred yards out. I could see lights— more than the usual that would warn passing ships of its presence. Someone was on board.

The ground became softer under my feet as splotchy reflections of rain hit the oily, polluted surface of the Arthur Kill. I scanned the water's edge, noticing one bright spot in the darkness, half hidden in the cattails: a yellow life raft that looked brand-new. To get to it I would need to wade out another fifteen feet, carefully, so I didn't make any noise that might warn the occupants of the *Eldia*. Fortunately, the raft had both an outboard motor and oars, so I could forge across the water stealthily.

Before I went any farther I dialed my cell phone. Hers rang only once. She'd been expecting my call.

"Where are you, Kill?" Kat asked.

"Knee deep in shit, where else?"

"I can call Burke and have him ping your cell and send the Feds right now, or you can stop fucking around," Kat told me. I knew she wasn't bluffing.

"Fine. I'm in the middle of the Arthur Kill boat graveyard. Just keep listening and if you hear anything sketchy, call Burke and get him down here."

"Maybe I should just call him now," she threatened.

I ignored her and slid my cell into my jacket pocket. I wanted to have Kat as a witness to what was about to happen, but I didn't want her rushing in with the cavalry, fucking everything up and getting everyone killed—and I certainly didn't want her telling Burke where I was too soon. He'd jump the gun so he could be the hero.

Something behind me moved the cattails, trampling over them. I had a massive sense of déjà vu. I would have run, but could feel the muck suck my feet in, and there was no way I was risking falling face first in the polluted water again. I knew from experience about the vicious eels here and that the water tasted like crap. The little that I'd ingested when I was a kid was probably already eating away at my intestines and would kill me in twenty years.

"Hands up! Don't move!" he shouted, with a gruff, smoke-etched voice that appeared to be heavy with mucus. I could hear him breathing heavily between words, so I was pretty sure of what I'd see when I turned around. I wasn't disappointed.

"Which is it you want me to do, put my hands up or not move?" I asked the hairy, portly man wheezing as he trotted toward me, a nine-millimeter pistol hanging heavy by his side.

"Don't be a smart ass. Get your hands where I can see them."

I raised my hands and noticed that his shirt was open, revealing a hairy paunch that hung over his unbuttoned pants. I'd interrupted him in the middle of something, possibly taking a piss, more likely pleasuring himself while watching late-night porn on his phone. Security in a boat graveyard had to be boring. I'm sure he got creative with how he passed his time.

"I have my shield in my jacket. You mind if I reach for it?" I asked, keeping my eyes on his pistol.

"Who the fuck are you?" the man demanded, catching his breath even as he raised the pistol to aim at my center mass.

"Detective Collins, NYPD. See?" I reached slowly into my jacket, pulling out my shield case. He moved closer, snatching it from me. After a moment he put out his hand again. I gave him my gun, not having much choice in the matter. Then he pulled out a shield case of his own, shoving it in my face.

"I got one of those too, genius." I looked at it closely—the ID of an NYPD sergeant.

"Good for you, Sergeant Weinberg. What are you doing here? Night security? In case someone tries to pirate a sinking ship?"

"Don't be a smart ass. What are *you* doing here?"

"Working a case. I need to get out to one of those boats."

"They're ships, not boats—and you're not goin' nowhere without a warrant."

I nodded, agreeable. I wanted to get on board the *Eldia*. Weinberg could help me do that if I worked him the right way.

"You work for the owner?" I asked.

"I work for the guy that owns the owner," he answered as I saw something move behind him, a pale white girl no more than nineteen, moist with mist, her shirt mostly open and too damp for anything near modesty. A hoodie had been hastily thrown over it, but that wasn't closed either. She was obviously cold—and curious. Sergeant Weinberg hadn't been taking a piss after all.

"Who's she?" I asked, distracting Weinberg, but not for long enough to make a move on him.

"A friend."

"Part of the compensation package? A little perk?"

"She's my fuckin' girlfriend, asshole," Weinberg said, pointing the gun at my face. He sounded as if he actually believed it.

"Let me guess. Markov introduced you, she keeps you satisfied and never, ever, ever tells him every single thing you do. She ever ask you about ongoing cases? Police business?"

"Fuck you. I trust her."

"Who is this, David? Why is he here?" the girl asked.

"Go inside, Ariana," Weinberg ordered, but Ariana didn't move.

"You ever wonder why a girl that looks like that would want to *schtup* you in a swampy boat graveyard, Weinberg?"

"Ariana, go back to the shed. Now. Stay there." Again, Ariana didn't move. She was too interested in what was going on—almost as if she'd have to report back to someone about everything she saw.

"Ariana, run. Now's your chance. ICE and the FBI will be here soon," I told her, and I caught her eye. She believed me, and that got her motivated as she started off into the shadows. I'd say that it was a fifty-fifty shot that Sergeant Weinberg would never see her again.

Relationships are so hard.

"I'm calling this in," Weinberg told me as he glanced back at Ariana, who was hurrying to leave, walking out of his life for good.

"Good, ask for Lieutenant Demetrius."

"I'm not calling the house, moron. I'm calling my boss." He was already dialing, and I was pretty sure that I was going to get the chance to meet Markov one more time before the night was over.

*

I got my ride to the *Eldia* in the life raft. It was at gunpoint, but at least I didn't have to row since the noise of the engine no longer mattered. Weinberg watched me nervously on the way over, probably never expecting any more excitement as a night security guard than Ariana's blowjobs. I'd upset his cush gig and made him come out in the rain. He wasn't happy about it.

"So, what was it? Why'd you need this job? Was it the divorce? Child support?" I pressed, talking to fill the nervous void.

"Divorces. Plural, not that it's any of your business."

"Of course. So, what do you do for him, break in the girls?" I asked, and a look of genuine disgust fleetingly crossed the old cop's face.

"I don't do nothin' illegal. I just keep people out."

"So you've never seen girls come through here?"

"Girls, boys, sure. Mr. Markov's trying to give them a chance at the American dream over here. Finds them jobs," he said. With a straight face.

"Seriously? You buy that? He transports teen girls here out of the goodness of his heart?"

"He says he has connections at the State Department. Gets them work visas."

"And that's why he brings them in through here, a boat graveyard?"

"He says it's Congress's fault. They can't pass a damn immigration bill. Better all these white kids than the spics and Africans, that's the way I figure it. Besides, why would a billionaire have to traffick kids?"

"For the *money*?"

"He's a billionaire, not a criminal," Weinberg said simply— and I realized that he was either an extremely simple human being or in deep denial. Either way, he was stupid.

"Billionaire criminals are the worst kind."

"I don't buy it. If he was a criminal, wouldn't we all know? And my girl there? Markov saved her from the street… Said she'd be hooking if it wasn't for him."

"So, she's doing you for him instead?"

Weinberg looked at me sharply, and I think if we weren't already in the shadow of the *Eldia*, he might have come at me. He knew that his "girlfriend" was part of Markov's livestock— but we were already looking up at three silhouettes hanging over the rail of the ship and he couldn't.

"You got a smart mouth, you know that? I'd keep it shut if I were you," he told me, letting the motor idle as we coasted into the side of the *Eldia*, just under a rusty steel ladder. "Now get the fuck up the ladder."

"You got it. But, Sarge, word of advice? Don't be here in twenty minutes. Not if you expect anyone to believe that story."

Weinberg's eyes met mine and I saw a flash of the instincts that allowed him to survive on the job. He'd be halfway to the Poconos in twenty minutes. Maybe he *was* dirty, or maybe he was the dumbest cop on Staten Island—which, as you might guess, is a highly competitive category—but at least now he got it.

I grabbed the ladder, but before I could even get out of the life raft, Weinberg gunned the engine and took off, spraying me with the oily detritus of the dying ships. One last fuck-you. He couldn't help himself.

With nowhere to go except up, I climbed the rusted and flaking side of the *Eldia*. Looking at the three men hanging over the side forty feet above me, I could make out that at least two of them held guns. Despite the fact that they were barely even silhouettes, I recognized both Pete, the man with the mangy mustache, and the Russian who had fled with Alina after Kat killed his partner.

It was nice to have familiar faces greet me.

As I got closer, I took in the PP-2000 submachine guns both of them held, complete with the spare forty-four round magazine. It was the standard of most Russian police forces because it was compact and light, and the ammunition loaded in them was probably armor-piercing or hollow-point rounds. That was the good news, in a way. If they decided to shoot me, I wouldn't need to worry about my wounds since I would be very dead. The third man had no gun, possibly because his right hand was heavily bandaged. He was missing a pinky. I decided not to tell him that I knew where it was, or comment on its unusually hairy nature, but I did smile as he winced in pain, helping me roughly over the rail.

"How stupid are you to come here?" asked Pete the Mangy Mustache.

"Don't know. How stupid am I? Do I get a prize if I answer right?"

"What do you want?"

"I know where the Swamp Pink is," I told him in a faux whisper. Guys like Pete hate it when they're trying to intimidate you and you joke with them. That's why I do it.

"What the hell does that mean? What the fuck is 'Swamp Pink'?" asked the pinky-less Russian.

"It means he knows what we're looking for and can get it, right?" asked Pete.

I smiled, mostly to annoy him. "You're smarter than you look, which is obviously very easy, but still—" I stopped, cut off by a jab to the gut. I probably deserved it.

"Shut up. Where is it?" Pete asked.

"I'll tell Markov. No one else."

"You'll tell us," said the wannabe-rapist Russian, the one that had been groping Alina.

"Nope. Sorry. Can't tell. You can shoot me if you want, but Markov will just shoot you for being an idiot, because you'll never find the cash his Uncle Mikhail was accused of stealing. You won't find his uncle either, for that matter."

The three men traded looks, knowing how important his uncle and the money were. They were all more afraid of fucking up for Markov than they'd ever be of me. It must have pissed them off that I was holding out, because I got a boot to the knee that sent me to the deck. I landed on my elbows and face, hard. A second and third kick caught me in the ribs in quick succession, and I swear I heard a couple of ribs crack.

I just lay there, since my lungs refused to inflate. When they finally did, it felt as if the splinters of a cracked rib were trying to punch holes into my left lung, and the heavy, moist air made it hard to breathe.

I swear to God, I hate the rain.

Maybe this wasn't such a good idea. Maybe I could have come up with a better plan than meeting with Markov alone at night on an abandoned freighter without backup. I was never great at plans. I started to get up as I caught my breath, and then saw a boot swinging again, this time aimed at my head. I rolled away, grabbing it and twisting it sideways. I heard the cartilage in his knee tear as the idiot with no pinky fell hard to the deck. I had a split second of satisfaction as he screamed, and then two guns were shoved in my face.

Thankfully, we were interrupted.

"Enough. Search him. Bring him downstairs where it's warm," I heard Markov say. He was standing by an open hatch, watching us calmly. Then he was gone, knowing his orders would be followed. They were. They patted me down, but luckily I disconnected Kat before they found the phone. I didn't want them to know anyone was coming.

I just hoped Kat called Burke as soon as I got cut off—like before my phone even hit the water.

CHAPTER TWENTY-FIVE

"Detective Collins. Good to see you again... I was told that you were, how do you say? 'Half-a-retard'? But to come here, alone, at night? I think maybe half is too little a retard," he said with a smile.

"My mother would probably agree with you. But you shouldn't say 'retard'—it's not polite." I smiled right back. Fuck him.

"This is funny?"

"On Staten Island it is. It's a local sense of humor."

"So I should laugh now?"

"Or cry. They're in close competition here," I told him, looking around, hoping to be inspired about what to do next. There was nothing. Nowhere to run, no cover if a gunfight started. Markov had the hold lit with portable lights and a gas-operated generator that powered heaters and stank up the place, but hadn't yet built up enough carbon monoxide to kill the fucker.

The fucker in question was seated incongruously in a canvas camp chair with a drink in his hand. The heroin, in the same crates I had seen on Markov's yacht during the storm, was also there. Anton had told Markov where it was before he died, obviously.

"Why are you here?" Markov asked, cutting through the bullshit.

"Morrigan Kelly and the two girls. You have them. I want them. You give me them, I'll tell you where the cash is." Saying it out loud made it all seem so reasonable. It was a simple trade—a long-lost payment for an arms deal in exchange for two teens I'd met just before they stabbed me—and a woman I dreamt about my whole life and slept with once before she ran out on me.

"You have the cash with you?" Markov asked, hopeful.

"Do I look like that much a retard? I hid it a long time ago, but I remember where now."

His face gave me the answer. He thought I was *that* much a retard. "What makes you think the cash is worth three women?"

"It's almost ten million from what I understand, and you've risked everything to find it. Is that because it will clear your uncle? He's dead, you know," I told him, purposefully taunting him.

"You don't know that."

"I saw him die, when I was just a kid, right here in these woods," I said simply. "Your father spent seven years in jail because they thought your Uncle Mikhail defected with that money. He lost seven years for nothing, and you can prove his innocence if you deal with me."

"Fair enough. But why do you care? Women are the most renewable resource on the planet. Twenty women are not worth that much in cash. This trade makes no sense."

"Maybe I'm a full retard—or maybe I think that money is cursed and fucking with the Markovs isn't worth it," I answered honestly.

"Get me the money, and then you can have them. Do whatever you want to them."

"Fuck you. I want to see them first."

Markov smiled and nodded toward Pete the Mangy Mustache, who disappeared into the shadows. I heard his footsteps echo on the steel deck after he'd gone, and then I heard a hatch open. I heard a slap and a short gasp, then:

"Touch me again and you'll lose more than a finger, fucker."

So, Dariya was fine, at least. Four sets of footsteps shuffled across the metal deck, as if tired and beaten down. Gradually, the soft penumbra from the work lights illuminated Rigan, Alina, and Dariya, all three of their faces so similar in structure and coloring, and all wearing the same expression of wary vigilance. Alina looked the worst, with a black eye, a nose that was almost surely broken and one side of her face so swollen that she was hard to recognize. Rigan was limping and holding one arm close to her side, as if her ribs were sore, but her face was unblemished except for a cut across one high cheekbone. Somehow the injuries made her look younger and more fragile, closer to the way I remembered her from my dreams.

Dariya, in comparison, looked much better. Her hair was as wild as a banshee's and her eyes glowed with fury. She appeared to be completely unharmed, and Pete was keeping well out of her reach.

"What was done to them?" I asked, knowing all the dark possibilities. I didn't really want to know, but I had to know. There is a difference.

"Nothing. Torture wasn't worth the bother," Markov replied flatly. "Jakob lost a finger, and none of us wanted to lose any other pieces to these lying bitches," he said. I wasn't sure that I believed him, but I was relieved anyway.

"I never lied to you. We had a deal, and you didn't deliver," Rigan snarled at him, her speech mumbled as if her mouth was swollen.

"You stole my drugs off the *Chistota*," Markov answered. So, Burke was right. Rigan had known what was on board, and she'd dumped me at the hospital before going back to get it—but it seemed like Markov didn't know she had a partner who had actually taken the heroin off the *Chistota*.

"Wait, *you* were buying the kids?" I asked, trying to follow what was going on.

Rigan turned to me as if I was both an idiot and a distraction.

Markov chuckled, amused that I was so far behind. "Your friend here has contacts in international trafficking, it seems. She's the one who contacted me. She knew I had these повій, wanting to make them disappear from the Ukraine as a message to the others. A side business to the heroin you Americans love. She said she would return the money my Uncle Mikhail had lost and would tell me what happened to him if I brought them to her," he explained, amused that I didn't know.

I looked at Rigan, confused. Why was she trafficking kids?

"I told Markov he could keep the money and I'd tell him where Mikhail Markov was if he delivered the kids safely. He didn't. He killed them."

"I didn't kill them. It was carbon monoxide. You stole my drugs before I could deliver the survivors."

"Those children were handcuffed. Abused. I said I wanted them untouched," Rigan snarled. Pete and the wannabe-Rapist Russian stayed between the two of them, wary.

"That little bitch killed four of my men. Would have killed me, too, if she could have. I should have sold them as whores. Fucked them all when I had the chance –"

Rigan exploded at that, furious, but before she could get close to Markov, the Russian stopped her cold with a fist to the ribs. I went after him, launching my right fist to his head, connecting just behind his ear. He went down hard, sprawling on the cold metal deck. I was about to kick him in the ribs when I caught Pete out of the corner of my eye, his gun pointed at my face.

"Enough," Markov muttered, "If I get the money, I'll let them live."

"He doesn't know where it is," interjected Rigan.

I glared at her, but she didn't seem to care that she was screwing up my negotiation.

"It seems he's begun to remember," Markov smirked, happy that Rigan was angry.

She turned toward me pointedly as she spoke to him. "No. He doesn't. If he really remembered, he'd never give it to you."

"So. She thinks you are half-retard too." he said, smirking.

"I don't care," I answered honestly. "Get the rafts, but those three go free before I show you anything," I told him. Markov just smiled.

*

We all fit in two life rafts. Markov, Pinky, Rigan and Alina were in one—and me, Pete, the Wanna-be-Rapist Russian, and Dariya in the other. As we approached the shoreline, I scanned in vain for silhouettes and movement, hoping that Kat had called Burke and he had arrived while I was having my friendly chat.

Sergeant Weinberg's guard shack was now dark, and I assumed he'd gotten smart and taken his little perk home with him. The rafts both grounded in deeper water than when we left, due to the extra weight in each one. We had to get out and wade in through the reeds and muck. Nobody was saying much, which worried me, since it's a proven fact that you generally don't make idle conversation with guys you're about to kill.

So I made some.

"When we get into the boatyard, I want Rigan and the two girls to go ahead of us to my car. Until they do, I'm not telling you anything."

"They stay with us through the boatyard," Markov ordered.

"Fine, but my car is right on Arthur Kill Road. I'll watch them get in and drive away. The four of you will stay with me. Anyone goes after the women, you'll never get the money, understand?" I looked over at Markov, who didn't seem very impressed with my idea of how to negotiate this.

"You're not in a position to make demands," Markov snarled. "But it doesn't matter. I can find them again if you let me down."

I was sure that he could, which meant that either Burke had to show up with the cavalry soon, or I needed to find a way to overpower these four in the woods before they killed me. Somewhere in that damaged place inside my head that was wired to be optimistic, I expected to get to the road and find Lieutenant Burke waiting with a dozen uniforms and an Emergency Services Team armed with automatic weapons.

I was highly disappointed.

The road was empty. My mother's car was where I had parked it. I stopped in the middle of the road, under a streetlight, about twenty feet away. Turning back to face Markov, I put up my hands.

"I'm going to reach in my pocket slowly to get the keys. Then I'm going to toss them to Rigan, all right?"

"Stop talking. Do it."

I put my hand in my pocket, catching Rigan's eye as I did. "Just go. Get to somewhere safe. He won't get out of the country," I reassured her, tossing the keys at her.

She snatched them out of the air without missing a beat.

"Killian, please—"

"Just go."

Rigan didn't listen. She was distracted by the sound of an engine approaching—the high-pitched hum of a performance machine, not the sound of any of the cars used by the NYPD. That meant it was not Burke. I pegged him for an American-made snob, even off duty.

"Off the road, all of you," Pete snapped, pushing Alina with the barrel of his gun. The girls shifted to the soft shoulder of the road without a word as Markov and Pinky herded me to the other side, away from the Accord.

"Don't move, and don't say shit," Pinky warned me.

"Can't I say damn or fuck?" I asked without thinking, and got the butt of his gun to my right kidney for my trouble.

"I said shut up."

The high beams of a black BMW were already illuminating us and reflecting off the fog as I got my breath back. Markov was staring at it, his pistol slowly coming up, aiming right at the driver's side.

"Beamers automatically call nine-one-one when they're in an accident. You're better off letting it pass," I warned him, hoping he'd listen and that this particular BMW would just pass us by. Markov grunted but lowered the pistol. The BMW wasn't slowing down at all. It would either pass us in a second—

– Or it would plow through us. When I heard the engine race, I knew which way it was going, and I knew exactly who was behind the wheel. Before I could react, the BMW swerved suddenly—

– Right into Pete and the Russian, just missing Rigan and the girls. It never braked, just plowed into Pete, cracking his legs at the knees and sending his body up over the hood, his head smashing through the windshield. The wannabe-rapist tried to dive out of the way but went down, underneath the car, a front wheel rolling over his head, his body dragged along until the underbrush scraped him off. The car finally stopped with the help of a sugar maple and everything settled into an uneasy silence.

The brake lights had never lit up. Maybe if I hadn't been so stunned, I could have taken advantage of the distraction, but by the time I moved, Markov had his pistol pointed at my head.

"Who is that? What did you do?" he demanded. I shrugged, and he pushed me into the road as the Pinky-less Russian limped over to the wrecked car. I noticed then that Rigan, Alina, and Dariya had disappeared, fleeing into the woods. I felt my shoulders relax, sure that Rigan would get away, and crossed the road in front of Markov, approaching the totaled BMW. I had to step over blood smears and bone fragments, but that wasn't the worst of it.

I could see Pete's head, inside the car, the windshield around his neck like a glass collar. His mangy mustache and entire upper lip had been sliced clean off by the glass, and his dead eyes stared at the driver, who had multiple piercings in her ears and dyed jet-black hair. She sat motionless, dead or unconscious.

I could always count on Kat.

"Let's go," Markov told Pinky, unaffected by his friends' deaths.

"Shouldn't we do something?" asked Pinky.

"Like what? Call the police maybe? According to Detective Collins, the BMW has already called them." Markov pushed me away from the car, its broken radiator hissing out steam that only thickened the fog. "No, we get what we came for," he continued. "How far is it, Detective?"

"A two-minute walk," I managed to respond, still staring at the back of the driver's head.

Kat was breathing. I could see the slight rise and fall of her shoulders.

"Start walking." Markov pushed me again, and I almost turned on him. I wanted to stay and help Kat, but if I tried, I knew he'd kill her just to get me moving. The Beamer was equipped with Intelligent Emergency Call, so I knew help would be coming.

I started walking, thinking about how to get out of this. Kat had given me better odds, taking out two of the Russians, but now I was on my own, one man against two with guns. I tried to think of what I had going for me. Staten Island was my home turf, I knew where I was going... and I had all my pinkies.

So, not much. They still had the guns, and Burke was nowhere in sight. I know Kat had to have called him by now.

So where the fuck was he?

CHAPTER TWENTY-SIX

Alone with Markov and No-Pinky, I was walking between the sporadic streetlights of Arthur Kill Road and the deeper darkness of Clay Pit Ponds. We were wet and cold, moving through fog that was coalescing into a misty rain. No-Pinky was tense and angry at the loss of his fellow Russian and the pain from both his knee and missing finger. Markov had little sympathy, struggling to walk in his expensive Italian shoes as they sloshed, full of water and grit from the swampy marshlands that gave the nature preserve its name. Personally, I was enjoying their discomfort, especially since it distracted them and might give me an opportunity as we got closer to our destination.

Through the trees I could see long-abandoned natural gas tanks gleaming white in the fog. I used them as a fixed point to navigate by, veering deeper into the nature preserve. I kept the line of the rusted chain-link fence separating us from the

Pioneer Bus Company lot to my right for another hundred feet, then veered for the ponds at the center of the wooded area.

For once in my life, I knew exactly where I was going, and even though the trees had grown and all the underbrush looked different, the boat graveyard, the LNG tanks, and even the bus parking lot were fixed points that had existed here for as long as I could remember. I could find the exact place that I was looking for—a place out of my dreams, which, like the fog, had been growing more solid and heavy as the night wore on.

"How far?" grumbled Markov.

"Another fifty yards. I'll know it when I see it."

"If you don't, I'll shoot you and leave you here."

"I'm aware of that," I answered. Actually, I expected him to shoot me no matter what happened. That's why I had been mulling my options. It was becoming obvious that I couldn't rely on Burke.

I was on my own, but I wasn't worried. If I could find a momentary distraction and run, I would either be dead or free within the first ten seconds. After that, the trees and underbrush would screen me from gunfire. I knew these woods better than either of them, and if I got a ten-second lead, I could get away. I'd make my move as soon as I gave Markov the box with the cash. His hands would be full. It was going to be then or never.

The moment was getting closer... Less than forty feet ahead I saw the edge of the water and the gnarled old oak tree that leaned over it. The tree was thicker around, but its bent form hadn't changed much over the years. I remembered the last time I'd seen it…

*

…The oak tree hung out over the water, its thick foliage impenetrable. I was freezing, shivering in the cold and the darkness, and a fine, misty fog gathered around me as I ran toward the old tree. I was almost there when I stumbled, falling into the water. I took a breath, trying to get to my feet when I heard someone, as large as an adult, running through the trees, cursing under his breath. I wasn't going to have time to climb the tree. He was too close.

I knew what I had to do, and I thrust my arms into the darkness of the water, digging my fingers into the bottom, pulling up thick gray clay. After a moment I'd dug a hole deep enough for the metal box. Checking to make sure that it was sealed with oilskin and wrapped tightly in plastic, I shoved the box down into the hole, carefully packing the clay around it again.

*

I stopped five feet from the water's edge, trying to gauge the distance between the base of the oak, the water's edge, and other fixed points to remember where I'd put the box in my dream/memory and hoped that no one had discovered it in all the years since.

"Give me a second. It's right here," I told him, buying myself some time to calculate my escape. "I just need to –"

The deafening sound of a gunshot went off behind my head,

and I flinched as the water rippled, the shot hitting its surface.

"Detective, I am tired. I am cold and impatient. Get it. Now."

"Shooting at me isn't helpful. I'm trying to concentrate. Not to mention that if anyone came to help the lady in the BMW, shooting will bring them here."

"I don't care. You'll be dead before they arrive. Move. Now."

I inhaled deeply, bracing myself to enter the water that I hated so much. The icy cold made my feet and legs go numb almost immediately. It was deeper here than I remembered, but Hurricane Sandy was probably to blame for that. When I was in up to my knees, about ten feet from a long root of the oak and fifteen from a large boulder on the shore, I knew that I was in the right place. I knelt down, getting wet to my waist. I felt my skin contract to retain body heat and as my knees hit bottom, they didn't sink into the muck as I had expected, but hit a hard edge of rock, giving me instant bruises.

I had forgotten about that stinging sensation, but now recalled that the same thing had happened when I was here last. So many years later, my heavier weight and older knees made the landing even more uncomfortable. I started to dig into the silt and vegetation above the heavy clay that lined the pond. The gelatinous ooze was cleared away easily, but when my fingertips finally reached the clay, clawing into it, the tendons in my hands tightened up from the cold and stretched with the effort.

"The cash is in the water?" asked Markov warily.

"In a waterproof box. It will be fine."

At least I hoped it would be. Markov might be slightly bent out of shape if I handed him a pile of pulp. I looked up at him, staring down the barrel of his gun, too cold and pissed off to filter my thoughts.

"You know, if there's as much money here as I think there is, won't somebody just knock you off you to take it?"

"Like who? Who would dare?" he said, confidently, giving me the perfect opening.

"Your bodyguards, maybe? Maybe even this nine-fingered numbnuts?" I asked, nodding at No-Pinky. Somewhere in the simian part of my brain I saw a way to use their power dynamics for my own purpose. Insecurity and paranoia can be great tools if you know how to use them.

"Three ounces of lead beat a bank full of gold every time. Power and money don't last," I said, glancing at No-Pinky again.

"Jakob, move where I can see you," Markov ordered, waving his gun to a point in the water closer to me and in front of him. It was working. I could see No-Pinky's distrust build as he stepped closer, into the water and on the wrong side of Markov's gun. If I moved fast enough, Jakob was now close enough that I might be able grab his leg under water and take him down. I grinned up at him.

"Careful, Jakob. Josef Markov doesn't like to share. You might end up dead in the water with me as soon as I find this box."

"I said shut up," Markov hissed, pointing his weapon at me again.

I did. Their paranoia would only grow with time. I'd planted the seed. When I looked back down, the water was calm and flat, reflecting everything. I could see Markov and Jakob behind me, both glancing at one another, neither one committing to pointing their weapons exclusively at me. I took a perverse pleasure in this as I dug deeper, hoping I would get a few seconds to make my break.

Soon my fingers scraped something a few inches below the surface of the clay, and I felt around its edges. It was that same hard, flat surface I remembered, a two-foot square box wrapped in a waterproof oilskin. I pulled it up as the clay and water created suction around it, making it feel heavier than it was.

"Is that it? Do you have it?"

"I have to open the box to know for sure. Let me get it to dry land."

I took a deep breath, trying to gauge the timing of what I was about to do. If I threw the box to Markov and took down Jakob as I did, I might get my hands on his gun, or I might be able to make it to the safety of the woods. I tensed, ready to make my move—

I heard leaves rustle, in a way that was too steady to be the wind. I didn't have a chance to turn before I heard the bellow of a shotgun, deafening me—two shots in quick succession and then twin splashes, almost simultaneous. I froze.

If I wasn't dead yet, I still had a chance.

I dropped the box and raised my hands. Tendrils of blood,

black in the moonlight, snaked out into the water and flowed toward the center of the pond from the two Russians' bodies.

"I've got the money right here," I told him, nodding to it. "I don't need to turn or see your face. You can take it and go."

"Sounds like a plan, Collins," he said, and I saw him move closer in the reflection on surface of the pond, where his features were obscured by the ripples in the water. It was a familiar voice, and a familiar reflection...

*

...A reflection of a shadowy face—the dark-haired man with the mustache and the shotgun. I couldn't move, could barely breathe... But then the moon cleared the clouds and I got a look at him, recognizing him as a cop my father worked with, back when he had longer hair and a mustache. I recognized Detective Burke...

*

...Who was now Lieutenant Burke, bald and older, and he was standing over me again. I tried to keep my expression neutral as I ignored the barrel of the shotgun.

"Damn, Burke, you could have arrested them. You had them dead to rights," I said, hoping I could bluff him into believing that I remembered nothing. Burke's eyes narrowed and he kept the shotgun pointed at me, but his finger relaxed slightly on the trigger.

"No, they had to die. If Markov lived, his father would just buy his way out and he'd be back to kill both of us before we could testify against him. Trust me, it's better this way." Burke stepped closer, motioning with one hand.

"Hand me that box and get out of the water. It's gotta be freezing."

I nodded, grabbing the box and trudging toward dry land. When I set the box on the ground, Burke just nodded to me, unwilling to put his gun down.

"Damn. It was right here the whole time… Unwrap it. Let's see what all this has been about."

I did, unwrapping the box to reveal its rusted metal lock.

"Where's the key?" Burke asked, his trigger finger twitching.

I shrugged. "No idea—but I think No-Pinky there had a knife. I could get it open if I had something to pry it with."

"Check their pockets."

"Sure. But why don't you get Markov? I'll get the other guy."

"Nice try, asshole, but I'm not stupid."

"Excuse me?"

"You can't bullshit me, Collins. If you remembered where this box is, you remember everything—don't you?"

"What the hell are you talking about? Rigan told me it was here." I feigned stupidity, searching Markov's pockets for something to pry the box open with. At the same time I was feeling underwater for the pistol Markov must have dropped somewhere close by.

"'Rigan,' huh? You got to know each other again?" Burke asked, eyeing the box lustfully but keeping the gun on me. "I'm not stupid, you know. Back in eighty-five I thought this was going to be my way off this thankless fucking job. I've spent all this time looking for it for the same guy who's been paying me to keep an eye on you. You think I'm going to let it slip through my hands now?"

"So you work for Markov senior?" I asked to keep him talking and buy myself some time as I held up the small knife I'd found on Markov.

"Toss it here on the shore. Carefully, or you'll be lying right next to him," he said as his knuckle went white on the trigger.

I tossed it at his feet, throwing it close enough to distract him, but it didn't stop him. He pulled the trigger—

And it all happened at once. I heard Rigan, somewhere close by yell, "Joe, no –"

—In the same instant I was hit by the impact—hurtled backward into the water. Burke smiled for a microsecond before his forehead erupted, spraying bone, brains, and blood from above the bridge of his nose.

…Then I was submerged in the water, looking up at milky moonlight through the murk of mixing mud and blood. Two silhouettes moved in the world above the water as I stared, wondering why I couldn't breathe, trying to will my muscles to move upward but unable to do anything but stare. One was Rigan, holding Pete's PP-2000 submachine gun…

…The other was the familiar man without a left eye. Their voices were muffled and carried urgency as Rigan reached toward me and pulled me up to the surface where I sucked in air, making the sharp pain in my chest so much worse. Rigan was looking at the man in the shadows behind her, yelling:

"He needs an ambulance."

"I can't be seen here. My cover can't be compromised," said her friend, hesitating.

"I'll deal with him. You just call 9-1-1 and go," she ordered as he started to fade into the forest shadows.

Then she turned back toward me, checking my wounds and keeping my head above water. Luckily, Rigan's yell had distracted Burke and I had a chance to dodge slightly to the right as he fired so the shotgun blast had hit me mostly on one side—in the shoulder and ribs. It hurt like fucking hell, but the bone had stopped any deep damage.

"Who… was that…?"

"No one. An old friend. Forget him. You're better off," she said, glancing after the man. I doubted that I could forget him again, but with my talents, I wasn't really sure.

"How's Kat?" I asked, trying to distract myself from the pain, noticing Rigan's eyes narrow as if the question annoyed her.

"She was alive when I left, cursing because the ambulance was taking so long," she answered, looking down at the box full of cash.

"You didn't help her?"

"She needed professional help, and you needed me more," Rigan said, glancing pointedly at the three dead men around me.

"I thought I told you to leave," I said.

"I didn't listen."

"I noticed."

"You're welcome," Rigan said with appropriate snark, pulling me with her so that my head and shoulders rested on dry land.

"Thank you," I grumbled reluctantly, slightly worried about how I was going to explain all the dead people to the department. Rigan turned away, pulling the box of cash closer, prying it open.

"We need to call this in. Turn that over to the police."

"No. This belongs to us, and to those girls—and everyone who was sold out by those bastards," she said with an ice-cold look in her eye.

"It doesn't. The courts can decide who owns it," I said, reasonably, in too much pain to reach for the box as Rigan lifted it out of the water. Her eyes were shining, although it was hard to tell whether I was seeing tears or rain.

"I'm doing what I should have done a long time ago … I'm sorry, Killian. I really am. I never should have left you behind in the woods... But they shot you in the head. I saw the wound. I thought you were going to die. I don't want to do it again, but I can put this money to good use."

"Rigan, you've been through a lot. I'm sure all of this has triggered whatever PTSD you might have." I spoke quickly, since she was walking toward the shore, carrying the box of cash away.

"Is that what you think this is? That I'm the crazy one?"

"Not crazy. Maybe just …it's Markov's money. He'll come after you. He's waited almost thirty years and now his son is dead, his money gone again."

"Let him come," Rigan said, moving closer, her breasts now brushing my chest as she leaned in slowly and touched her lips to mine. They were warm and soft, and in the cold damp air I could feel the heat of her body on my skin before she touched me. I let her kiss me and couldn't help but respond, aware the whole time that I'd sworn off crazy women and that getting involved with one who had just been involved in shooting and killing a New York City Police lieutenant—no matter how good a reason she had—was the height of stupidity. Still, the kiss was worth it…

"Good-bye, Killian. I really am sorry."

I was starting to fade as Rigan stood and cocked her head, listening. I heard what she did—the far-off sound of sirens. Help was on the way to Kat, and if I was lucky, they'd find me as well. The sirens were getting louder as she kissed my lips again.

"I'll make sure they find you faster this time. I have to go. Things are moving quickly now—but know that I wish this could have ended differently," Rigan told me, then kissed me again and turned away. I watched her fade into the darkness, not running this time, not a young girl, barefoot and in shorts, but a grown woman. Even so, I would have recognized her stride anywhere…

*

… I was somewhere else, standing in the warm sun, barefoot in long green grass. Rigan was running toward me, her auburn hair

streaming out behind her as she hit me full force, tackling me to the ground. We were young, no more than seven, and she was wearing a flowing white dress. Her skirt rose up her left thigh as she ran, and I didn't see a scar... As the sun filtered through her hair, she grabbed my hand, pulling me toward a rocky shore. I closed my eyes, trusting her to lead me, feeling the sun on my face, the breeze teasing my skin, and the grass below me, slightly dry and itchy... I was more relaxed and happier than I ever remembered being...

*

...When I opened my eyes, I was somewhere dark and damp—the only light coming in from my left... a windshield. The dim light framed a silhouette of a dead man, the pilot. I was in the plane. I could smell the coppery scent of blood and hear the rain on the aluminum skin, the loudest sound in the night until I heard her moan in pain.

"Focáil leat," *she said, struggling for breath. I turned to see Morrigan struggling to get out from under a body and the wreckage. I went to help her and put my hand in something warm and sticky, and I gasped. It was blood.*

I might have run out on her then, but there was another sound outside. Leaves rusting, branches snapping and a rhythm of movement. That's when I saw the flashlights, coming for both of us...

"Someone's coming. We need to go," *said Morrigan, pulling herself up from under the debris.*

"*Maybe they're here to help,*" *I reassured her, trying to move, only to find that my leg was pinned under something cold and metallic that still dripped with the blood of the body it had impaled.* "*I can't move anyway…*"

The flashlights were just outside now, and as the cargo door opened, one of them lit Rigan up, and I heard Big Jim Collins.

"*We got one. She's alive…*"

*

"…He's alive." I heard as sounds gradually started to come back. A radio crackled and wet leaves moved with shuffling feet. Finally, a voice reached me as if from a great distance.

"Demetrius. You got a dead lieutenant here—maybe a detective too," the voice said as I felt his breath on my face and his cold fingers on my neck, feeling for a pulse. "Goddammit. This one's still breathing. It's Kill Collins…"

…And then it all started to fade again…

CHAPTER TWENTY-SEVEN

I was laid up in the hospital for three days, to have shrapnel from the shotgun wound in my shoulder and chest removed. Kat was one floor down with five broken ribs, a broken nose, and cuts on her hands and arms. I heard later that she had tried to see me, but security escorted her back to her own room since she wasn't a relative. Soon after, Kat signed herself out because she had heard Demetrius was looking for her. She was afraid that he might charge her with negligent homicide in the deaths of Pete and the Russian.

It was never going to happen.

Things were too complicated for Demetrius. He had the Feds haranguing him about Josef Markov, the dead son of the oligarch Alik Markov; Burke, a dead NYPD lieutenant; three other bodies whose deaths were hard to explain; *and* the aftermath of Hurricane Sandy. Yes, Demetrius had bigger problems than Kat. In the end, he explained the way the whole situation was going to be resolved as I lay in my hospital bed, hopped up on Percocet.

"Your friend Pete and the Russians were looting the yacht in the aftermath of the hurricane, you understand?" he said, leaning in close and whispering, as if the nurses might be working for Internal Affairs.

"No, I don't."

"Burke was tracking them down, helping recover Markov's stolen goods. He was shot and killed by the thieves, as was Markov, while trying to recover them."

I glanced over at Demetrius, who was keeping a straight face as he told me the official story. "Really? This is a nice fairy tale. How does it end?" I asked, worried that his story wouldn't stick and that somehow I'd end up indicted for something—like lying under oath.

"*You* shot the guy that killed Markov and Burke... Please, Killer, don't give me any shit. I'm doing you a solid."

"And the two killed by the BMW? What about them?"

"That's an unrelated traffic accident," he said, as if that was obvious.

I smiled. The story wasn't half bad.

"What about the missing girls?" I asked, trying to eliminate holes in this story that could trip us up later.

"What missing girls? If they ever existed, the misguided Morrigan Kelly probably took them somewhere safe. We'll discuss it with her when we find her, if Markov's father doesn't find her first."

"And the plane crash? The cash that went missing?"

"A myth. That case was closed back in eighty-five."

I nodded. Demetrius was right. It was better off closed. Never found. If Alik Markov or anyone else knew the cash was still available, Rigan would be hunted down. She'd taken enough risks going up against the Russians, and didn't need the Feds, the NYPD, *and* Markov's father looking for her. Rigan would be better off if she were never found.

"Great. Since I'm apparently the hero of this fable, do I get my gun and shield back?" I asked. Immediately, I saw the hesitation in Demetrius's eyes.

"Yeah, well… about that. The brass is a little uncomfortable with this and Internal Affairs might be poking around. I was told to inform you that if you put in your papers for the gunshot, maybe even 'psychological disability'—or whatever the hell else you can think of—no one would stand in your way."

"They want me out?"

"It's easier than investigating and finding out that your lead detective in human trafficking was involved in trafficking kids and working for a Russian mobster. Think about it, Kill—you can get three-quarters pay the rest of your life. You just won the lottery."

"And if I don't put in my papers?" I asked.

Demetrius shrugged, his body language implying that the question was an indication of mental incompetence. "Maybe you get your badge back, maybe you don't. As of now you're suspended indefinitely. There are too many dead people and too many missing girls. You get that, right?"

I did. It was about the optics. The NYPD didn't want to look too closely at this, afraid of what they might find. To tell the truth, neither did I.

*

As soon as I was able to sign myself out, I went directly to Rigan's house. The crime scene tape still surrounding it was in tatters, blowing in the wind.

I went in the front door, still swollen with the moisture, smelling the musty dampness that had settled over the unheated old home. The floors creaked in the stillness as I wandered through, wondering what her days here must have been like, knowing that I lived less than five miles away, never remembering who she was.

The bedroom was where I found the photo album, full of old newspaper clippings and pictures—

They were all of me. She'd kept articles from the *Staten Island Advance* about my wins as a pitcher in Little League, my high school graduation, and even my appointment to the police department. In the back were other photos, stolen from a distance, pictures she or someone else had taken of me doing extraordinarily ordinary things: playing handball at I.S. 72 when I was in middle school; drinking beer with friends at Wolfe's Pond Park; working on my first car in front of my parents' house; at a barbeque; sitting on my front steps… Rigan had captured all of it.

There were even two photos that we were in together. In one, Rigan was seated right behind me on a set of bleachers. We could have been together, or maybe she just photo-bombed me… But the second one was on the Staten Island ferry, with the Manhattan skyline in the background at night, a few drops of rain on the camera lens… We both appeared to be in our early twenties and my arm was around her. We were both smiling. Happy…

I had no memory of it.

Maybe we were drunk, or maybe it was just one of my lost nights. One of the encounters that could have changed my life if I was ever able to hang on to them…

I took the album and paged through it as I lay on her bed, the smell of her still on the sheets. Eventually, I drifted off to sleep, and when I woke, the house felt different, a slight draft pulling the air down the stairs and outside…

I'd missed her.

I knew it as soon as I opened my eyes, but by the time I got downstairs, the only thing left of her was a single sheet of paper just inside the door. I picked it up carefully, seeing her handwritten letter:

Killian,

I am safe, as are Dariya and Alina. I wanted to thank you for all you did to protect them, and me. I'm sorry about all of this. Maybe I should have tried to reach out to you sooner, but

*people were watching. I wish I could explain more fully. Perhaps
later, when you remember more. I know you think this is all just
because I am a post-traumatic stress-induced survivor—and I
am—but I have also loved you for as long as I can remember.
Please, think of that when you think of me, think of what you
gave me on our one night together, and know that I will always
keep the memory of you safe.*

Love, always,

Your Morrigan

I'd just finished reading the letter when I heard a car engine
start somewhere out on Sharrotts Road. I ran out to the street,
into the rain, to try to catch her.

I was too late. All I could see were the red taillights of her
car as it took the corner and accelerated into the night. I didn't
bother to chase after it. She was already too far gone…

*

Two hours later, I walked into my parents' sunroom and
confronted my father, who was thankfully with us. I asked
him the big question—a tactic some detectives like to call the
nuclear option in an interrogation—putting it all out there just
to get a baseline reaction.

"Is Joe Corrigan dead, Dad? I asked without preamble,
watching his eyes for any tells.

"What kinda stupid question is that?" he demanded. His
voice never wavered, eyes never moved, and he gave no other
sign of deception.

"There are no stupid questions, and you didn't answer me," I pressed him.

"I was at his funeral, wasn't I?"

"Still not answering. Did you see him dead?" I asked, and got that heavy sigh he always used to buy himself some time. I was on the right track.

"He was shot in the head. The casket was closed, so no. I never saw Joe Corrigan dead," he answered, again in a way that made perfect sense unless you knew what an evasive fucker my father could be.

"Did you ever see him alive after October 23, 1985?"

"Joe Corrigan? No," he muttered, knowing that he himself had taught me how to spot conditional language in an answer. He'd added the words "Joe Corrigan" to that answer when he didn't need to.

"How about anyone who once went by the name 'Joe Corrigan'?" I asked, making it more specific so that he'd have to answer.

"Oh, for fuck's sake, Killian, can't you leave anything alone—ever?"

"So. That's a yes, considering you can't just say no."

My father looked away, out the windows at the fog and the hovering mist. He sighed and went on, never looking at me directly.

"Hypothetically, you relentless little shit, there was someone corrupt on the squad who'd killed Tompkins and Germanario—and now we had a dead KGB operative and people who were hunting down kids who were witnesses. Joe, *if* he'd lived, would've been a marked man."

"So that's who I've been seeing."

"You know who it is," he mumbled.

"I want to hear you say it."

"Fine, you stubborn little shit. It was him. Okay?"

"Aidan knew?" I asked, knowing the answer.

"Some of the other Corrigans, too," my father admitted reluctantly. "They had connections in Ireland. Joe went there for a while, but couldn't leave it alone. Had to know who did this to him... The bullet in his head fucked him up like it did to you. I thought we'd seen the last of him, and then he showed up a few years back, working for the Feds on international smuggling and trafficking. He'd been in deep cover—real deep shit, new identity, the works. He'd also become obsessed with the Markovs and whoever was dirty on our squad."

"And Rigan?" I asked.

My father looked up at me with something like compassion in his eyes. Maybe even regret.

"Joe asked if I knew where she was. I didn't. He thought she might remember enough to lure out whoever set him up... I guess he found her."

"Was the part about the psych ward true?" I asked.

"True enough. That girl was crazed. Wouldn't speak. After a few weeks we thought she was getting better and we were going to adopt her as well. Then one night she just bolted off the psych floor. We never saw her again until the other day."

"So all of this, it's been a lie? Joe's not dead, it wasn't a car accident, Rigan was always out there... My life is a lie?"

"Fuck off with the drama, Killian. If your life's a lie, it's a damn good one. It kept you safe, and you've become a good man. You fight the good fight, protect the weak, defend the defenseless. What more could you hope to be? What more could I ask for in a son?"

"What about who I could have been if I knew the truth? What about who I was?" Don't I deserve to know that? I asked.

"No. That's exactly my point. That's who you were." My father looked away again, voice drifting off as he stared at his own reflection in the window. "It's not who you *are*. Life isn't about chasing the past, Kill. It's about loving the people in your life—and you have people who love you. That's more than most have. You've got me and your mother and a beautiful friend who loves you in all the ways a woman should love a man. When are you ever going to wake up and know that it's enough?"

"Are you talking about Kat?"

"My God, you really are half-a-retard, aren't you," he said, then finally looked at me and took my hand. "I'm gonna say this once, in case I never remember to say it again—'cause we both know that you and me have shit for brains when it comes to remembering things. I've come to accept that there are very few things worth remembering, Kill. This is one of them—you are my son and I love you. Even when I've lost every last marble, I will know that in my heart."

I nodded. It's all I could do. There was no way that I could speak, since I was choking back tears.

I knew who I was, right now.

I could hang onto that. I could remember that much.

*

It was misting again by the time I got back to the site of the plane crash, the one connection I had to my life before the accident. I'd left my father at his place and promised my mother I'd go straight home, but I'd lied. I had to come back one last time.

I watched the skies as I walked out into the woods, since another nor'easter was predicted, but they were temporarily placid. Neither the cold nor the gentle rain bothered me. The weather suited my mood, as did the quiet rhythm of the raindrops.

A damp, mossy tree lay where it had been uprooted in some long-ago storm, or even in the plane crash, and offered a convenient seat. I rested there, letting the heavy mist envelop me. I'm not sure how long I sat there before I felt a slight warmth on my face and saw the sun trying to break through the solid gray sky, sending twisted rainbows of light glancing off the droplets of water that fell from the branches of the dormant oaks. I closed my eyes to enjoy the slight warmth and didn't turn as I heard footsteps so light that the leaves barely made a sound under them. I thought it was my imagination—and then the dead tree I sat on settled closer to the ground. She sat right next to me, so close that I could feel her body warmth without opening my eyes.

"She's gone, you know that, right?" Kat asked, her voice barely louder than the whispering leaves. She knew me too well, knew that in spite of all my history, she would find me here waiting in the rain for a woman who would never come.

"I know…" I admitted. Rigan *was* gone. I knew that, and I knew that Kat deserved better than finding me out here in the rain waiting for another woman. In all the time I'd known Kat, she'd been there whenever I needed someone. I'd never stepped foot outside in the rain for her, and yet here I was in the rain, in the woods where my worst nightmares became memories, waiting for Rigan.

"You know it's raining?" she asked, gently brushing the droplets off my hair.

"It's misting," I corrected.

"It's still wet. I'm beginning to worry about your sanity. Sitting out in the rain is not like you."

"Not like me? I don't even know who I am. I can't remember who I was, or people I've known that were important to me."

"Oh, fuck, here comes the melodramatic crap. Who cares about that shit? You're who you've always been, Kill. A prince among men, a white knight. Killian Collins. You know what that name means?"

"Please, Kat. Not now."

"Yes, now. It means 'little church' in Irish, but in ancient Gaelic a Cill wasn't really a church. It was a locked gate, a cell—

or even a graveyard, full of the dead and gone. Isn't that right?" Kat asked, moving so that I couldn't avoid looking at her face, wet with the rain, makeup free, fierce and perfect...

"It's just a name."

"You're a locked cell, Kill. That head of yours is a graveyard, full of the dead and gone. Time to open up. If not to me, then to someone."

"I don't need to hear this."

"Yes, you do. You know what 'Collins' means? Literally 'young dog.' The kind they use to track prey and hunt, or to protect their homes—you're a hunter and a fighter. Act like one. Get up off your ass and track that bitch down if she's what you want. Sail the seven seas to find her like your crazy friend Sean." Kat took my hands in hers, trying to catch my eye. She was the last person I wanted to talk to about Rigan and all of this.

"I'm not sure I want to."

"Then you're being a pussy—*or*—you don't really want to. Lie to me, but not yourself, Kill. Do you want this woman, or is it just the fairy tale bullshit of long-lost little girls that's got you hooked?"

"You don't know what you're talking about," I told her.

"No? You're a dreamer, Kill. You think you're a white knight. Tell me that as soon as you have time to think about it, you're not going to get obsessed with where those other kids that survived the plane wreck went and rush off to save them too."

"They might need help," I admitted, falling right into her trap.

"Exactly. You want to be their hero, just like you want to be hers. Well, maybe she doesn't need a hero. Maybe you should save the ones who want to be saved," she said, touching my hand. I looked up to find Kat still watching my eyes. She cared. I could see that. I had to tell her.

"You're right. She's not coming back. It's pointless to go after her... but I thought women who tell you not to chase them say it just to test and see if you will."

"You're an idiot. That's bullshit made up by men who are stalkers, trust me. Take me, for example. I'd never ask any man to chase me, and I'd never tell them not to. I don't have time for games. You know that—just like you know that when I say I'm here for you, it means I'm fucking here for you. Always."

"I know."

"Good. Then you know that I'm not going anywhere... And that this is enough for me," she said, losing me.

"What, exactly, is enough?" I asked, turning to face her, wanting to be able to read her expression. When I caught her eye, I saw that they were clear, solemn, and drilling right through me. She knew me too well for me to hide from that look.

"Being second. Being part of whatever this is... It's good enough."

"Being second shouldn't be good enough for anybody."

"Maybe it won't be later," she said, taking her hand off my back. "I plan on working my way up."

"To what?"

"First. You'll forget her sooner or later. I'm banking on sooner."

"I'm not sure it works like that, Kat."

"Maybe, but forgetting can be a way of healing too." Hope lifted her voice, a sort of life-affirming tone that I hadn't noticed before. She was hoping I'd forget, when I'd spent my whole life trying to remember.

"Kat, I don't think—"

I stopped, cut off by Kat's lips on mine. They were warm and soft and dusted with the dew that had settled there as we spoke. I couldn't pull away until she did. She didn't go far— our noses were practically touching as she put her forehead to mine, staring me down.

"Kill, I'm going to tell you something you need to remember no matter what else happens."

"Sure."

"When a girl lays it on the line for you, a word of advice— shut up and let her hope."

We both sat there in silence, and I stared out at the marshy ground, remembering and dreaming of things that would never be. It was the most peaceful time I can remember in spite of the warm rain falling through the leaves. The sound of it, syncopated and rhythmic on the ground, rustling the leaves to a murmuring whisper, reminded me of a thousand conversations locked away somewhere in my mind. They're in there, barely audible, just below the threshold of comprehension... the whispers of people I can't remember. Their words are the story of my life, the stories I can never tell, the loves, like Rigan, who I've lost and may never remember.

I miss them.

Without thinking, I put an arm around Kat, and the sun broke through the clouds. I still had Kat. When she was around, the world was always full, and alive, and somehow even warm and dry—even when it wasn't.

For now, that was enough. Maybe the rain wasn't so bad.

The End

ABOUT THE AUTHOR

Kevin Fox has been a producer and writer of television and film for over twenty years, writing films such as *The Negotiator*, starring Sam Jackson, as well as writing and producing television such as FOX's *Lie to me** and *Law & Order: SVU*, for which he was nominated for the prestigious Edgar Award. His first novel, *Until the Next Time*, was published by Algonquin Books to strong critical support. Born and raised in Staten Island, the setting of *The Killian Collins Series*, he is from a multi-generational Irish American family of police officers, and is a dual citizen of The United States and The Irish Republic.

You can keep up to date with Kevin via his website:

KEVINFOX.COM